DON'T

Jenny Diski was born in 1947 in London, where she lives and works. She is the author of seven novels: *Nothing Natural*, *Rainforest*, *Like Mother*, *Then Again*, *Happily Ever After*, *Monkey's Uncle* and *The Dream Mistress*, as well as a collection of short stories, *The Vanishing Princess*. Her first non-fiction book, *Skating to Antarctica*, was recently published to great critical acclaim. She is a regular contributor to the *London Review of Books* and the *Observer*.

D0995508

ALSO BY JENNY DISKI

Fiction

Nothing Natural
Rainforest
Like Mother
Then Again
Happily Ever After
Monkey's Uncle
The Vanishing Princess
The Dream Mistress

Non-Fiction

Skating to Antarctica

DON'T

Jenny Diski

Granta Books
London

Granta Publications, 2/3 Hanover Yard, London N1 8BE

First published in Great Britain by Granta Books 1998
This edition published by Granta Books 1999

A CIP catalogue record for this book
is available from the British Library.

1 3 5 7 9 10 8 6 4 2

Typeset by M Rules
Printed and bound in Great Britain by
Mackays of Chatham PLC

For my friend Sam Frears, with love

Contents

Ever Thus in England

Madness and its Uses

Taking Off

Preface

On my paper I trace a straight line with occasional angles, and this is Agilulf's route. This other line all twirls and zigzags in Gurduloo's. When he sees a butterfly flutter by Gurduloo at once urges his horse after it, thinking himself astride not the horse but the butterfly, and so wanders off the road and into the fields. Meanwhile Agilulf goes straight ahead, following his course. Every now and again Gurduloo's route off the road coincides with invisible short cuts (or maybe the horse is following a path of its own choice, with no guidance from its rider) and after many a twist and turn the vagabond finds himself again beside his master on the main road.

'The Non-Existent Knight'
Italo Calvino

One of the great pleasures for me of writing is starting out in the wrong direction and discovering how all points can eventually lead to home. It isn't just a desire to be awkward, although there is that, it's also the fact that writing is about surprise – not so much for the reader as for the writer herself. At school I tried virtuously to plan essays as instructed, and as a teacher I passed on handy tips about making essay plans. But the truth is that the more remote my starting point, the more I enjoyed working my way round to what I was supposed to be saying. Writing ought to be a devious business, a game played with yourself and your reader. Gradually, you learn to trust digression. I did, and consequently failed my English Language O-Level exam. Examinees should take that as a warning, aspiring writers as encouragement. Or vice versa.

Most of the essays in this collection were written for the *London Review of Books*. They would have had to have been; no other journal that I can think of would have allowed me to spend so much space meandering on my way to and from the point. I think on the whole I get there in the end, although occasionally it has been a close call. My warmest thanks to the editor, Mary-Kay Wilmers, and the other staff of the *LRB* for the opportunities they have given me to digress from so many intriguing starting points.

Looking at
Monsters
in the Dark

A Horrified, Lidless Stare

For as long as I can remember, I've had trouble with monsters. When I was very small, adults tried to alleviate the terror by opening the cupboard and shining torches under the bed to prove to me nothing was there. It made things worse, of course, because the monsters' invisibility gave them absolute power. If they couldn't be seen, they were all the more invincible, and capable of taking on distorted shapes beyond even the wild imagination of a child. Worse than all my fear of seeing them, was my fear of never seeing them, of never being able to look at them hard enough to make them go away.

Plato was only half right. The shadow we see on the wall of the cave is not just a pale reflection of the Light, but an equally pale reflection of the Dark. The perfect form is less than half the story without its misshapen shadow.

Civilisation may be the art of looking away, but there have always been some who choose to look directly at the darkness. The cinema, more than anywhere, is where we find ourselves face forward in the dark, having to stare back into the eyes of the murderer, the vampire, the nightmare mutation, because the lens of the camera refuses to blink and look away on our behalf.

So on a gloomy bank holiday weekend, I pulled down the blinds, and indulged my taste for excess in a private video festival on the theme of the halt and the lame, the misbegotten, and the damned. A student of the psyche might find it instructive to spend a little time working in a video shop, where people like me scuttle back and forth, revealing, as in a Rorschach test, the twisting and turning of their minds.

The unswerving gaze (so different from the polite looking away, which is, in reality, more a stare than any staring we might do) goes back to cinema's earliest days. Lon Chaney's Quasimodo in *The Hunchback of Notre Dame* is a horribly misshapen, wrongly made gargoyle. He is a black hole of biological accident to match the equally arbitrary accident of beauty, which his single seeing eye looks on with longing, knowing it to be impossibly out of reach. It is his *looking* that moves us and frightens us because the camera holds steady on his gaze, and, for all his twisted frame, won't let us imagine he is so different from us that he is without desire.

We cannot look directly into the eyes of another and feel entirely unrelated. That is the trump card of the cinema. The child murderer in *M* is another kind of monster, as mysterious as the modern child batterer of whom we shake our heads, perplexed, and ask each other, 'How could they do such a thing?' The answer is in Peter Lorre's horrified, lidless stare, directly into the camera, as he articulates a familiar truth: 'I'm always afraid . . . Always I am followed, soundlessly. Yet I hear it. It's me pursuing myself. I can't escape.' For a black, bleak moment, watching his face, you look into the void and know there is a place close by where such things can indeed be done.

The truth is that monsters are always with us, very near. They live in the dark, hating the daylight, like the vampire who has no reflection. But nowhere in the world is darker than the recesses of the human imagination. We might walk in broad daylight, on the sunny side of the street, but still the monsters have the perfect hiding place, protected in the shadowy nooks and crannies of our minds, and, perhaps, deeper and darker still, in our very cells. No getting away from them. Father Sandor, vampire hunter, explains, in *Dracula: Prince of Darkness*, that a vampire can't cross a threshold unless he's invited by someone already inside.

The makers of the movies have always known that they display the monsters for the twin human need of voyeurism and understanding. Tod Browning's *Freaks* would not be made today. Watch it at your peril; your modern, liberal sensibilities shaken, your wide-eyed curiosity and fascination barely beneath the surface. There are no special effects, no technology to keep you at a distance. The Siamese twins are Siamese twins, the Pinheads are called 'Pinheads' in the cast list, the man without pelvis or legs is more fortunate than the man with nothing but a head and a torso. He displays his skills at lighting cigarettes; the Pinheads chatter and chortle incomprehensibly; the Siamese twins joke elaborately about the sexual quandary of one being married, while the other doesn't like her brother-in-law and keeps dragging her sister off on the grounds that she needs a pee. 'Aw', says the hubby, who can't get his hands on his missus, 'You always make the same excuse.' Sometimes they all just stand still and look at you from the other side of the lens. The challenge is not to look away, but to watch another kind of normality. But more than that, it's to confront our own, non-liberal disgust at the abnormal.

At the wedding between the dwarf, Hans, who forgets his place in the world, and Cleopatra, the perfect woman he fatally falls in love with, the community of freaks feasts and welcomes her, chanting, 'One of us, one of us'. Certainly, Browning's tale of exploitation shows us the hideously deformed soul of the physically perfect specimen, but the truly honest moment is the sight of the horrified stare of Cleopatra, faced with the possibility of being part of the deformed community. She is not *just* a wicked person, she is one of us. You realise gradually as you meet her stare that your own eyes have taken on the same appalled expression. Her fear is yours, and the monsters in our dark places are getting restless.

The more recent movies let us off more lightly, at least in the sense that they offer us monsters so stunning to look at that we can distract ourselves with wonder at their making. We may recognise the abject weariness and despair of Klaus Kinski's *Nosferatu* as something to do with us, damned and doomed to walk in the darkness, but we can't help noticing how beautifully blood-drained the lighting is. And while John Carpenter, in his bio-fantasy, *The Thing*, threatens us with the possibility of being mere imitations of the humans we think we are, the monster is so brilliant, you keep having to freeze frame to see its gory and glorious fleshiness better.

This century has brought us a new era of darkness and we are, with reason, haunted by our biology. It isn't just that we have discovered we are not God's best and favourite creatures. It isn't evolution that threatens us with the void, but the discovery of DNA, and the possibility that we may be no more (and no less) than vehicles for that microscopic, seemingly inhuman stuff which was floating around in the primal soup. The horror has come down to our very cells, although we've always suspected that flesh is the source of trouble.

David Cronenberg knows it is. The fly in the human ointment is not really the fly in the telepod, but the terrible possibility that we are, finally, no more than the sum of our biological parts. Shake and stir the components a little, and we become any kind of horror. Once that becomes true, we will have dispensed with conundrums of beauty and ugliness, perfection and deformity, and all the rest of the dreams and nightmares of being human. God and the Devil will have no use, in their eternal battle, for beings which are no more than the result of the meaningless, random firing of electrical connections. Then the dark will close, finally, over our heads.

Good Housekeeping

> *The Shrine of Jeffrey Dahmer*
> by Brian Masters
> (HODDER, LONDON, 1993)

By the age of 31 Jeffrey Dahmer had killed 17 people, all men, none of whom he had known for more than a few hours. He masturbated with the bodies, dissected them, had sex with the viscera and performed fellatio with the opened mouths of severed heads. Not long before he was caught, and while in the process of yet another killing, his flat in Milwaukee contained two corpses in the bath, a headless torso immersed in bleach, several severed heads, hearts and genitalia in the fridge and freezer, and the body of a man killed two days previously under a blanket on the only bed, where, presumably, Dahmer slept until he discovered the head crawling with maggots, and was obliged to cut it off and prepare it for freezing.

Do we need to know about this man and his activities? Is he of intrinsic interest? Wouldn't it be enough to catch him, account for 17 missing people, and prevent any more deaths by locking him securely away for the rest of his life? It could be useful for specialists – criminologists, psychiatrists – to have the details of Dahmer's life and doings with a view to learning about the causes, and therefore the prevention, of such aberrant behaviour. But is it useful for you and me, with no more than a window-shopper's interest, to know about Jeffrey Dahmer? Brian Masters says yes, not only is it useful, it is vital to examine this human being in detail, because he is one of us.

I suppose the world divides into those who look and those who look away. Looking away is easiest, of course, because it requires no justification, implying, as it does, decent sensibility. Looking is altogether a more difficult activity. I doubt that it's ever entirely free of prurience, but the decision to gaze on the abominable – starving children in far-away countries, death and destruction in vicious wars, images and accounts of the Holocaust – might also be a conscious decision to bear witness to the monstrous possibilities of our own humanity. Part of Primo Levi's final depression centred on his belief that fewer and fewer people were listening to what he had witnessed on our behalf. 'Nothing human is alien to me' is more than an affirmation of a species' togetherness: it's a warning that by denying kinship with the worst of our kind, we may never know ourselves at all. There have been others like Dahmer, but he'll do as the worst.

Masters quotes Colin Wilson: 'The study of murder is not the study of abnormal human nature; it is the study of human nature stained by an act that makes it visible on the microscopic slide.' This is a seductive argument for insatiably curious creatures like ourselves, but why then don't we pick up (or review) with equal relish books about the good, the gentle or the kind? If wickedness is a black hole we peer intently into because we are unable to comprehend it, isn't goodness, actually, as mysterious? Why isn't it as interesting?

Masters is severe with his readers, there is a touch of the moral tutor about him. His study of murder and psychological mayhem is a philosophical enquiry which we are bound to contemplate if we seek the truth. 'I realise, of course, that this is a dangerous undertaking, and there are many who will take refuge in any manner of evasions rather than face it . . . The reader must have something of the therapist who "draws on his own psychotic possibilities", or he will flounder in the reassuring soup of "objectivity".' In spite of quoting the dubious authority of R.D. Laing, there is no questioning Masters' intention, which is serious, as it was in his previous book *Killing For Company*, on Dennis Nilsen, another killer whose behaviour was inexplicable to most people.

Murder is the borderline between society and the wilderness. It is the irreversible act which must make the killer an outcast, for ever set apart. But this does not mean he (or she) is inexplicable to the rest of us. The taking of another life is always terrible, but it is also sometimes understandable. Even the most dreadful of murders, infanticide, is not beyond the comprehension of parents who remember the power that the cries of small babies have to distress. From time to time we have all had to use self-control when faced with the rage other people can create in us. But such feelings, even when acted on, are still *feelings*, and connect us with others. Murder is usually a social crime.

Jeffrey Dahmer is extraordinary (although not alone: Nilsen's affect and motivation are remarkably similar) in that absence of feeling is at the root of his crimes. So absent is the feeling that murder is hardly the crime at all. It only happens to be what he has to be charged with because the law does not recognise his real transgression. The death of others for Dahmer was merely a necessary stage on the way to what he really wanted: lifeless bodies deprived of all volition. Depersonalised from childhood, he needed to subtract the person from individuals in order to make a relationship with them. In this sense, Dahmer (like Nilsen) was not destroying, but creating: he was making dead bodies which he then, and only then, could have and hold. Before he began habitually killing people, he drugged them insensible even when they were willing to have sex with him. And later, when dead bodies proved so unsatisfying because they could not be kept for very long, he tried, a crazed and ill-informed Dr Frankenstein, to create a living zombie by drilling into a sleeping man's skull and injecting the frontal lobes with acid. Death was not his object: objects were his object.

If we are looking at Dahmer to see our own distorted reflections, there are two essential questions: how did he come to be the way he was? And: was he mad, a monster or evil? In order to answer the first question, Masters details Jeffrey Dahmer's upbringing. A tranquilliser-addicted, neurotic mother, a distant, though not uncaring father, a country-town boyhood. It is not a happy childhood, and like many children of disturbed families, he became withdrawn. The problem here is to make a distinction between Freud's 'ordinary unhappiness' and the devastating turmoil of this particular individual. Masters pinpoints details which, with hindsight, look powerfully significant. The game he invented at the age of 11 was called the Infinity Game, where stick people were annihilated if they came too close to each other, and tightly drawn spirals called Black Holes were the entrances to Infinity, from which nothing returned. He had an early addiction to being drunk. He vented his unhappiness by smashing at trees with an axe in the woods, rather than speaking to anyone. At four, he had the experience of a double hernia operation, and a (presumably subconscious) memory of having his viscera handled, then of waking in such pain that he asked his mother if his penis had been cut off. And he dissected dead animals.

This last was Dahmer's single boyhood enthusiasm. He took road-kills apart, examined the internal organs, let the flesh rot and then tried to reassemble the skeleton. He never killed anything, or took pleasure in giving pain. It's tempting to think that, finding a void within himself, he was taking living things apart to see what it was he was missing. When he began to kill men he picked up, it was with the intention of keeping them, of not letting them go away. There was something he wanted from them, and in all probability it was life. But like taking a watch to pieces in order to see where the tick is, the thing he was looking for vanished in the searching.

None of these aspects of Dahmer's youth really explains what he became, and even if the combination of all of them signals what he was, there is still no clue as to why. Which, of course, is the real mystery. An early interest in form and structure might turn an adolescent into a sculptor, an architect, a butcher, a biologist. Young boys who have had hernia operations don't regularly become the kind of necrophiliac even necrophiliacs shy away from. Drunkenness might make it easier to do unspeakable things to human beings, but most people who get drunk to overcome their inhibitions do not want to do what Dahmer did. And might not the young inventor of the Infinity Game become an astro-physicist or SF novelist? Masters does suggest (nerve-wrackingly for the inhabitants of North London) that Dahmer's kind of withdrawal has two possible outcomes: if it doesn't make a killer of you, 'it promotes the creative isolation of the artist, who is, in this respect, the antithetical twin of the murderer'.

If we must confront wickedness, we may also have to confront our inability to grasp it in a simple cause-and-effect way. Not long ago someone suggested I read Alice Miller's case study on Hitler, because, she said, 'the way she analyses his childhood makes him completely understandable'. Do we want Hitler's childhood to make him understandable? And could it ever? The fact is, the range of unhappiness in childhood is so vast and so dreadful that I doubt Hitler's home life was worse than that of many another infant who did not grow up as he did. But it is not Hitler, really, who we need as comparison to Jeffrey Dahmer. It is the concentration-camp guard we need to wonder at, the man who looked human beings in the eye while he performed the acts which Hitler merely ordered. The mystery is in the absence of shame and humanity on the small scale of Dahmer and his visitors, or you and me. It's at that singular point we can find no other word more appropriate than evil.

The question the jury at Dahmer's trial had to decide on was not guilt or innocence, but whether the man was a mad devil or a sane monster. Technically, did he have a mental disease? Did he have any control over his impulses? Dahmer spoke of being 'compelled' or 'possessed' by the hunger to have bodies. He did not only use the bodies for sexual gratification, but had a black table with skulls and a skeleton arranged on it, which he called his 'shrine', and he also ate human flesh.

Masters makes a good deal of anthropological evidence on the cannibalism/primitive religion nexus, citing the Aztecs, the Windigo psychosis of Canadian Indians who became eaters of human flesh, and of course, the Catholic Mass. Certainly, Dahmer seems to fit in with these notions, as well as the dark area of the psyche which includes were-wolves and vampires. The sacrifice of humans and eating people as an act of love, or a desire to partake of their qual-ities has a long history. Masters speculates on the spiritual plainness of Dahmer's Lutheran religion, and how it might have created a vacancy which hankered after Dionysian excess and primitive ritual. (You almost get the feeling Masters is suggesting that had Dahmer been a Catholic – of the Southern European variety, it would have to be – he might have been all right.) It's important, says Masters, that Dahmer is not a moral idiot. He knows right from wrong. But that is no proof against possession. The Devil only tri-umphs over a man capable of putting up a fight against him. Corruption must have a decent medium in which its bacilli can multiply. Dahmer was finally taken over, but there were periods when he tried for normality.

In the end the labels seem transferable: what we might call multiple or schizoid personality and feel comfortable with, is surely no more than a current transformation of the ancient idea of possession of spirits. In either case, what the individual feels is that his ordinary social self has been overcome by a force, a will, beyond his control. Call it devilry, call it madness; either way Dahmer was obviously not very well.

Which is not what the jury decided. On all counts of murder Dahmer was found, by ten votes to two, *not* to have a mental disease. It suggests, since there is no death penalty in Wisconsin, that the ten were those who choose to 'look away'. They decided not to have his condition examined, but to lock him away out of sight.

Masters is very likely right to suggest that Jeffrey Dahmer's crimes were extreme versions of our own unacted-on fantasies, on which we prefer not to dwell. A desire to explore the internal labyrinths and possess the interior of a lover's body is not beyond the sexual imagination. Indeed, it is implied in the various acts of penetration people perform with one another. Sexual hunger is visceral; though, unlike Dahmer, most of us settle for dark dreams and do not go beyond the limits of reason.

The danger in this line of thought is that Dahmer becomes an existential hero, the outsider who dares to act on what ordinary mortals can barely think about. But the reality of Dahmer is otherwise. Finally, I doubt that his actions can tell us more than we know already from myth, story and fantasy. The strongest and most awful image of both Dahmer and Nilsen is that of housekeeping in hell. Both come to a point where the bodies pile up around them – Dahmer taking a shower with two corpses in the tub – the smells are intolerable, the logistics of disposal impossible, and they are condemned to a seemingly unending task of dismembering, eviscerating, dissolving, and scrubbing away at the disorder and putrefaction they have created. All the classic images of hell are present in each of those flats, inhabited by the ghost of Hieronymous Bosch and the two increasingly bewildered, dull-minded men, who finally long to be caught so that their nightmare can stop. The question of whether Jeffrey Dahmer is, in the end, of vital interest is addressed by Dahmer himself, and I'm inclined to agree with him: 'This is the grand finale of a life poorly spent . . . How it can help anyone, I've no idea.'

Bob and Betty

> *A Mind of My Own:*
> *My Life with Robert Maxwell*
> by Elizabeth Maxwell
> (SIDGWICK, LONDON, 1994)

Those given to hasty judgments might find the title of Betty Maxwell's autobiography something of a logical contradiction. Even leaving aside the strangeness, to feminist eyes, of the title's construction, just a passing knowledge of the dynamics of Robert Maxwell's ego would seem to preclude the possibility of having the one while being with the other for 47 years. Yet, when one has read the book, it becomes clear that the colon is, after all, perfectly placed between the two propositions, and that the initial judgment turned on a very narrow and possibly rather transitory definition of having a mind of one's own. If living with Robert Maxwell provides satisfaction, however specialised, then to do so is perfectly in keeping with having a mind of one's own.

Betty Maxwell got her heart's desire from the start of her relationship with Robert Maxwell, and, what is more, she kept on getting it, in her fashion, for the duration of the marriage. Some desires override the independence modern women assume to be the *sine qua non* of a free spirit. Indeed, some are inimical to a strict definition of independence, and who is to say that such desires are not to be satisfied?

There was a curious novel published a few years ago by Robert Coover called *Spanking the Maid*. It was a slim volume, because essentially it dealt with only a single scene in the life of a master/narrator and his maid. He calls her in to clean his room and make the bed. She does so, but some careless or clumsy detail – a wrinkle in the sheets, a drop of water spilled on the floor – spoils her efforts. The master is obliged to punish her before ordering her to begin again. Each plays their part with consummate awareness of the requirements of their role. The effort to make immaculate, the inexorable failure, the ritualised punishment are repeated, word for word, sentence for sentence, unvarying except for the nature of the maid's error. The tone of the narrator and the demeanour of the maid are dull and despairing since they understand the necessity for error and punishment and the terrible circle of banality and repetition in which they are both caught up. Not that I'm suggesting for a moment that spanking had any place in the relationship between the adults in the Maxwell family, but there is something about their married life, as it is described by Mrs Maxwell, that brings to mind Coover's book on the structure of domesticity and desire.

Robert Maxwell had very firm ideas on how a wife ought to behave:

He would constantly revert to the same old theme – that I did not look after his material needs to a standard he considered acceptable and was therefore incapable of ensuring his happiness. Sometimes there would be a button missing on a shirt, or I would forget his evening shirt studs or black tie when I packed his bag. He would complain that his cupboards were not impeccably tidy or that I hadn't got his summer clothes out early enough . . . What he wanted me to do was 'assist, bolster and serve him and the children'.

This was not just a man demanding that all his physical needs be attended to. Right from the beginning of their marriage, domestic detail is inextricably linked to love and loyalty. Letters stating their intent and reiterating the themes of their passion fly back and forth between them throughout their long marriage:

Betuska my love,
You most certainly have made big strides towards becoming the perfect partner through the things you have done like washing my clothes, or darning my socks . . . Although by themselves they may seem trivial and matter-of-fact, do not be deceived by that because they constitute the demonstration of the love which we have for each other, and to me they are of the highest value, for without them our love could not live.

Betty, like Coover's maid, clearly understands that his wishes are not trivial, that her domestic attentions are central to their mutual desire:

I want to live for you, I want to drown my soul in your desires. This requires all my attention and all my strength, there is no time to do anything else. You will only need to say what you want and it will be done, or to express a desire and I will satisfy it. Perhaps you will discover that the half-flayed creature you have stripped naked still deserves to be loved.

For all the berating on his part and the grovelling on hers, Betty Maxwell comes across, not as a domestic doormat, but as a fully collusive partner in a very complicated relationship, which, right from the start, is powerfully sexual. But the power is not, as it appears or as it is portrayed, entirely one-sided.

The key to this kind of partnership is not actually the dominant member's demands, but the submissive one's power to elicit those demands while seeming to remain docile. 'I never felt belittled by deferring to his authority . . . He was for ever searching for that indefinable "something" which he sensed I was holding back. For my own part, I was convinced it was precisely that very *chasse au bonheur* – the chase for love so clearly depicted in Stendhal – that would keep him interested in me.' Holding back is exactly what Coover's maid does in failing every time to perform perfectly. Every slip-up she makes is essential to the fulfilment of the narrator's happiness, and a gift she freely brings to the relationship. She is the only one who can break the contract by performing her duties in such a way that no punishment is called for. Betty Maxwell, not tied to Maxwell for want of alternatives or money, is perfectly correct in attributing to herself a mind of her own.

She was a virgin when they first made love. 'Although he was ablaze with desire, he did not rush me. I was ready for love, eager to be at one with him . . . But despite my readiness, it was a painful first experience. He was in tears at the thought of having hurt me. Nothing was ever to move me more than my husband's tears.' If you are disturbed by the mental image of Robert Maxwell in the throes of love, it might (or might not) help to bear in mind Betty's description of him as a young man: 'There was an overwhelming impression of dominance and masculinity, reinforced by the resonant speaking voice from deep down in the diaphragm, confident and self-assured. When he spoke, his swift-moving lips, thick and red like two ripe fruits, evoked luxury and youthfulness; yet sometimes, thin as filaments of blood, they depicted death and carnage.'

In addition to the nature of the hankerings, the prose style holds an important clue to Betty Maxwell's character. There is a marvellous mixing of respectability and libido. She is the perfect suburban lady honeycombed with dark subterranean desires. She loves to remember the sparkling, bourgeois social life and travel opportunities afforded to the wife of a tycoon ('people tell me that my dining room was rather like one of those celebrated Parisian salons') and shares them with us in prose similar to her description of Elizabeth Taylor's eyes: 'of a deep, rich velvety purple'. Istanbul is encased in its geographical surroundings like 'a jewel in lapis lazuli'; the Taj Mahal, 'one of the Seven Wonders of the World', she saw 'at dawn, when the main dome was iridescent in the pink rays of the sun, then at midday in golden sunshine and beneath the most glorious blue sky and finally at midnight . . . when the full moon was at its brightest and picked out the marble of the dome and four minarets in a translucent pearly white'. On the other hand, the land and people of Australia were found to be 'too vast, too rough, too brash, too uncouth, too wild' for her refined taste. She is vaguely conscious that there are some who are unaccustomed to her way of life: 'All but the uninitiated will be well aware that in foreign waters, most yachting transactions take place in cash.'

It looks to me as if we can expect Betty Maxwell to climb out of her financial difficulties with one of those monosyllabically titled best-sellers filled with fashion tips ('The Queen would not agree to extravagant expenditure on her clothes and neither did I'), wine-dark prose and exotic settings, as others on their uppers have done before her. She writes to Bob in 1981 after their final flare-up: 'You have always refused to recognise my deeply creative instincts, the poet, dreamer, writer, storyteller within me . . . when by preference I would have liked to write, draw and make music under the warm Mediterranean sun, breathing in the scented fragrances of the garrigue and pinewoods.'

Poetry, refinement and good manners are essential qualities for the French-born Mrs Maxwell and in some way they seem to help her when the old animal threatens to break out. It was only by her side and under her tutelage that Maxwell managed to pass himself off socially: 'Sadly, in the last few years of his life, when I was no longer at his side to remind him constantly that "manners maketh man," he tended to overlook this aspect of social intercourse.' Discovering that her husband and his personal assistant were having an affair, she comforts herself with the knowledge of her own impeccable propriety: 'Nor could I understand how a girl would allow herself to fall in love with the father of six children under the age of eight, whatever the circumstances. It was not the kind of moral code I had been brought up on, and I can say in all honesty that I have never allowed myself to fall in love with a married man.' In 1969, 20 years into their marriage, a solitary safari provokes the two strands of Betty's sensual and straitlaced character into expressing themselves. In a tented hotel at the foot of Mount Kenya, with guards around them for protection, she sat 'beneath the starry African sky' and explained to the curious hotel manager and guests why 'a white woman like me', finding herself alone in 'darkest Africa', wasn't afraid. She told them she could 'call on God who could see me, as he now saw them talking to me. My words seemed to impress them and gave me confidence to go back to my tent, reasonably sure I would not be raped, but I must confess that the Ashantis [*sic*] guarding that camp frightened me much more than those herds of elephants poised to charge the car a few days before.' She was alone because Bob, anxious to be back in the world of commerce, had upped and offed, leaving her to complete their holiday alone.

The next day she wrote a long letter to Bob: 'For some years now, I have realised, at first with bellicose sadness, then with hurt pride and at last with victorious serenity, that

my usefulness to you has come to an end . . . As a supreme
act of my love for you, I will make no more demands on
your physical and mental love and I relieve you as of now of
any sense of guilt that might creep in.' Luckily, Maxwell still
wanted his buttons sewn on, so their final separation was to
be postponed for another 20 years.

Throughout the Eighties they grew further apart, with
Maxwell spending more time in his London flat and behaving
outrageously when he was in Oxford – increasingly it looked
as if he had had enough of family life. Even then, Betty found
something positive about their relationship: 'Yet the separa-
tions also helped our relationship to survive: as soon as we
were apart, we would both forget reality and recreate in our
minds the love we had first known.' Until 1990 there were
regular reconciliations with Maxwell writing: 'I love you,
only you, I adore you for ever my untamed, wild but fasci-
nating creature.' It wasn't until July 1990 that he announced
that he wanted a legal separation and that it had to be adver-
tised in *The Times*. (It wasn't.) 'I don't want to see you again,
I don't want you to phone me, I don't want to talk to you any
more. I no longer love you,' he told her, which was, that
time, four decades into the marriage, as definite as it sounds.
By then the financial panic had started, and press baron status
had inflated his ego to gigantic proportions.

A passionate dyad is perhaps not the best basis for a
happy family life. The relationship between the two of them
was all-consuming and it seems odd that they chose to have
so many children (there were nine in all, of whom seven survived) to clutter their self-absorption. Perhaps hostages are
necessary in such a relationship, so that notable sacrifices
can be made as test and proof of sincerity of intent. When a
choice was to be made between her husband's overweening
needs and her children, there was never any contest. When
Maxwell wanted her to campaign with him in his
Parliamentary period, the children were packed off to the

grandparents in France for six months so that Betty could devote her time and energy to canvassing for her husband. She feels now that he might have gone too far when he persecuted his children, as he did every Sunday, reducing them to tears, each in turn, week by week. But although 'my own heart was torn to shreds . . . I felt it was important to maintain a united front before the children.' Still, she was not above a little disciplining herself. After he had misbehaved, she offered Ian, at 15, the choice of taking 'three of the best' from herself or waiting till his father came home: 'After momentary reflection, he decided to take the beating from me . . . I hated doing it and needed all the courage I could muster to perform such a hated punishment with the twins' riding crop.' However, 'from that day on . . . Ian always showed me the utmost respect, and never once ventured a word of insolence and we have remained the best of friends.' Betty could play the dominance/submission game from either end of the pitch.

Betty Maxwell's account of her life with Robert Maxwell is not the best place to look for a description of Maxwell the businessman or Maxwell the crook. For a detailed account of the wheeling and dealing and finagling (or is it finessing?), you are better off going to Tom Bower's biographies of Maxwell. As she sees it, Maxwell made mistakes because he was 'rash', a word she uses repeatedly about his trickier business dealings. His faults are essentially over-enthusiasm and naivety. Whether she really believes this or is merely distancing herself from the taint of his dishonesty is unclear. In her book she has it both ways: Maxwell carries on his business outside the house, but when the chickens come home to roost, Betty stands by her man.

Her considered opinion about the Leasco scandal is that Saul Steinberg and his wife (guilty of working on a tapestry during lunch with 'Nicole de Bedford' at Woburn Abbey) were 'self-opinionated and ill-mannered'. The failure of

Simkin Marshall, the book wholesaling business that crashed under Maxwell's ownership, was due to publishers 'stabbing the new enterprise in the back'. The report of the DTI into the Pergamon mess which concluded, 'he is not in our opinion a person who can be relied on to exercise a proper stewardship of a public quoted company,' is dismissed as 'merely an opinion'.

You have the feeling that Betty was always out, or having her hair done, when the most scandalous and illegal events took place. When she expresses pity for the Maxwell Group pensioners whose retirement income was stolen by her husband ('the loss of financial security in old age is cruel indeed') you suspect she is reminding you of her own newly straitened circumstances. They are not the only ones who suffered, she seems to be suggesting; she, a pensioner too, is reduced to living 'temporarily' in a two-bedroomed house in London, although her interior decorator, loyal to the last, has loaned her 'some of his own furniture to add a touch of the elegance to which he knew I was accustomed'. Actually, although she mentions the losses the pensioners have suffered there is no precise reference to the fact that her husband embezzled the money during the last months of his life to keep his tycoon dream afloat. A Martian might conclude the pensioners had been careless with their funds and left them on an omnibus.

Curiously, while Maxwell tried to sue the socks off Tom Bower, it is his book that provides the more sympathetic picture. If Mrs Maxwell's longings and evasions preclude much sympathy, her husband is another case altogether. Maxwell seems to me to be the businessman capitalism deserves, and I have to confess to a certain pleasure at his vulgarity in the clubbable world of bankers. As an innocent in the world of high finance, I have trouble seeing why the financial games he played were any worse than the games played by those he was dealing with. Almost everything he did (with the exception of the overtly illegal appropriation of the pension funds) was within the incredibly elastic rules of making money out of money. Even the pension fund fraud was financed by the banks, who were falling over themselves to make a packet out of a man they despised. In fact, he lost most of his takeover battles because he was too emotional a player when pitched against the cool-headed likes of Rupert Murdoch. And, of course, he wasn't English. You might say that Rupert Murdoch isn't English either, but for all Betty Maxwell's distaste for things and people Antipodean, the English understand that an Australian is more nearly one of them than an upstart Jew from somewhere unpronounceable in Mittel Europe can ever hope to be. In a world of commerce where ambition and greed for more than is necessary are essential and admired qualities, he just wanted to shine. But he didn't understand the underlying rules that require ambition and greed to be overlaid with acceptable evidence of breeding. When he was outmanoeuvred by Murdoch and the money-men in the *News of the World* takeover, he complained of the Norwich Union boss who switched sides: 'Mr Watson threw a googly at me.' Mr Watson replied: 'Every Englishman knows you "bowl" a googly.'

There seems to have been enough of that sort of thing to have driven Maxwell's ambitions to manic extremes. Doubtless the boy from the *shtetl* had a burning desire to belong. He loved shaking hands with the rich and famous and cavorting ludicrously on the pages of his own newspaper, bought, very likely, because he knew he'd never get a respectful press from anyone else. He was a monster, of course, consumed with avarice and the desire to be in control, but he had help in the burgeoning of his monstrousness. He was, by any account, extraordinary, and perhaps, in another place, might have been something quite different.

Betty Maxwell believes he was driven by a need to atone for his survival: 'He was convinced that had he stayed at home, he could have saved the lives of his parents and younger siblings' – who died in concentration camps: 'Nothing he achieved in life would ever compensate for what he had not been able to accomplish – the rescue of his family.'

His Jewishness was not just a problem for the English establishment, but for Maxwell himself. Betty Maxwell suspects that in marrying out of the faith he felt he had betrayed his family. In consequence, she devoted herself to working 'towards Jewish–Christian reconciliation' and bringing the knowledge of the Holocaust to the attention of the world. 'In some ways,' she writes, this 'brought us together, in others, it widened the gulf between us as I gradually became more recognised in my own right.' The Maxwell tensions remained taut right to the end.

Ever one to make the best of a bad business, in her time of trouble after her husband's death when people were riffling through her bank accounts, she found comfort in what she learned of Maxwell's family history. 'Through all of this I was sustained by my respect and love for the memory of Bob's mother, this woman I had never known but to whom I felt so close . . . She and her family had gone through far worse, along with all their fellow Jews, who had been humiliated, vilified, degraded and finally murdered. How did I dare complain, even to myself? I felt supported by sharing vicariously, even in a small way, an appalling fate and being punished for alleged deeds I had neither committed nor been aware of.' Thank God, it wasn't all in vain.

He Could Afford It

> *Howard Hughes: The Secret Life*
> by Charles Higham
> (SIDGWICK, LONDON, 1993)

This is the story of a man who insisted on having precisely 12 peas on his dinner plate every evening. He threaded the peas all in a row on to his fork and ate them, but if one of the peas was too big to fit on the prong with the rest, it was returned to the chef to be replaced by a pea of standard size. Once you know this everything else follows.

Howard Hughes's life is a series of obsessions, each over-ridden in its turn by a bigger and better fixation. It begins with 12 peas on a plate, and ends with urine stored in Mason jars. Actually, it's not an unusual story as such – the world is full of people dogged by ritual obsessions. What made Hughes remarkable was that he had the money to give absolute licence to every desperate whim. There was no practical reason for him to try to control his madness. The rest of us have to make our neuroses fit in with the world around us – a touch of reality that may trim our unreason. The rich are different from us not just because they can afford to indulge their madnesses, but because they can pay other people to sustain their nightmares.

This is a practical, rather than a moral point, and not one made by Charles Higham, whose moral fervour in telling this wretched story twangs with self-righteousness. There's talk of 'moral cesspools' and 'man-hungry, tweedy heiresses' – it's a world where God and Charles Higham sit in judgment and everybody gets their just deserts. You might think that a man whose lovers include Katharine Hepburn, Ava Gardner, Claudette Colbert, Bette Davis, Lana Turner, Rita Hayworth, Marlene Dietrich, Tyrone Power, Robert Ryan and Cary Grant must have had some kind of good time, but no one gets to have much fun in Higham's book. He explains with nice elaboration that, with women, Hughes 'preferred intermammary intercourse – making love between a woman's breasts – or fellatio to vaginal intromission. With men, he also preferred oral sex.' On the other hand, we're told later that after marrying the virginal Terry Moore on a yacht outside the five-mile limit so that the marriage wouldn't be legal, he 'massaged her clitoris, using a Japanese technique of arousal that overcame her inhibitions'. Unfortunately for inhibited women everywhere (except in Japan), Higham doesn't amplify.

Women are either virgins or sluts to Higham, and he doesn't give much for their strength of character whatever their moral state. Here's how he describes Katharine Hepburn: 'She was no stronger than any other woman when it came to meeting an immensely powerful and wealthy young man with stunning good looks and a lean, hard body who looked vulnerable and anxious to be mothered.' Do you hear the weird sound of simultaneous salivation and teeth-grinding? As a final thrust we're told: 'It never seems to have occurred to her, in her extraordinary state of selfcentredness, that she would be sharing Hughes with Cary Grant, Corinne Griffith and any number of unnamed beauties of both sexes.' The slurping and gnashing reach ear-splitting proportions.

But however loud the voice of the moral majority, the tale

of Howard Hughes comes across for the miserable, sad thing it was. Not a tragedy. That would require a poor, talented boy who hungers for success, makes good and can't handle it. What we've got is a rich, talented boy who starts off with everything, wants more and handles it well enough, but is unfortunately also a fruitcake. It wasn't just the peas: during the same period he took to conducting his business conferences on the lavatory. Severe anxiety about constipation had set in. Apparently, the business associates of rich young men do not refuse to meet wherever the rich young men require them to.

What made Howard run? Was it that wicked Uncle Rupert who sodomised young Howard? The late *Photoplay* publisher James Quirk told his nephew Lawrence (who decades later told Mr Higham) that Rupert put pressure on Hughes to go to bed with him. Higham says *they* say that Rupert owned a circular graveyard in New England in which he kept the bodies of people he'd murdered, drowned his daughter, replaced her with a double and made love to his sister. Which is pretty conclusive, and who knows, maybe that was where the funny stuff with the peas – not to mention the constipation – began. Then, thank God, we've got an explanation for the whole sorry mess and we can go about our business safe in the knowledge that once again child abuse is to blame for it all.

Then again, perhaps it was the family holocaust that happened when Hughes was in his late teens and, over a period of less than two years, his germophobic, hypochondriac mother died under an anaesthetic, his alcoholic aunt hanged herself, and his father fell off his chair and died of an embolism. Or did Hughes's congenital deafness so isolate him that his world shrank to the peas on his plate? Actually, there's no indication that Higham cares to explain why Hughes was the way he was. The family background and tales of his youth are not developed as psychological causes,

but are merely tossed on an accumulating pile of corruption.
Everybody is doomed because everybody, past and present,
is contaminated. This is quite Greek, except the Chorus is
that of the tongue-clicking virtuous – no hint of pity attends
this drama.

Of course, sex has nothing to do with Hughes's life.
Women were conquests and in that sense not very different
from planes – Hughes had a number of record-breaking
flying exploits to his name. When one – sadly unnamed –
movie star refused to go into his bedroom after weeks of
being wined and dined, he went in by himself, leaving the
door open so that the astonished woman could see him
having sex with a life-size, anatomically correct, rubber
replica of herself which he had had made. But by the early
Fifties he had given up the real-ish thing and was spending
days at a time locked in the Goldwyn studio's screening
room, peeing into bottles and masturbating to the bad
movies he had RKO make for the purpose. This ended when
Preminger screened a rough cut of *Porgy and Bess* in the
room, and Hughes, as anti-black as he was anti-Semitic,
refused ever to go there again.

All along, it was about power, and although he seemed not
to be very good at business (luckily he was rich enough to
stay rich whatever messy deals he made), he had a real talent
for buying influence – with Nixon, the CIA, Somoza, the
Mafia and any passing local politician. He was involved in an
assassination attempt on Castro, the Watergate break-in and
had the US weapons establishment in his pocket. Power is, of
course, control, and Hughes accumulated it from the
moment he had access to wealth. But it was at the peak of his
influence that the obsessive anxieties really took flight. As he
wrapped up control of the macroscopic world, the microscopic universe began to control him. His mother's fear of
germs re-emerged and he sat naked in air-conditioned hotel
suites, touching nothing – doorknobs, telephones – unless his

hands were protected by a Kleenex tissue. Sometimes for days on end he'd sit like this, staring at the light bulb in case a fly landed and deposited its germs. Three Mormon aides were employed to work eight-hour shifts exclusively to deal with the threat – which has had the happy result of allowing one of them to write a memoir entitled *I Caught Flies for Howard Hughes*. Magazines were brought in on a trolley by other aides who had to move one step at a time to Hughes's signal so that no dust was disturbed in the room. There had to be three copies of each magazine, and when, eventually, they were within arm's reach, the Kleenex-covered hand picked the middle copy.

If, from the word go, you have power, but want more and have the means to get it, eventually you get all the power an individual can have. But flies still fly, and germs remain invisible – and so long as something, somewhere in the cosmos is beyond your command, you don't have everything. Nothing you've got is going to make up for the control hole, once you've spotted it. Perhaps there's another way of looking at it: when a man has everything, what is going to keep him alive except the discovery of some recalcitrant aspects of the world he can go on wanting? Hughes needed the flies that didn't need him.

Higham reckons that he has two main contributions to make to the sum of human knowledge: the first is that Hughes died of an early form of Aids. There are certainly coincidences of symptoms over Hughes's long, slow deterioration, though these could be the symptoms of any kind of auto-immune disease. He cites evidence of an English sailor whose frozen blood proved to have been HIV positive when he died in 1959, which might indicate something, but not that Hughes had Aids, since he refused to allow blood to be taken. Higham asked a retired forensic surgeon if, with his symptoms, Hughes could have had Aids, to which the surgeon replied that he could. In fact, Hughes died of kidney failure brought on by taking too many analgesics in his attempt to control the permanent pain he had been in since a flying accident. Case not exactly proven, I'd say.

Higham's other theory is that, contrary to the rumours of Hughes being *non compos mentis* and under the evil influence of his Mormon aides, he was meanly and miserably in control right up to the time of his death. This sounds more persuasive. A man as control-hungry as Hughes wouldn't let a small detail like dementia or insanity prevent him from keeping tabs on things.

There may have been a moment when Howard Hughes had the chance to be a human being. In his twenties he walked out on his life and hoboed around America. Preston Sturges based *Sullivan's Travels* on the adventure. But what Hughes found out in the real world didn't please him. He came back and settled into his penthouse seclusion. And Preston Sturges, of course, went mad.

Stinker

> *Roald Dahl: A Biography*
> by Jeremy Treglown
> (FABER, LONDON, 1994)

It goes against all the currents of current wisdom that a public man should be just what he seems to be. Is there anyone left in the world who doesn't believe at some level or other in the disjunction between appearance and reality? I suppose somewhere deep in the forests where no white man has trod; in the highest, most inaccessible plateaux of some far-flung mountainous region, there might be a few primitive folk left who still think that what they see is what there is. But the rest of us are not completely astonished to discover that nice, ordinary MPs who take decent girls to Tory fund-raising dances prefer stockings and electric flex in the privacy of their own kitchens, or that our favourite English poet of quiet suburban gloom had a nasty sense of humour and some unfortunate habits. We know that beneath all exteriors lie subterranean streams and caverns where the private, unknowable self contradicts the stated desires and achievements of the visible life.

A biography, these days, must be a tale of the unexpected. Wouldn't modern readers feel cheated to find that Antonia

White and A.A. Milne were wise and devoted parents, or
that Larkin only released his bicycle clips in order to sip
cocoa in striped pyjamas and have gently sad, humane
thoughts before bed? But an authorised biography has little
to offer a post-Freudian readership. Isn't it autobiography in
disguise: a ventriloquist act where the subject, or their family,
pulls the strings and keeps the subterranean firmly underground? The approved biographer is not likely to be the
surgeon we require, slicing through the superficial layers
with his scalpel.

The prefaced justifications of unauthorised biographers
are no more than pious mouthings; who, really, wants to
read an authorised biography? So take Jeremy Treglown's
apologia at the beginning of his Dahl biography with a pinch
of salt. Ophelia Dahl plans to write the authorised version of
her father's life, with the approval of his second wife, Felicity,
who asked friends and relatives not to co-operate with any
other project. Should we worry then that Treglown lacks
sources? Hardly. Apart from Felicity and Ophelia, everyone
talked, as people will.

Roald Dahl is, however, a different case from the public
achiever who turns out to have feet of clay. Nobody who had
read his books or heard his opinions could ever have supposed him to be a comfortably wonderful human being. On
the whole, it seemed that Roald Dahl was not a very nice
man who wrote not very nice, though hugely popular, books
and short stories for children and adults. If this biography is
disappointing, it is because, in reverse, it offends our
assumptions about appearance and reality. Roald Dahl, it
emerges, was exactly what he seemed to be, and Jeremy
Treglown is hard put to come up with anything surprisingly
endearing about the man.

The last time I read Roald Dahl was to my seven-year-old
in 1984. I'd got to page 46 of *George's Marvellous
Medicine*, beyond the first description of Grandma: 'She

was a selfish grumpy old woman. She had pale brown teeth
and a small puckered up mouth like a dog's bottom.' I'd
managed George's later depictions of Grandma as 'a grumpy
old cow', 'a miserable old pig' and his remorse at not being
able to cover her with sheep-dip: 'how I'd love to . . . slosh
it all over old Grandma and watch the ticks and fleas go
jumping off her. But I can't. I mustn't. So she'll have to drink
it instead.' By page 46 George's medicine is ready and I was
about to read: 'The old hag opened her small wrinkled
mouth, showing disgusting pale brown teeth.' But I'd had
enough.

I explained that since she could now read herself, this
bedtime story thing ought to be a pleasure for both of us. I
turned down the corner of the page, offered to read her anything else and promised to continue buying her books by
Roald Dahl. Only she'd have to read them herself. Separate
development in the Dahl department worked out well
enough. And I now have a handy 16-year-old, close enough
to back then to recall what it was like being a child and
reading Dahl's books. With a surprised blink of childhood
pleasure recollected, she explained: 'They were *exactly* what
I wanted to be reading. Every one of them. They filled me
with . . . glee.'

Multiply that pleasure by 11 million paperbacks sold in
Britain alone, between 1980 and 1990 (not to mention a
print run of two million of *Charlie and the Chocolate
Factory* in China) and you get a notion of what Dahl meant
when he spoke of his 'child power'. He claimed, probably
rightly, that he could walk into any house with children in
Europe or the US, and find himself recognised and wel-
comed. Compared with that, having his books banned by
librarians on the grounds of racism (the original Oompa
Loompas were black with fuzzy hair and thick lips), misog-
yny ('A witch is always a woman. I do not wish to speak
badly of women . . . On the other hand, a ghoul is always a

male. So indeed is a barghest. Both are dangerous. But neither of them is half as dangerous as a *real witch*') or ageism (see above), was pretty small potatoes.

Children love his stories. They speak to the last overt remains of the disreputable, unsocialised, inelegant parts of themselves the grown-ups are trying so hard to push firmly underground. If they are coarsely written, structurally feeble, morally dubious, so much the better. If the adults can't bear to read them, then childhood nirvana is attained. Adults are to be poisoned and shrunk into nothingness, dragged unwillingly on their deathbed to live in a chocolate factory, and outwitted like the murderous farmers who wait outside Mr Fox's lair only to be trounced by his cunning. Quite right. Dahl has a proper relationship with childish desires and best we keep out of it. Except, perhaps, for the recognition that there are other more gracious childish desires which can also be catered for.

Given that special relationship between Dahl and his readers, and the fact that he wrote two volumes of self-dramatising autobiography for children, what is the function of an adult biography of the man? Jeremy Treglown quotes the American children's writer Eleanor Cameron's attack on *Charlie and the Chocolate Factory*. It's necessary to sort good books from bad, she says, but goodness in fiction is also a moral matter depending on 'the goodness of the writer himself, his worth as a human being'. This would seem to be an extraordinary basis for deciding the value of adult fiction; people, like books, are a matter of taste, and if I would find it tiresome to have Dostoevsky round to tea, that doesn't mean *Crime and Punishment* should be swilled down the waste disposal along with the old tea leaves. But perhaps intention *is* important. There is something in us that wants good writers to be good people. There's also something in us that knows pigs can't fly.

Treglown paints a portrait of a young man delirious with

his own promise. As a wounded RAF war hero (who actually crashed his plane through inexperience on a routine flight) he was sent to Washington and New York to gossip and gather intelligence about American intentions towards the Allies. He was better at the gossip and excellent at self-promotion. 'He was extremely conceited, saw himself as a creative artist of a high order, and therefore entitled to respect and very special treatment,' says Isaiah Berlin. Brendan Gill remembers him: 'The most conceited man who ever lived in our time in New York City. Vain to the point where it was a kind of natural wonder.'

His attraction to conspicuous wealth and for women resulted in his flashing gifts of gold cigarette cases and lighters at his friends, as well as a gold key to the house of Standard Oil heiress Millicent Rogers. No one, except possibly the heiresses, seems to have had a very high opinion of the young man, apart from Charles Marsh, an older oil tycoon who became a sort of mystical father to Dahl, though not to either man's benefit according to a dining companion: 'Roald and Charles both did a job on each other . . . The *bullshit* that washed across the table.' They vied with each other to keep up what Treglown calls 'the high gibberish quotient' of their relationship.

Dashiell Hammett was appalled to hear of Patricia Neal's planned marriage to Dahl, while Leonard Bernstein told her she was making the biggest mistake of her life. Treglown met and interviewed Neal, divorced from Dahl after 30 years of a marriage during which she survived a series of strokes and a Dahl-enforced recovery, and bore five children, of whom one died and the only son suffered irreversible brain damage in a street accident. Wisely, he did not ask her if Bernstein's prognostication had turned out to be true.

But it is in the domestic life that those contradictory elements we look for are generally found, and Dahl's family life was not short of the kind of challenge that shows up public people for what they really are. Treglown offers a suggestion that the death of his father when Dahl was just four, leaving him to be brought up surrounded by sisters and an adoring if physically remote mother, might have resulted in his perpetually yearning to get back to the power and desires of his childhood. If millions of children all over the world love the subversive, prurient and emotionally capricious stories he told, could that be because he never left his infantile self behind? Those of us old enough to have found out that no one ever really grows up can be grateful to Treglown for the comforting thought that some of us are more grown up than others. Dahl's gambling, boasting, sexual flightiness and public tantrums all point in the direction of arrested emotional development. And look how the anti-semitism ('even a stinker like Hitler didn't just pick on them for no reason') comes with a childlike vocabulary. He displays a reaction to personal disaster in which desire to gain control over the situation often appears like a flight mechanism. When his son's life is endangered after his accident because the valve to drain the water from his brain keeps getting clogged, Dahl more or less absents himself in a search for a new model. When Neal is crippled and rendered speechless, he organises a six-hour daily rota to force her to learn to speak again, though he is not on the rota himself. When she is sunk in despair at her depletions, he insists she goes back to work as an actress, although she has terrible trouble remembering lines and walks with a limp. Somehow, the children become his, and she becomes a depressed and depressing presence to them. Friends felt uneasy at the controlling zeal he displayed, and remarked on his lack of simple kindness to his wife.

But Dahl was a good and attentive father, claims Treglown, with relief you feel at having found some quality to admire in his subject. Even so, this potentially benign quirk is tempered by the adult lives of his daughters, which according to their own stories have been blighted with addiction to drugs, drink and self-destructive neurosis. They speak of him still as god-like and powerful and cast around, apparently, for men who can live up to their fantasies of him. But there is a moment when he becomes human, and Treglown wrenches something moving from his subject. He quotes Tessa Dahl explaining: 'Daddy got so caught up in *making things better*. He used to say: "You've got to get on with it" . . . He used to shout, "I want my children to be brave."' There's a note of despair and a touch of courage about this which gives Dahl a shade more substance.

The writing career was curiously sporadic and sparse for one of the world's best-selling authors. There were no adult novels, except for a very early effort he later disowned, and even after the first volume of short stories, *Someone Like You*, he was struggling to come up with ideas to fill the next book, telling Alfred Knopf he feared running out altogether. The *New Yorker* and the BBC turned down more short stories than they printed or broadcast, and for a long time British publishers resisted the charms of his children's writing, which he turned to in the early Sixties after the adult fiction seemed to have dried up. Those stories for adults are clever, cruel and sometimes satisfying in the same way, I imagine, that George poisoning his grandmother is to children. But they are, as Treglown points out, stories that can be extracted from their writing and told, all of them, like bar-room jokes. More than anything they are like those urban myths that go around, which have ghostly hitchhikers stopping a friend of a friend on a dark country road. They are indeed *tales*, which lose their capacity to shock in their desire to do little more than just that.

The publishing history is hilarious, and happy young Dahl readers should not be told that their favourite books (*Charlie*, *The Witches*, *Fantastic Mr Fox*, *The BFG*) were almost entirely replotted and sometimes rewritten by his various editors, who sweated over his first drafts until such time as his imperious vanity was no longer tolerable. Robert Gottlieb of Knopf finally had to invoke his 'Fuck-You Principle', which held that he'd put up with difficult authors only until he could take no more, and then, business or no business, fuck them. The final straw for Gottlieb was an offensive stream of letters from Dahl in England, announcing he was running out of pencils. They were to get him six dozen Dixon Ticonderoga 1388 – 2–5/10 (Medium) and send them airmail. Unable to find the essential pencils, they sent the best they could find, but received a diatribe. Gottlieb cracked. 'In brief, and as unemotionally as I can state it . . . you have behaved to us in a way I can honestly say is unmatched in my experience for overbearingness and utter lack of civility . . . unless you start acting civilly to us, there is no possibility of our agreeing to continue to publish you.' Apparently, everyone at Knopf stood on their desks and cheered as the letter went off.

Brimstone
and Treacle

> *Fight & Kick & Bite:*
> *The Life and Work of Dennis Potter*
> by W. Stephen Gilbert
> (HODDER, LONDON, 1995)
>
> *Dennis Potter: A Life on Screen*
> by John Cook
> (MANCHESTER UNIVERSITY PRESS, MANCHESTER, 1995)

The death of Dennis Potter may have been authored by God, but it was adapted for television by Potter himself. It began after a brief report in the *Guardian* suggested that Potter's terminal cancer related to his lifelong addiction to nicotine. By return there was a gleeful letter from Potter revelling in the Potteresque fact that far from his 'beloved cigarettes' being the culprits, his forthcoming death from pancreatic cancer was probably iatrogenic: the result of years of lethal medication. The *Guardian* letter assumed its readers knew that he had suffered all his adult life from psoriatic arthropathy, which, of course, they did. But tellingly, so did the readers of the *Sun* and the *News of the World*, who were more familiar with Potter as the 'Dirty Drama King' and 'Television's Mr Filth'. Very few playwrights have had this kind of reach, and none has put it to such dramatic and manipulative use as Dennis Potter in his leavetaking broadcast to the nation. Though Potter was a Methodist, it was a final performance worthy of the archetypal Yiddisher momma having her guilt-laying, emotional-blackmailing finest hour. He may, as a lad, have gone three times every Sunday to a chapel called Salem, but it's not for nothing that one of his plays was entitled *Schmoedipus* – as in the old Jewish joke, 'Oedipus, schmoedipus, what does it matter so long as he loves his mother?'

Nobody was fooled, but everyone loved it and cheered Potter to the end, as he swigged morphine from a hip flask, forced BBC's Yentob and Channel 4's Grade into a graveside wedding, introduced his lethal tumour as 'Rupert' (after Murdoch), and kept the nation engrossed with a will he/won't he finish his final play before death overcomes him cliffhanger. It was a *tour de force* in which he didn't fail to include a Dostoevskian eulogy to the nowness of now and the blossomest of blossom, and even managed to gain the disapproval of his old primary-school teacher who, according to Stephen Gilbert, admired his final interview but was not pleased when 'he said "God the old bugger" . . . I didn't like that.' It was such a successful finale that I still expect the credits to roll and Potter to pop up again to instruct us not to assume that what a writer says is simple autobiography.

If you've got to have self-referential fiction, you might as well have it in the form of Dennis Potter announcing his death on his chosen medium and going on to describe his imminent posthumous work about the dissemination of a dead writer's memories via a TV hook-up between pickled brain and screen. It gets the whole recursive tangle – creation, authorship, death and readership – wrapped up in one neat package so intricately knotted that we can pick it up, feel its weight and then chuck it in the back of the drawer where it belongs. We might judge the final episode of *Cold Lazarus* an appropriate moment to draw a line under self-referential fiction, raise our glasses to Dennis Potter for providing a good deal of entertaining mischief and move on – not, I think, back – to the not, after all, so innocent view of fiction in the days before the intrusion of the authorial voice became a blinding authorial vice.

Potter himself was, in some moments, of this opinion. 'One of the reasons I chose to write "drama" rather than prose fiction is precisely to avoid the question which has so damaged, or intellectually denuded, the contemporary novel: *Who is saying this?*' But being a Godlike Author, and therefore an inconsistent old bugger, he then went on to poke his authorial voice into every crack and cranny of his novels and plays so as to provide them with the intellectual finery he feared was missing from television drama. The me/not me card is a joker in any writer's pack, fun to play and providing just the right degree of equivocation for someone like Potter who claimed reclusiveness while being the most publicly visible of authors. He played the identity card for considerably more than it is worth. Writers who are not self-obsessed and wriggling through what they hope are their own labyrinthine psyches are very likely not writers at all, and the torpefying quest of the public and critics for simple autobiography deserves the run-around it gets. The trouble is that the side-issue of autobiography can become a dead end for the writer as well as the reader.

The 'Who authored this?' question is probably one that should be asked only once in the history of literature, then shelved. Sterne pretty well took care of the issue with *Tristram Shandy*, since when it has become the clunkiest way of expressing the central doubt of human experience. It begins to look like an insult to the intelligence of an audience, who, having, as Potter scoffed in a *New Society* article, 'solved the equations between the writer, the writing and

the world . . . simply by taking them for granted' may be
waiting for the author to provide something more than a
lesson in how to suck eggs. Stephen Gilbert and John Cook
(along with just about everyone else) would agree that Potter
reached his reflexive nadir with *Blackeyes*, in which the story
of the eponymous model based on the central character,
Jessica, is related as a novel authored by Jessica's uncle, but
rewritten by Jessica, both of whom, in the third episode,
turn out to have been authored by a journalist called Jeff,
who turns out himself, in the final scene, to have been the
invented creature of a writer who is none other than 'Dennis
Potter'. Cook makes the interesting point that the audience,
who had stayed with quite intricate Potter works such as
Pennies from Heaven and *The Singing Detective*, showed
its feelings about the authorial revelations by falling from a
record seven million for episode one, to five million for
episodes two and three, to 3.8 million for episode four. This
means that 3.2 million people never discovered that 'Dennis
Potter' was the author of it all, but perhaps they are the 3.2
million who felt it was sufficient to know that Dennis Potter
without the quotation marks wrote the piece and made a
quality decision to do something else with their time.
According to Richard Loncraine, who directed *Blade on the
Feather*, Potter 'got lazy and recycled the same ideas too
many times. I think he looked down on his audience, he
thought the world was full of arseholes and he patronised
them.'

Still, Cook finds Potter's self-revelation enthralling, using
it to trace a unifying theme throughout his work, but he
does not do Potter much of a service in failing to perceive the
poverty of what became by the end little more than a device.
Find-the-Potter is an arid game to play over an entire writing
career, and one that may have clouded rather than illumi-
nated the substance of his work. Cook is a media studies
lecturer and his study of Potter began life as a doctoral

thesis. Potter, with his commitment to television drama, is a gift to media studies, one of television's very few intellectually respectable gifts. For Cook, the fact that his death was covered by national TV news, obituaries in both broadsheet and tabloid press, and 'even a tribute from the then Heritage Secretary Peter Brooke MP' was 'final proof and vindication that Potter as television writer had been successful in his aim of trying to cut across the lines in British society. Through television, his writing and ideas had reached out to a far greater range of people, communicating with them and touching their lives to a far greater extent than if he had been a figure predominantly of the theatre or of literature.' With Potter, television comes of age and provides reputable material for academic study. Good heavens, the man even deconstructed his own work.

However, considering the tabloid media's attitude and, indeed, the response of 'the people', it's doubtful whether the televising of Potter's work touched the generality of lives he hoped to touch. Gilbert, denied access to the estate by Potter's children, managed to get an interview with his mother, now in her eighties, and sister June, who still live in the Forest of Dean. 'The foresters,' according to June, 'didn't like his plays very much. They didn't understand them. We didn't either, let's be honest.' Potter necessarily left the forest early in his life and he may have forgotten, as people do, how powerful are the constraints of society beyond the boundaries of Oxford and the BBC. Leaving the narrow locale of childhood we're inclined to think we've landed in the big wide world, but usually, we've got it the wrong way round.

A local man told Gilbert that 'he must have had horrible, nasty things in his head'. They were often and agonisingly all over his body too. His psoriasis was hereditary but its frequency and extent were, he acknowledged, related to stress and anxiety. He shared affliction with Job, but the degree to which it was self-inflicted was more Freud than God-given. The physical pain and crippling effects had their psychic shadow in increasingly insistent suggestions of sexual abuse and guilt. A ten-year-old child, sexually interfered with or disturbed in the forest, became a motif, beginning with his description in his 1972 novel *Hide and Seek* of a man with 'eyes that later always seemed to be the colour of phlegm'. Potter spoke of this to Cook in an interview: 'I was . . . sexually assaulted when I was ten years of age . . . People endure what they endure and they deal with it. It may corrupt them. It may lead them to all sorts of compensatory excesses in order to escape the nightmare, the memory of that.' If this sounds like a summation of Potter's themes – abuse, guilt, corruption, excess – he is at pains to obscure any such simplicity. 'It's important but it's not *that* important' because still 'you're left with your basic human striving and dignity.' The having it both ways was essential Potter.

In *Stand Up Nigel Barton* the hero confesses to a public meeting that he has slept with 136 prostitutes; in the novel *Hide and Seek* the number of these encounters rises to 156. As Gilbert says, 'Potter sought to create very bad persons – bad men, of course – who yet repent perfectly.' They have the capacity to repent perfectly because their 'crimes' are invariably the outcome of crimes committed on them, they are twisted out of shape by a world beyond their childhood control. The bad men are to be forgiven because of their capacity to suffer for their misdeeds, and because these misdeeds are essentially no fault of theirs. This is a good enough description of the effects of the Biblical Fall to explain Potter's use of women. His characters' guilt about their adultery is a consequence of the fact that they choose to use prostitutes – the prostitutes are a given, available either to utilise or turn down. The good man passes by, the bad man employs them and then pays again with a searing of his flesh and conscience. The whore simply is.

Potter's view of women in his fiction as whores or frustrated and frustrating housewives caused considerable complaint from his feminist critics. His depiction of the depth of his ambivalence (a man's ambivalence) to women had the virtue of transparency, of showing how each sex, like each individual, must implicate and accuse the other in order to find itself essentially good – though whether that was Potter's intention is less clear. Potter's fantasies about women were unoriginal: if they were sexual they were punished, dying nastily at their own or the protagonist's hand; if they were virtuous they were usually responsible for the murderous rage of their partner.

Potter described in detail the scabs on his skin and in his mind, but he was interested in more than that, and Cook's vindication of his use of women as whores or angels deserves the contempt even Potter, I think, would have had for it. 'It is important to note that such a dichotomy is simply a function of the much wider schism between "flesh" and "spirit" which . . . runs right through Potter's work and which "tears" at many of his male protagonists. Moreover . . . notions of "whore" versus "angel" are also simply "conventional stereotypes", embedded deep within our culture. They are, in fact, Western society's traditional way of looking at women.' Well, that's all right then. Though I had thought that art was supposed to do something with stereotypes beyond reproducing them for our further perusal. Cook concurs with Potter's excuse for what seemed like the irredeemable salaciousness of *Blackeyes* by telling us he was 'investigating the nature of patriarchy itself' and how in '*Blackeyes*, it is the female not the male characters who are emphasised as the "suffering martyrs" of patriarchy'. If that's what Potter thought he was up to in the serial, and he did say something very similar, then not only his dramatic skills, but his intellectual honesty were gravely in question. As an example of Potter's empathy with women, Cook reminds us of the moment when Blackeyes/Jessica 'cries to heaven: "Jesus, why weren't you a woman?"' I remember it well: it was the moment when I lost all control of my derision centres and fell off the sofa laughing.

Stephen Gilbert's critical biography is rather more stylish and far less deferential than Cook's. He acknowledges Potter's blankness about half the population, and does not pretend that archetypal symbolism can account for it. He quotes Gareth Davies, who directed several early Potter plays: 'All these women you write,' Davies, said to him, 'they're always somebody's mother or somebody's wife or somebody's mistress, that's all they're there for, to serve some sort of male.' 'That's right,' Potter replied. 'All my own fantasies . . . Boring characters . . . they don't *work*. I find them rather dull.' It was Nancy Banks-Smith, in a review of *Stand Up Nigel Barton*, who, according to Gilbert, put her finger on the flaw which 'would run right through Potter's work: "The women were weird. The witch, a bitch and a fool. The schoolmistress was a nightmare to frighten little children with. The girlfriend a tart on tranquillisers."'

Gilbert traces much the same thematic development in Potter's works as Cook finds. Potter's concerns were those of his time and place: the new fluidity of social class in his youth, the desire to bring art to the masses, the foregrounding of sexuality as a key to discontent, the loss of faith and certainty in what seemed like iconoclastic times and an attempt to reclaim a God of some sort as life proceeded. The threads linked and were transformed over time into a personal mythology. Guilt and frustration were the major themes that emerged as he made his way from rural innocence to a self-conscious post-war world. He was well placed to make his subject the Fall.

Potter had a good enough brain to eject him out of his class and society, into Oxford and the BBC, at a time when the effects of separation from one's background were under scrutiny by the sociologists, and Richard Hoggart was affirming in *The Uses of Literacy* that a young man like Potter is 'cut off by his parents as much as by his talent which urges him to break away from his group'. Alienation was all the rage and Potter took on the role of outsider on the inside with relish. At Oxford he was a working-class radical, while at the BBC he made a half-cooked documentary about his estrangement from his family ('even at home with my own parents I felt a shame-faced irritation with the tempo of a pickle-jar style of living') which to his astonishment caused considerable resentment among his family and neighbours. His shame at the headline 'Miner's Son at Oxford Ashamed of Home. The Boy Who Kept His Father Secret' made his Oedipal treachery clear to him and fed his drama for decades.

The ideas were large and juicy – God and the Devil, guilt and innocence, betrayal and redemption, the provocative outsider, childhood as a lost landscape – but very often by the end of one of Potter's plays there was a feeling of disappointment, of the drama not having made the most of the ideas. Potter himself said in later years that *Son of Man* was evasive. By dramatising Christ as a political hero and excising all reference to the Resurrection and the transcendental intention of the Gospels, he simply sidestepped the area that poses the main obstacle for agnostics. Much of what he wrote took a single, rather abstract notion and developed it thinly to the exclusion of difficulty. Plays that look complex are often too neatly dialectical. It makes it easy for Cook to render them down to their bare bones. To Cook, *The Singing Detective* marks the apotheosis of Potter's theme, as Marlow, the embittered sick man (and writer), creates an alter ego to investigate an intolerable moment in his past which split him between spirit and flesh. The re-integration comes when his creature, the detective Marlow, kills off his creator, the

defective Marlow. It is, says Cook, a religious play about
redemption, which suggests that Potter's reclaimed religion
was little more than the notion of a healed psyche, with a
popularised Freud as the Messiah.

The Singing Detective used wit and humanity in its hospital scenes and memories of childhood. The
transcendental-dressed-as-pulp-detective sections were the
least successful, looking far too much like a nervous search
for profundity. The sense of a truthful story burdened with a
less than interesting mystery was common with Potter. When
he allowed himself to work in a more direct way, trusting his
material, the results were much more effective. *Blue
Remembered Hills* was about the line that children walk
between play and persecution. The story was uncluttered
and chronological. *Joe's Ark* followed with close attention
the rage and sadness of a man whose young daughter was
dying. *Where Adam Stood* took a chapter from Edmund
Gosse's *Father and Son* and dramatised the moment when
the boy gains the strength to challenge the blindness and
bigotry of his father. None of them required complex sub-
plots, actors talking direct to camera, or even miming to
evocative old songs.

Which is not to say that Potter shouldn't have innovated
(using adult actors for the children in *Blue Remembered
Hills* worked for the play), but that he became too caught up
in the innovation. The evocative old songs certainly did their
bit in the early episodes of *Pennies from Heaven*, but as
Gilbert points out, the script is 'overwritten, overlong, repet-
itive and undisciplined', and more and more songs were
used, as the narrative drive fell away, until every time the
band struck up it came to seem like panic. The device was
cunning because the music is so seductive, but sometimes it
induced foot-tapping at the expense of the drama. It became
a Potter trademark, and writers like Potter shouldn't need
trademarks.

The group of people who produced and wrote *The Wednesday Play* and *Play for Today* in the late Sixties and Seventies were men (almost exclusively) with a calling to make television into a catalyst for social debate. They were prelapsarian liberals and socialists from a variety of backgrounds who saw the potential of television as a dynamic tool for widening education and culture, a force for the good, which might use the excitement of art to unify a rigidly stratified nation. The BBC bureaucrats, for their part, looked on the likes of Potter and David Mercer, Peter Nichols and David Rudkin as the means of fulfilling their commitment to public service broadcasting, which, of necessity included 'the arts'. Somewhere in between, the executive producer Sydney Newman, the playwright Troy Kennedy Martin, the producer Kenith Trodd, the script editor Roger Smith and others, had thoughts about creating a new form of drama, not dependent on theatrical traditions, but written and directed for the strengths of the television studio. While Potter's early *Nigel Barton* plays criticised the poverty of political life and Ken Loach's *Cathy Come Home* created a social services scandal, everyone could feel that television was a power for the general good. The pressure was not, then, to maximise viewers, but to produce enough thought-provoking programmes between *Double Your Money* and *Juke Box Jury* to allow Lord Reith to sleep easy in his bed. Reithian sensitivity, however, worked both ways: thought-provoking was one thing, but tasteless, anti-religious, sex-obsessed stuff was quite another. What are fondly remembered as the golden days of TV drama lasted only until it was discovered by Reith's successors that some things were not for broadcasting to the masses. With *Brimstone and Treacle* Potter found the edge of television liberalism. Alasdair Milne, Director of Programmes, viewed it at the last minute and pulled it from the schedules. The play centred on the brain-damaged daughter of a family shrouded in guilt who makes a miraculous recovery when raped by a passing devil. It was, Milne wrote to Potter, 'brilliantly written and made, but nauseating. I believe that it is right in certain instances to outrage the viewers in order to get over a point of serious importance, but I am afraid that I believe in this case real outrage would be widely felt and that no such point would get across.'

Potter threw himself into battle, making his commitment to radical television drama clear, where others made their way into the theatre or films. He made television his cause and was prepared to make a fuss about it, and much credit goes to him for doing that. Staying with it, he wrote what he felt he needed to write and made innovation part of his crusade. But still it was only possible because the ratings war hadn't hotted up to the point where a small audience for a drama series – even on the BBC – would mean its cancellation and the likely sacking of those who commissioned it. According to Gilbert what the BBC Drama Department under Sydney Newman offered its authors was above all 'the right to fail'. That right has now been rescinded. But it has to be said that, uniquely, television's commitment to Potter was at least as strong as Potter's devotion to it. Potter was allowed to fail frequently and was always recommissioned. After *Blackeyes* died the death, Channel 4 financed *Lipstick on Your Collar*, and although that was received with less than a tumult, the BBC commissioned *Midnight Movie* and *Karaoke*. For all Potter's complaints, many of his contemporaries who went into the theatre, such as Peter Nichols and Alun Owen, languished, while his work went on and will go on being produced and performed.

Oh, the Burden,
the Anxiety,
the Sacrifices

> *Anaïs Nin*
> by Deirdre Bair
> (BLOOMSBURY, LONDON, 1995)
>
> *Conversations with Anaïs Nin*
> edited by Wendy Dubow
> (MISSISSIPPI, JACKSON, 1994)

Although it's counter-intuitive, neither sex nor the pursuit of self were inventions of the 20th century. In his snatch of *vérité* during the film *Reds*, Henry Miller hazarded the view that people have always done a lot of fucking. Montaigne settled to his solitary task of reflective self-examination in the mid-16th century. Sex and the self as subjects for investigation share the characteristic of always making their examiners feel like pioneers in uncharted territory. Either because of this, or because what there is to know is naturally limited, the data don't so much accrete over time as repeat themselves.

It could be said that in this century the invention of psychoanalysis has changed the study of sex and of self by providing a structure in which the two can combine (in the

manner of DNA, as it were) to produce a boundless variety
of understandings. Or it may be that psychoanalysis has
merely provided us with an excuse to remain stuck in the
revolving door of self-absorption. According to Deirdre Bair,
'sex, the self and psychoanalysis' are three of the concepts
that have brought 'sweeping societal change' to our century.
She doesn't say whether we should rejoice over this, or
wonder in dismay if solipsism hasn't become the plughole
down which this century will gurgle. It is, however, her
reason for choosing Anaïs Nin as her third biographical subject, after Simone de Beauvoir and Samuel Beckett.

Bair is not making a case for re-evaluating Nin's fiction.
Her claim is that although Nin was 'not an original thinker'
and a 'minor writer whose novels are seldom read these
days', she nonetheless merits a substantial biography because
a life as 'rich and full' as hers enables 'the rest of us to understand the chaotic century that is now winding down'. This
argument might apply to any number of individuals whether
disregarded novelists or not, but very few were so compulsive in their anatomising of self as to leave, as Nin did,
250,000 hand-written pages of diary for a biographer to
trawl through.

What does the notion of a rich and full life spanning the
years from 1903 to 1977 conjure up? Being at the centre of
great political and economic movements? Witnessing two
of the most cataclysmic wars in history? Synthesising the
experience of these into illuminating work? This isn't Nin's
way. Wars, economic collapse, holocaust and revolution
barely rate a mention in the quarter-million pages of her
diary. The world is outside her remit. Nin's universe, like her
fiction, terminates at the boundaries of her own skin, like
nerve-endings; the outside environment exists only where it
stimulates or articulates her private sense of identity. The
rich and full life that merits our study is the daily emotional
and sexual life-story of an ego, self-consciously honing itself

to represent interiority as the discovery of the age. As an adolescent, Nin was writing in her diary that school was a waste of time: 'I learn things that I don't want to learn, and sometimes I am afraid of losing entirely the delicate and exquisite mental picture that I have of the beauty of things around me.' Which is as it should be at such an age. The problem is that the tone of the diary doesn't alter over the decades. The world never develops beyond its function as a mirror for her own exquisite and distorted mental processes.

Nin's vivid life consisted largely of having affairs, in Paris and New York, with notable people and of recounting them in exhaustive detail in her diaries; or as a student put it to Deirdre Bair, 'Nin had a lot of sex and lied a lot.' If Henry Miller was her most famous paramour, there were also encounters with Otto Rank, Antonin Artaud, Norman Bel Geddes ('the P.T. Barnum of design'), George Barker and innumerable sub-luminaries of the literary world. Like Miller, many of them were supported financially by Nin, or more accurately, by her besotted husband Hugo, who on marrying Anaïs had the great good sense to become a banker rather than the poet he had hoped to be. Even with a sub-stantial salary, Hugo was unable to keep up his wife's payouts without eventually falling into massive debt. This translates at the height of Nin's popularity in 1969 to the fol-lowing description in the *Boston Globe*: 'Although poor herself, and living on a pittance, she supported materially and emotionally a whole extended family of down-and-out artists, musicians, writers and revolutionaries, some geniuses, others sponging wastrels.' Nin had a somewhat unreconstructed notion (considering that she became a hero-ine of the early feminists) that it was a woman's role to provide support for creative men, but at the same time understood very well the power of the purse strings. When Miller briefly found himself earning money as an analyst in New York he resisted returning to Paris as Nin wanted him to; but according to Bair, 'Henry's fear of losing Anaïs's steady stipend proved stronger than his confidence about supporting himself,' and he sailed back to Europe.

Seduction was victory. In 1933, her first analyst, René Allendy, one of the founders of the Société Psychanalytique de Paris, was moved by her graphic descriptions of sex with Miller to provide her in their next session with a diaphragm. She returned it, used though clean, a week later. He was soon enough her lover, however, and she was able to confide to her diary that his body was 'white and flabby'; and she was obliged to fake an orgasm. 'Laugh it off,' she wrote. 'Conquer it. Make the man happy. That is all. A gift. I make a gift in return for the tribute of his love. And I feel free of debts. I walk joyously away, debtless, independent, uncaptured.'

All the while, her husband paid up, and until her death, suffered what was doubtless a delicious agony. Hugo was devastated on discovering her first infidelity ('Today I died') but soon found a way to live with it. '*She is the definition of art*. Therefore, she cannot make mistakes. Whatever she does with that instinct burning in her is right, becomes right, for it is she who does it.'

The first love is always self-love and the first offence is always against the omnipotent 'I'. We may never quite forgive or forget the wounding, but as a rule, we dust ourselves off and try to find a way to rub along with the world. It's a practical matter. Though we always know, secretly, that we are all and everything, the dead centre of the only circle, we learn to keep it more or less to ourselves. That way we make a living and avoid excessive loneliness. An alternative, if the initial wounding is very great (and in Nin's case it was), is to turn inwards towards what we might call madness. What makes Nin's life exceptional is that she contrived to turn in on herself but also to find abundant support (or collusion) in the world around her. Reality, for some reason that never becomes quite clear, keeps turning itself around and con-forming to her vision of the universe in a manner that seems outrageous to anyone familiar with the way personal narratives are supposed to turn out. We all know, don't we, that a life committed to self-indulgence, uncontrolled sexual adventuring and deceit will come to a thoroughly bad end – the flesh will rot, the mind will curdle, the world will pass by in contempt as you suffer a terrible retribution of social isolation and a dismal death. But Nin's story, although all the factors for ultimate disaster are present throughout her life, keeps coming out wrong – or rather, right – in the most improbable way. Though she must have been one of the most self-centred women who ever lived, she was adored and remained adored for a lifetime by her husband, and at the end both by her husband and her final lover.

The initial cause of her involution is clear enough. Nin's father, Joaquin, was a talented pianist, handsome and considerably younger than his wife, whom he married in Cuba for her inheritance. That he beat her and his three children is confirmed by the surviving youngest son, Joaquin Nin-Culmell. The confirmation is necessary because Nin's capacity to fudge reality is monumental. Anaïs's recollection at the age of 17, 'I would do anything to keep him from lifting my dress and beating me,' is embellished thirty years later: 'He begins to hit me with the palm of his hand . . . But he stops hitting me and caresses me. Then he sticks his penis into me, pretending to be beating me. Oh, I enjoy it. I have a violent orgasm.' But the passage continues: 'I believe this really happened. I do not believe my father penetrated me sexually but I believe he caressed me while or instead of beating me.' Building an accurate biography out of Nin's material must have been like trying to make the Taj Mahal out of mercury.

Her father stopped beating the children when Anaïs was ten or 11, but substituted photography, making them stand naked in the midst of dressing or bathing while he focused and changed lenses. Then he abandoned the family, staying in touch only with Anaïs in letters filled with his successes as a lover and pianist, telling her that everyone loved him and therefore she should too. Which, of course, she did. In a note Bair explains, a touch unnecessarily, that the psycho-analytic term for Joaquin's behaviour is 'the seductive father'.

Added to the burden of the sadistic, seductive father, was a near-fatal illness at the age of nine during which her mother prayed to Sainte Thérèse of Lisieux, and her father expressed real distress. Her unexpected recovery gave not only her mother, but Anaïs herself, the impression that a miracle had occurred. It's probably quite bad for people to believe themselves saved; living up to the implied promise of a destiny may be too great a load to allow them ever to be satisfied with everyday reality.

The diary began when Anaïs was 11, on the boat to New York, where Rosa took her abandoned family. The first entry in the notebook her mother bought for her was an unsent letter to her father. Later she would define the nature of the diary (which others refer to as 'the liary') and of the conduct of her life more accurately. Her untruths were 'mensonges vital': 'different kinds of lies, the special lies which I tell for very specific reasons – to improve on living'. The truth, she concluded, was 'not always creative' or 'more right than untruth'. But even the view of her diary as a life-improver is confounded as she recollects times when she had deliber-ately not done certain things so she would not have to face 'the shame of writing them down'.

It's doubtful, however, that shame played much part in determining the actions of her life. If the unconscious, as defined by Freud, is the mechanism by which we hide our darkest, most shamefully unsocialised desires from our-selves, then it's entirely likely that Anaïs Nin didn't have one. Quite apart from the extreme doubts that arise about any therapeutic technique which allowed both Henry Miller and Anaïs Nin to become, however briefly, practitioners with patients, Nin's conscious life surely provides a convincing argument against the central tenets of psychoanalytic theory. There doesn't seem a lot of point in you and me spending 20 years on the couch coming to terms with the intolerable fact that we want to do it with our fathers, when Nin, aged 30, is writing in her diary after a summer of incest with her father: 'I love him . . . love him . . . I want nothing else, nobody else. He fills my life, my thoughts, my blood.' She 'wants to die with joy' at their affair. Just before Joaquin makes her nipples hard and inserts his finger in her vagina, Nin has her father cry out: 'Bring Freud here, and all the psychologists. What could they say about this?' Not much, I suspect. At the time she was sleeping with her analyst Allendy, her protégé Henry Miller, her eternally devoted husband Hugo Guiler and trying very hard to seduce Antonin Artaud, though he was a confirmed homosexual. It's not just her conscious that leaves you gasping: so does her stamina. Still, it is not without problems: 'It is getting more and more difficult to make four men happy,' she moans. 'Oh, the burden, the anxiety, the sacrifices, the gifts I must give!'

Nor did she utilise what unconscious she may have had to restrain herself from confronting other dubious motivations. Her pleasures sunbathed fully naked on the surface of her awareness. She seduced Otto Rank in New York in 1935, when he was analysing her and preparing her to receive patients herself. She had no real interest in any of it, admitting to a friend that she liked watching Rank 'undermining the psychoanalysis from which he lives. I would not mind doing him harm.' When the friend suggested that if she couldn't have God she might as well have all the analysts, she replied 'I don't give myself to them. I keep myself.'

Though it very nearly doesn't matter whether the affair with her father actually happened or not, Bair does bear the liary in mind, qualifying the description of the incestuous 'non-stop orgiastic frenzy' with 'if Anaïs Nin the diarist is to be believed'. And she certainly doubts Nin's later account of a two-day shipboard affair with her middle brother Thorvald. It only gets a single diary mention, which makes Bair wonder: 'Did it happen at all?' Was it, she asks, a '"screen memory" for something else so deeply hidden that she was never able to pull it into her consciousness long enough to write about it?' The brain aches with the attempt to imagine what that unadmittable something else might be. If there was anything more that was possible to think, there's no doubt Nin would have thought it and written it up.

Then she would have rewritten it – because the diaries were artefacts she reworked over the years. The untruths she told herself as a diarist were not quite the same as the lies that she believed might turn fiction into something more truthful. She makes the sculptor Lenore Tawney incoherently say: 'You are a great artist, Anaïs, for you I would give you my work in exchange for what your books meant to me.' Years later, on reading this, Tawney claims not to have known Nin was a writer until she turned up at her studio. 'Anaïs paid me too many compliments. I didn't like them.' And Bair doubts that an evening spent arguing the literary toss with Lawrence Durrell and Henry Miller in fact ended with both men saying: 'We have a real woman artist before us, the first one and we ought to bow down instead of trying to make a monster out of her.'

These are lies that 'improve the reality' and 'make the dream real', but they are not the kind of lies that improve and nurture lasting fiction. Most of those who knew her believed the diaries themselves prevented her from becoming what she most wanted to be – a creative writer. 'The "I" has become a terrible habit,' she confesses. 'I note everything down. Why, why can't I write a novel, objective, with all my inventions? It is such a round-about method [to] write a diary which I will have to transform later into a novel.' Husband Hugo, Miller, Otto Rank, all believed she had to stop writing the diary. In 1934, at Rank's insistence, she tried to cold-turkey from it by checking into a hotel without her diary and favourite pen, but she only lasted a few hours before cadging pencil and paper from the manager and writing what Bair describes as 'a series of feverish notes'. The fictions she finally achieved were largely obsessive reworkings of diary material whose doubled unreality creates characters who seem to hover several feet above the ground. The diary became the only landscape Nin needed to express herself so that when she comes to writing fiction it has no world in which to exist. Having designated her own interiority as the central subject, she fails to find an environment on which the achings of the soul might act.

In an interview with Judy Chicago in 1971 Nin asserts that women 'are speaking for the first time'. 'What this suggests,' says Chicago, 'is that women will lead the way into a kind of outpouring of the spirit and the soul.' 'Yes,' agrees Nin. 'They will lead the way in a fusion of them.' If a fusion of outpourings is what you're after in fiction, then Nin's the writer for you. If not, you may find, like me, that the inescapable hyper-sensitivity of *Cities of the Interior* has you wandering around the house every 20 pages or so, looking for a dirty teacup to wash up or a neglected saucepan to scour.

At the age of 44, in 1947, she met the 28-year-old Rupert Pole, who was to become one half of the double life she would lead until her death. Gradually, the other lovers fell away or transformed into gay acolytes, and Nin set up two independent households, one with Hugo in New York, the other with Rupert in California. Neither man knew, or was prepared to know, that she spent half the year with the other.

Although Hugo financially supported Rupert, he chose to believe that Nin retired for the summer to a spiritual ranch for a dose of solitude. Rupert, receiving an income which enabled him to build a house for himself and Anaïs, was prepared to accept her story that she and Hugo lived entirely separately in New York embroiled in a complicated divorce. When Rupert finally phoned Hugo in the middle of the night and Nin answered the phone, she palmed him off with a lie. In 1955 she told Rupert that the imaginary divorce had at last gone through, and married him. She had felt 'so deeply married to Rupert so many times' over the past eight years that the illegal ceremony was merely another such moment.

The great frustration of her life eventually came right: the novels and finally the diaries were published, and along with keeping her two love lives going, Nin also began to conduct a literary life. Her novels and diaries found an admiring young audience in the university campuses of the Sixties and early Seventies. The cause of her fame was as duplicitous as the rest of her existence. Many saw her as a proto-feminist, as having lead the life of a free, sexual woman, a pioneer of the new spirit of independence. But she never was exactly that. When asked at Smith College about the feminist nature of her writings, she replied that her aim was to give the world 'one perfect life', meaning her own. The more radical students hooted and hissed. An article in *Village Voice* a year later described how Nin 'showed her nipples and the rest of her beautiful shape through a clinging silver dress, held a mask in front of her face, lowered it, and began to read from her diaries'. Time and admiration were running out for 'a woman who . . . seeks to be feminist . . . speaking primarily on the thinkings and doings of men'. But she won the race and death came before disregard.

Between 1974 and early 1977 when she died, Nin kept a journal of her cancer. It was painful and physically humiliating, but Rupert Pole remained her devoted lover and carer. She was aware, in spite of the awfulness of the disease, how fortunate she was, 'grateful, grateful to have attained a great love, and gained love for my work'. According to Bair, Rupert nursed her through the ravages of surgery and chemotherapy, bought her wigs, changed her colostomy bags, 'raised and lowered her into the swimming pool each day, and even made love to her there so that she would not dwell on the loss of her beauty'. When she confessed the truth about her continuing marriage to Hugo, Rupert 'understood the motivation for the double life' immediately and since she found it difficult, dialled Hugo's number for her so she could speak to him frequently. When she became too ill to speak, he phoned Hugo himself and reported on her condition.

Rupert Pole is 75 now and still devotes himself to Nin. He selects themed excerpts from her original journals and publishes them as separate volumes of 'unexpurgated diaries'. According to Bair, critics and scholars believe they present her in an unattractive light 'as a monstrous narcissist if not a pathological personality. But Rupert is unfazed by negative criticism and remains so devoted to the memory of Anaïs Nin that he usually speaks of her in the present tense.' Hugo Guiler died in 1985 aged 86, believing that the spirit of Nin visited him every morning and sat on the edge of his bed waiting to 'guide him over' when his time came. By the end of the biography it is hard to see in what way exactly the life of Anaïs Nin might assist us in understanding this 'chaotic century' as Deirdre Bair hoped it would, and you can't help feeling there's something that has not been explained, some missing element in the pathology that begins to account for the passionate affection such a 'monstrous narcissist' managed to accumulate.

Icons of
Perfect Light

The Illusory Game

Here's a game for the lengthening evenings. You are the Archangel Gabriel, halo gleaming, wings aflutter, with a less than angelic smile on your face. In front of you, all looking a bit down in the mouth, are the unborn souls of Michael Jackson, John Kennedy, Marilyn Monroe, John Lennon, Woody Allen, David Mellor and assorted graduates of the Betty Ford Clinic. 'Cheer up,' you tell them. 'It may never happen. That was just foretaste processing – a service we provide for prospective earthlings. Now you know how it's going to be, hands up who wants to be famous when you get down there.' Who goes through the door marked anonymity?

Try another angle: this time you're the soul who has to answer the question. If reason had anything to do with it, it would be preferable to sit in a barrel up to your neck in horse manure than to opt for fame. But it does seem that, a few brave souls like Thomas Pynchon excepted, given the merest sliver of a chance, we take the notoriety and run.

Statistically, being famous isn't good for people. At best it causes disappointment, at worst it makes them prematurely dead, mad, drunk, drugged, debunked or scandal-struck. It's hard to think of anyone really famous who has ever got clean

70   J e n n y   D i s k i

away with it – apart from those to whom nemesis hasn't happened yet.

The fantasy of fame originates as a way of consoling ourselves for the sense of isolation brought on by dawning self-consciousness. Children dream of being famous when they stand on the brink of discovering they are their own unique selves. They want that uniqueness to be registered, to make their mark. But the thrill of individuality is double-edged; the moment you recognise that you are only you, you also have to know that you are lonely you. Around the same time, children begin to get an inkling of death – not of their own (does anyone get that far?) but their parents'. One thing about parents, even the worst, is that, at least part of the time, you can count on being on their minds. When they've gone, who will keep you in mind? And if no one's keeping you in mind, how will you know you exist? What if you're only a figment of your imagination?

Well and good for children, the dreams and reassurance of fame, but once we've put away childish things, how come we still cling on to the idea of celebrity, as if it were the last floating splinter in a death-dealing sea?

Perhaps, if people you have never heard of have heard of you, it could make you feel a little more substantial. If you see your photograph in the newspaper over breakfast and it bears any resemblance to the face you saw in the bathroom mirror, you might have reasonable grounds for presuming that it wasn't just a ghostly apparition glaring back at you. It's the Tinkerbell syndrome: now, children, clap your hands three times and say 'I believe in fairies', and Tinkerbell will live to see another day. Every Christmas some imp of perversity (or solidarity with the ill-used Wendy), had me yearning for a resounding silence, but the noise was always deafening and Tinkerbell tinkled on.

Eventually, the truth about fame is inescapable: all the millions of people you don't know, don't know you either.

The you who's on their minds from time to time is nothing more than a construct of their imagination. Their thoughts of you are actually their own private thoughts; projections in the game they're playing with their own reality. Nothing to do with you. Blink twice, and this morning's reflection disappears into thin air. People aren't known by strangers, only what they do is known. Of course, grown-ups are satisfied to have their paintings, movies, books and discoveries appreciated, but I've never met any of those happy souls. When deconstructionist theory suggests the work has nothing to do with the individual who creates it, it confirms the suspicion we all have that what we do and how we are doesn't touch the us inside our own heads. They could have papered the walls of the Louvre with Van Gogh's canvases, but chances are he'd still only have had one ear when he shot himself. Monroe could have won the Nobel prize for acting and been promised eternally firm breasts, but she'd still never have made it to serene, grey-haired old ladydom. Fame doesn't work, it's an self-concealing itch – you never find out where to scratch.

Am I being unduly moralistic, or even a little romantic? There might be some egos so colossally narcissistic that none of these troubling thoughts ever alight, the Faustian deal they've struck might preclude rats of doubt gnawing away at their entrails. But the infrastructure of fame is the mass media, which has its own preordained rules and timetables. The regard of the interviewer, the glare of a flashbulb, the red light above the TV camera have a powerfully seductive intensity when they are pointing at you, but their brightness is neutral. It isn't love, it's wattage. They focus just as strongly on the next object of interest. Suddenly, the interviewer's back's to you and he's engrossed in someone else. When Grace Jones whacked Russell Harty, she struck a blow for every narcissist whose time was up.

The feeding frenzy of the chat show gave us another

warped angle on the search for stardom. Fame became a kind of consolation prize for the unfortunate and afflicted. Cancer patients (though only young ones) sat and chatted to Wogan to wild applause from the studio audience ('She's a very brave girl. Give her a big hand'), and millions suffered when a few weeks later the damp-eyed host announced their death, before moving on to beam on the latest star in town. Disaster survivors appeared so regularly I began to wonder if this wasn't some kind of trauma training against giving up when all seems lost: 'Keep your head above the water, auntie, if we get out of this alive we'll be on Wogan.'

Nobody's safe. Just when they think immortality (that's strangers thinking about you after you stop existing) is there for the taking, it's debunking time. It turns out the paintings, poetry and novels aren't as good as we'd thought – you're off the reading lists. Someone shouts 'child abuse', and you're dead; Pepsi doesn't want to know you any more, and no one's giving you the money to make the next sub-Bergman movie. Meanwhile, the rest of us shake our heads knowingly, because we're the smart souls who settled for obscurity.

Perfect Light

Diana: Her True Story
by Andrew Morton
(MICHAEL O'MARA, LONDON, 1992)

Shared Lives
by Lyndall Gordon
(BLOOMSBURY, LONDON, 1992)

Antonia White: Diaries 1958–1979
edited by Susan Chitty
(CONSTABLE, LONDON, 1992)

One of the mysteries of our time is the hunger we have to know details about the lives of people we have never met. Years ago, walking down Heath Street, I saw, at the bottom of the hill by the station, the most extraordinary glow in the air. I was still too far away to see what was causing the strange disturbance, but as I got closer the picture resolved itself into two figures encased in a golden shimmer, the light zinging around them. Naturally, I was thrilled to be getting my first authentic sighting of extraterrestrials – and in Hampstead, too. Sadly, my vision firmed up quite soon, as they and I got closer to each other, and I recognised the not-quite-extraterrestrial, dumpy, middle-aged forms of

Elizabeth Taylor and Richard Burton panting their way up the hill. The glow was not, of course, from their outward perfection, nor their inner beauty and wisdom, but the result of years and years of attention from precision-ground lenses and high-wattage lights being focused and shone at them. They had absorbed the energy, and like fully charged batteries, radiated it back.

This must account for some of our obsession with the lives of the famous. We invest energy in them and then mine them, as if they were natural resources, warming our chilly everyday selves with the glow we have created.

Imagine a world where, every time you turned on the television, you did not see an actor giving his recipe for world peace, before laying before us his deep emotional feelings (yes, I *know* that's tautologous) about fatherhood. Imagine a world in which one-third of every newspaper (I mean, of course, the quality press) was not devoted to in-depth interviews with dressmakers and novelists, so that you were not obliged to know their attitude to contraception and the wall-colouring technique of their favourite room. Difficult to imagine so many blank screens and empty pages, I know, but it's worth the effort to achieve the rush of serenity to the frontal lobes, where before there was only brain ache.

In a hundred years or so, I suspect that our time will be described, not as the age of Marx or Freud or Darwin (anyway, one has toppled, one's shaky on his pins, and the last hasn't got a chance in hell of surviving the Age of Aquarius), but as the age of the personality. 'Whatever that was,' they may well add.

For posterity, let me explain about personality. It might be supposed that in order to *be* one, an individual ought to *have* one. If this was true in the past (was it? Was drinking too much and killing big fish evidence that Hemingway was someone we needed to listen to?), the reverse is true now. Ideally, a personality should have no more to say than would take up ten minutes of *Wogan* or *Aspel* air time, they should wear the clothes of a handful of authorised designers (Armani, say, or Westwood), and they should be falling over themselves to reassure us that any past misdemeanours are regretted and, in any case, not nearly as exciting as we were led to believe. I'm thinking here particularly of a recent interview with Paul McCartney where he explained that when he and Mick smoked what he described charmingly as 'pot' together (after dinner, with a nice glass of wine apparently) all that happened was that they 'discussed art'. I remember '68, and let me assure you, he's right, that's *just* how it was.

So where, in the personality stakes, does this leave a 30-year-old woman with two kids, a minimum of education and no qualifications, trapped in a dead marriage to an absentee husband? Nowhere, of course, if she happens to live in a housing estate in Leeds: but right bang on top of the interview list if her old man happens to be the next king of England.

Early on in *Diana: Her True Story* (isn't that a nice title?), I find myself vindicated in my zinging light theory, by best friend Carolyn, who assures us: 'I'm not a terribly spiritual person but I do believe that she was meant to do what she is doing and she certainly believes that. She was surrounded by this golden aura which stopped men going any further, whether they would have liked to or not, it never happened. She was protected somehow by a perfect light.' And this before anything more momentous had happened to her than finding herself with Barbara Cartland as a step-grandmother. Diana, apparently, concurs with this: 'I knew I had to keep myself tidy for what lay ahead.'

This magical piece of gynaecological imagery makes Andrew Morton's book almost worth reading, but it might not be enough to make it worth buying. Diana is constantly quoted, the key phrase being, 'As Diana says . . .' But it is never clear to whom she is speaking, or even when. It gives

her a mythic quality. She exists like a genie in a bottle, whose
stopper is occasionally lifted, and lo, she speaks. Obviously,
she is not speaking to Morton; you can almost feel the pain
of the missing 'to me' at the end of the stock phrase.

There are a few other exciting moments, as when Morton
combines the sartorial with the mystical: 'The most obvious
outward sign of the inner development was her new shorter
hairstyle which signified the liberation she feels from her
past life.' Clearly, Morton has taken a leaf out of Diana's
own book and consulted a spirit medium who put him in
touch with Barthes for this insight. In fact, the suggested
spiral of her spiritual development is such that we might
shortly be privileged to see her (just before her canonisation
along with her pal, Mother Teresa) with an entirely shaved
head. I await the moment with quiet excitement.

Tempered steel is emerging from the nondescript little girl
whose marital suffering has made a woman of her. Once
praised merely for 'being, not for doing', she has decided to
allow the world to know all that she has to put up with.
Prince Charles is a cad – he walks away when she flings herself head-first down the stairs, he mocks her when he finds
her reading Jungian texts on death and holding the hands of
dying friends, he is petulant about her popularity with the
population. Worst of all is his persistent liaison with the sinister Camilla Parker-Bowles. (We are not told if this is a
sexual relationship, but no doubt the lady gives good-enough
Jung and Van der Post to satisfy the seeking Prince.) All this,
according to Morton, has made Diana increasingly her own
woman. With the help of astrologers and metaphysically
inclined masseurs she is carving a niche for herself in suc-
couring the halt and the lame, while knowing (in that way
one *knows*) that she won't become queen of England. The
premonition is never quite explained. Does she think that
death is beckoning, or divorce, or is she planning to become
a nun? It is not clear.

In truth, if things are as described between the Waleses, it is a miserable marriage and you can't help but be sorry for that. But since when were royal marriages supposed to be happy? In the history of British royalty, when was there ever a sexually and mentally fulfilling official coupling? It's not supposed to be like that, I had thought. Princes of Wales have mistresses and peculiar social theories, and Princesses of Wales give themselves up to dignified child-bearing and weird waving in nice frocks from open carriages. *That's* a royal destiny.

The trouble seems to stem from that terrible wedding business. Having read (or been forced to read) too many of her step-grandmother's books, Princess Sweet Pea-Brain was caught up in the fabulation, and believed she was actually participating in a fairy-tale. This fantasy, of course, was only meant for the hoi polloi, who were, at the time, being distracted by the Brixton riots, IRA hunger strikes and trouble in the mines: but young girls' heads (those not born to it) *will* be turned by an overdose of petticoats and lace. Only now does Diana appear to have understood that she was merely an actor in a long-running show, whose cast, unlike that of *The Mousetrap*, never changes. Naturally, waking as she has from a dream, she's a bit grumpy, feeling a little cheated by reality. Either she will adjust to it (a Mars Bar is always a good way of getting fast energy after a long nap), or we may look forward, in years to come, to ghosted memoirs and to a stream of chat-show appearances by the personality of all personalities: the one that got away from the innermost sanctum of the Royal Family. Fergie, eat your heart out.*

It's hardly surprising that some will revolt against all this, and search for meaning in ordinary, un-spotlit lives,

---

* This was a review of the first edition, written five years before the Princess of Wales's death.

demanding to know, with Virginia Woolf, 'whether the lives of great men only should be recorded. Is not anyone who has lived a life, and left a record of that life, worthy of biography – the failures as well as the successes, the humble as well as the illustrious? And what is greatness? And what is smallness?' And what, one might ask V.W. in a whisper, is humbug? Still, finding meaning in the ordinary life is the stated purpose of Lyndall Gordon's biography of her three girlhood friends, Romy, Rose and Ellie, who never became famous for anything before they each died, younger than people are supposed to these days.

Of course, an early death is almost as sexy as fame and riches, especially if it's the death of a woman who is unhappy, confused, unfulfilled. Little lives rounded with a sleep are given their shape, and therefore a special significance, which little lives that linger on into tetchy, dismal old age don't have. Just a question, but what if Sylvia Plath were alive and well, along with Anne Sexton, and the two of them met over occasional lunches to tut-tut over the sloppy rearing of their grandchildren?

Death, in any case, has a cachet which lends weight to even the featheriest of lives. A cynic might suppose that Lyndall Gordon was fortunate to have such friends, their brief lives a biographical gift to the surviving fourth, who was the only formal achiever in the group. The time and place, too, were serendipitous: South Africa in the Fifties has the retrospective air of Pompeii before Vesuvius went pop, Pudding Lane just before someone dropped a match, the *Titanic* as the bottle of champagne crashed against her bows.

Apartheid was in full bloom throughout their youth, with Sharpeville at its dead centre. All of them, from politically liberal families grew to dislike the regime and finally left the country. Yet you can't help wondering to what extent the political outrage was fuelled by the perceived glamour of

New York and Paris, beckoning in glossy magazines to the young women who felt themselves to be stuck in a provincial backwater. And the problems of virginity and marriage seem to loom largest in the story of their lives.

Of the four friends, the star is Flora, whose name mutated with the years to a more glitzy Romy. She seems to exist in the book almost as the shadow self of Lyndall Gordon, who herself married young, travelled to America where her husband worked, had children, post-natal depression, and finally got down to a career in academe, and the writing of two literary biographies.

Meanwhile Romy – who was the plump schoolfriend, Flora – flits furiously around the world pursued by lovers, but staying single and virgo intacta for an inordinately long time. She diets, cuts her hair and her hemlines according to the needs of the decade, but remains in permanent flight from the social and cultural necessity of settling down. Romy is presented as a free spirit, inevitably damaged by the changing demands of the times she is living through – by the past and her family, who so badly want her married and bearing babies, by the future and the outside world, which wants her an independent carefree career-woman. Yet she comes across as irritatingly neurotic rather than heroic – though the two conditions are perhaps much the same. Eventually, she does get married – to the man to whom she finally loses her virginity, although not the man she loves. Her death not long after, from viral pneumonia, colludes in keeping her from the dull satisfactions of the future.

There is undoubtedly a bond of time and place between the women, but the often over-wrought prose Gordon uses to describe it is not very convincing. This is the response to a letter from Rose suggesting she and Gordon were never all that close: 'I had shared with Rose a sense of a submerged being, like some deep-sea creature swimming and diving beneath the surface. Nothing of this had we put into words, but meeting Rose or Flora beneath the sea, had been for me, and I believed still was for Flora, the truthful moment.' There's no one left to argue the point, and Rose's cool words are left to flap uselessly about in someone else's record of time past. And, in the end, it's hard not to feel that the story which started out as an attempt to retrieve the value in invisible lives has become a faintly triumphal account of Lyndall Gordon the survivor, the achiever, and the one, out of all of the promising friends, who has the power to choose to make them visible.

The other side of the personality conundrum is how much do we really want, or need, to know about the lives of those who *do* achieve something memorable? Clearly, we want to know quite badly, if the plethora of biographical material on Antonia White is anything to go by. Since her death, squabbles and law suits have busied her offspring, and trees by the dozen have been felled in the cause of discovering the real Antonia White. The second volume of her diaries takes her from the age of 60 up to her death at 81, a period in her life when no new books were written, though not from want of trying, and those written years before were re-issued as 'classic women's writing' by Virago.

The diaries are edited by Susan Chitty, White's eldest daughter, in the teeth of her half-sister Lyndall's opposition. Antonia White herself seemed not entirely sure if she wanted them published or not. 'All I can say is that they *are* a record of what I was thinking and feeling at the time. On the other hand, there are things in them which it would hurt Sue, and perhaps Lyndall to read . . . and I know they are a horrible exposure of myself.' In the same passage she advocates burning the diaries, but also thinks they might be useful to other writers and to Catholics. A nice little problem to leave for your descendants to argue about. Their use to writers is limited, I should think, to their description of what all must either know or fear already: the agony of the The Block. And for Catholics, White's relationship to religion, in this period, would, I imagine, be dispiriting.

The entries tell the story of a terrible aridity, desperate displacement obsessions about painting and decorating (problems with the right kind of chintz loom large), sentimental religiosity and the sad business of waiting for death. Not that the unhappy declining of powers and the struggle to keep them alive isn't a story to tell, but perhaps it is one better told in fiction, where the sharp eye of a novelist such as White herself can cut through the miasma of self-deception and silliness. Her desperate attempts to overcome her writing block are painful to read. Over and over she asks herself if she's *meant* to be a writer, spends months working and reworking a single paragraph, then decides it would be better to do another book altogether. It is a state of panic which nothing can alleviate: 'three weeks ago I said to God "If you really want me to write this book, give me some idea *how* to handle this chapter."'

God isn't much help here, though he does come up trumps financially from time to time. He assists her in the housing department, too, when she moves into a new flat. 'All the astonishing things that have happened ought to convince me God *wants* me to have it! I will never know what I owe to my friends' prayers and generosity . . . think of Phyllis, so poor herself, giving me that £100.'

It is curious that the author of *Frost in May* should have so infantilised her relationship with God. The child in that novel, which White herself calls autobiographical, has an infinitely more profound understanding of the power and sensuality of the Catholicism to which Antonia White returned in later life. Nanda, the child in the novel, struggles with the grip of the Church over her imagination and spirit, all the while loving and fearing its terrible coercive power of ceremony and guilt. The elderly woman, however, wonders, when she wonders at all, what parts of the Garden of Eden

story she is supposed to take literally. It is in the fiction that
we see most clearly what White increasingly doubts the existence of through the period of this diary: the 'core' of herself.
I can see nothing to be gained from reading about the
pathetic private confusion of her last months, but it is true
that up to that point you sense a great tenacity, an almost
noble determination to struggle on despite the brick walls of
writer's block and increasing infirmity. But that strength is
precisely what is most strongly seen and felt in the novels
and stories.

Fiction is what she did in the world, and what she thought
of herself as doing. Isn't it odd that, admiring the work, we
want to possess the worker – happy, apparently, to exchange
her carefully thought-out intention for the everyday inade-
quacy of a life which is, of course, just as humdrum and
confused as the life of anyone else. What we own of Antonia
White is her published fiction, stories and novels, and that is
all we can ever own, unless we were personally involved
with her. And perhaps it's also true, conversely, that those
personally involved with writers can never quite own the
fiction. To look to the life, of Diana, Romy or Antonia
White, for what fiction does so much better is to seek out a
phantom which cannot fail to disappoint.

Homage to
Barbara Cartland

I could have left well alone; read the new autobiography
and a novel or two and got stuck in. I'm not a great believer
in the principle that talking to people is the best way of finding out who they really are. I'm not sure I'm even a great
believer in the notion that there is a who-they-really-are to be
found out. So why I petitioned for an interview with Barbara
Cartland still baffles me, except perhaps that I enjoy improb-
ability and (occasionally) being in situations that are entirely
beyond my ken.

In preparation for our meeting, I was sent a package, the
contents of which spilled out on the kitchen table, making an
otherwise ordinary morning sparkle. It had proved impossible to find any of Dame Barbara's novels in local bookshops
or even W.H. Smith, though I was lent a copy of *Lovers in
Lisbon* by Portuguese friends on condition that I cherished it.
There were two novels in the package, *A Nightingale Sang*
and *The Disgraceful Duke*, as well as a small pink booklet
on the cover of which is a drawing of Dame Barbara looking
very like Zsa Zsa Gabor in her youth, resting on a globe. The
booklet enumerates all her doings and works. After listing
her 600 novels, there is a heading: 'Her Other Wonderful
Books', with sub-headings such as Philosophy, Sociology

and Historical. Finally, and most movingly, there was a type-script bound in pink ribbon tied with a bow. The handwritten stick-on label reads: 'How I Want to be Remembered'. After elaborating on the 16 numbered life achievements of which she is most proud, she writes: 'I am very thrilled by what I have achieved in my life and if nothing else, I would like to say a prayer of gratitude because I have helped a great number of people, both physically and spiritually, to find love.'

We spoke on the phone, and she explained why I had to sign an indemnity form before meeting her. 'You see, my dear, people come and see me and then they go away and write that I wear too much mascara and that I am ugly.' My heartstrings twanged, as they would faced with any 93-year-old who has been ill-used by the grown-ups. People can be so unkind. We negotiated and came to a compromise about the indemnity form: she could not have a veto over anything I wrote, but she could reject anything I quoted directly from our meeting. After reading the typescript Dame Barbara did, in fact delete several passages and expanded all spoken contractions.

Camfield Place is a large gloomy house which was Elizabethan until Beatrix Potter's grandfather ('rich and without much taste') demolished it to build himself a proper mansion. It's dark and shadowy inside, so far removed from the world outside that you feel alarmed at stepping across the threshold and leaving the light behind. The dimness is relieved only by a scattering of gleaming rococo occasional tables, all cherubs and curlicues, but which look at first glance as if Jackson Pollock has been let loose with some-one's up-chucked lunch and pots of gold paint. The room in which she received me was the green the Nile is supposed to be, but almost certainly isn't. Not, alas, pink, though the dozen or so urns of flowers – two held spiritedly aloft by a pair of life-sized gilded satyrs – were symphonies of pink carnations, lilies and the like. But in common with the threadbare, taped-up carpets, the blooms had seen better days, and sagged with the effort of living up to the complexity of their arrangement.

Dame Barbara, on the other hand, was remarkably fresh and vigorous, in a multi-coloured silk tea-frock, tripping along on her sandals and smiling quite a lot. She has a very nice smile, and hair like cumulus clouds, billowing white, tending upwards, and, being rather sparse, transparent enough to see the light from the window behind her scintillate through the wisps. The false eyelashes *are* a mistake because, being heavy, they tend to make her lids droop, concealing a pair of vivid green eyes, alert and interested, which you'd like to see more of. Still, we all need protection from the stranger's glance. Me, I leave my spectacles on when I'm not sure of the company I'm keeping.

There is very little difference between the way Barbara Cartland writes about herself and the way she talks. In either mode what occurs is stream of consciousness, the like of which I haven't encountered since Molly Bloom had her final say. One thought follows another, though rarely consequentially. Occasionally, it's possible to glimpse an underlying connection, if not logic, as ideas hurtle along bumping into one another and doffing their hats. There is a chapter in her latest, fifth autobiography, *I Reach for the Stars*,* which seems for half its length to concern her memories of her great friend Lord Mountbatten. They were in the middle of writing a novel together (*Love at the Helm* – 'he was to do the plot . . . then I would do the love') when he was killed. She mentions, in case we had forgotten, that he was Viceroy of India and swerves suddenly into an account of her own achievements in connection with the subcontinent: 'When I first visited India in 1959, I stayed with the

* Robson, London, 1994.

Governor of Bombay. He said: "Oh do speak to my women and tell them about your vitamins, I am sure they will be interested."' They weren't. Indeed, they had 'no idea what I was talking about'. Indira Gandhi, when she came to power, did appreciate the vitamins and distributed them to her staff, and so in 1988, Dame Barbara went to open a health resort in Delhi. 'The weather was lovely and I was able to wear a large pink hat and a thin dress.' Next thing you know, it's back to 1969 and she's on a trip to Vienna, where the Mayor gave her a special dinner party because of her contribution to health. But miraculously it does come back to Dickie for a moment. She wrote a biography of Elizabeth of Austria, and 'it was taken by the Elizabeth Club, who said it was the best biography ever written about her. They told Lord Mountbatten how pleased they were with it when he visited Vienna.' You see? What goes around comes around.

When she speaks there is a problem about the ends of her sentences. The words come very fast, bubbling over to be released, but by the end of the sentence something goes – energy, the original intention, perhaps – and the last words dribble away, seeming to drop off and plummet into some deep underground cavern where all the words of all the ends of sentences lie tumbled and tangled together. It's likely that the speed with which the words are delivered is an attempt to get as many as possible out before coming to the edge of the word precipice.

The Dame is full of advice, and some of it is to be treasured. Only the personal pronoun distinguishes the title of Dame Barbara's autobiography from the title of the film about Douglas Bader, he who lost both legs as a fighter pilot. I supposed at first it was accidental, but in the book, after describing the death of her second husband, who had been badly wounded during the war, she explains: 'Few people realise that when a man has been wounded and his blood circulation has been shortened, he is far more passionate than is normal.' Though the Amazons 'never had any use for men' they nevertheless broke the legs of their prisoners because it made them better lovers. And according to Dame Barbara, Admiral Nelson of the single arm, was, not coincidentally, a virtuoso in the art of love, as was a very ordinary Guardsman in the Twenties to whom no one paid much attention until he fell from a station platform and damaged both legs. 'After this he became one of the most sought-after men in London.' No wonder Toulouse-Lautrec got all those girls to pose for him.

However, sex is no part of Dame Barbara's art. In the romances, men may be bad and experienced ('*Someone* has to know what they are doing,' she confided to me over tea), but girls are pure and redeeming. Her novels are light-years from the Brontës', yet they twinkle merrily at *Wuthering Heights* and *Jane Eyre* across the chasm. The Disgraceful Duke is dark, dangerous and cynical, having to be horribly burned, his thrilling sinfulness purified by fire, before he can receive the consoling love of the innocent Shimona. So I was surprised when I read the following sentence in that novel: 'Only a stupid woman would be overwhelmed by love.' It had a dissonant ring of modernity, even modishness, about it. What did she mean, I asked her. She looked baffled. 'Yes, well, I do not know quite what I meant by that. I was talking to the Prime Minister and what we are trying to say is that we are trying to get back to romance. Nowadays, it is sex, sex, sex.'

Dame Barbara frequently uses the word in a set of three. Earlier she explained: 'Gradually, we are just getting back to romance, and that is what the Prime Minister calls getting back to the beginning. What we are trying to do is get rid of this sex business. In America the only thing that sells is dirty sex, as dirty as possible. Sex, sex, sex.'

What about 'the beginning'? In the beginning 'the Greeks believed that God made first of all, as I say, a man, and because he was lonely, He cut the man in half and the soft, sweet, gentle spiritual half became the woman. The man was the fighter and protector. So now we are always looking for the other half of ourselves.' Dame Barbara would seem to have Gnostic tendencies. Love is the mystical search for and sudden recognition of the completing other-gendered side of yourself. Like three-quarters of the world, she says, she believes in the wheel of rebirth. Those, like her adored brother Ronald, killed at Dunkirk, who are 'so advanced, so up', go on to the Fourth Dimension (it sounded very upper-case). The rest of us get reborn in incremental stages. 'They say to me how can you bear India when you see them living on the pavement? They are perfectly happy, much more happy than they would be in England, because they believe they are going to have a better body next time.'

I imagine this is her solution to a moment of moral difficulty she encountered in 1926. In an earlier, reissued, autobiography, *We Danced All Night*,* she describes her part in saving the country from the 'unknown dangers' of the General Strike. She went, one of the Bright Young Things, on an errand from strike-breaking headquarters to a vicarage in the Harrow Road. She had never been to this part of London, nor ever seen 'the dirty streets, the dilapidated, mean little houses badly in need of repair, the ragged children running about with insufficient clothes and bare feet'. The poverty struck her 'with surprise' and she wondered for the first time since the strike began 'if the miners were not justified in refusing a cut in their wages'. At the vicarage with its 'inevitable smell of cabbage' (positively Orwellian, that) a woman bumps into her on the stairs, drops her shopping bag of meagre groceries and bursts into tears. Young Barbara is embarrassed and apologises, assuring her that the potatoes

---

* Robson, London, 1994.

will be all right. 'It isn't that, miss, and you 'aven't done any 'arm.'

She tells bright young Barbara about her striking husband, five children, the overdue rent and there not being enough to buy medicine for the little one who's been so ill. Barbara gropes for her purse, and finding 22s 3d (I wonder if there wasn't an odd halfpenny she's forgotten over the past seventy years), gives it to the woman. '"God bless you, miss," she said, the tears starting to her eyes . . . But going home I knew that 22s 3d had not salved my conscience. How long would it last to feed a family of five children? And how many families were there without help, without hope?'

Easy enough to sneer, and it's true that after that we hear only of the heroism of the strike-breakers and the violence of the strikers, but here was a moment when a shaft of reality impinged on the pink dream. Then the curtain fell, and the world became for ever more a place where 'you cannot get a woman to come and clean the house because the dole pays them too much'. Maybe that moment in 1926 was Dame Barbara's chance to move into a better body next time round. I fear she may have failed the test.

In any case, she'd moved on from the wheel of fortune to the subject of women priests. 'I do not like women priests. Ach, pushy women. You are not allowed to say God's a man now.'

'You don't think women are the equal of men?' I managed to get in.

'Men have a much greater . . . sense . . . of what is right and what is wrong than women. Women always think, well, perhaps I can get round it, do you know what I mean?'

'Men are more moral than women?' I asked.

'Morally, I think men are much stronger. Why? Because women are weaker and less intelligent.' She giggled. 'That will make me popular. You know perfectly well they are not as intelligent as men, and they have awful squeaky voices. Why do we now have to have a woman reading about the games?' She makes a series of mimsy high-pitched squeaks mimicking a woman commentating on the cricket on television.

'You don't like women much?'

'Women are very sweet and nice, but you always have to be rather careful that they do not run off with your husband or your best lover. They are rather inclined to do that. Don't you see, you have got to be careful of women. The men do not make trouble, at least not with me.'

I've noticed, I say, getting on to the writing, that you write in paragraphs of one sentence. 'That's journalism,' she tells me. Lord Beaverbrook taught her. Always write in short paragraphs, he told her before asking her for a kiss which she refused saying she was saving her kisses for the man she would marry. He respected her for that. As to inspiration: 'When I want a plot, I say to God, please give me a plot. And it works.' Though sometimes God is not immediately obliging. 'The other day He was a bit slow; I thought perhaps He is bored with me. I asked my secretaries, bring me up all my research on the Restoration . . . you know, George V . . . and as it was coming, a voice said, absolutely clearly: "Panama Canal." I knew nothing about the Panama Canal, but as I read about it, it was absolutely riveting. Disraeli would not let us join in building it because they used slave labour. Later Lord Rothschild bought a great number of shares back from the French and Disraeli was able to go to Queen Victoria and say: "I bought you the Suez Canal, Ma'am!" It gave us a quick way to India.' Since she takes only two weeks to dictate a novel, we may expect the Panama/Suez Canal book very soon.

In the autobiographies she harps continually on physical beauty – hers most of all, but all the other well-bred girls are described as terribly beautiful, as if it came with the inherited land. Oddly, looking at the photos it's hard to discern the jaw-hanging nature of their loveliness. It's as if I do not have the key to it, and see only rather round-faced, unremarkable-looking young women. In much the same way one has to take on trust the astonishing oratorical power Hitler was supposed to possess: such film as remains of his speeches leaves you shrugging.

There is a brief insight. While pregnant with Raine, she determined that her child would be beautiful. She bought a picture of a very attractive baby and looked at it every day. She was concerned for her child because she had 'suffered so much myself by hearing people say I was plain when I was young'. When I asked her about this, she did not hear me, then when I repeated my question she said: 'Yes, yes, I became very beautiful.' Perhaps, after all, what I see in the old photos is what there is, and what she remembers is what they told each other.

She describes the young people of the Twenties as rebels, dancing madly against the memory of the war and all those lost young men. 'What we danced in those days,' she told a journalist who phoned her to ask about the revival of the tango, 'was swinging round. And we danced round and round and round. I did not do the tango, it was rather . . . complicated.' It sounds almost tragic, very Scott Fitzgerald, until you remember the woman on the stairs with the five children and the sad sack of groceries. Perhaps all that going round and round prevented her from going forward and she came to an emotional end of paragraph. She has known sadness: the death of her father and two brothers in the world wars, and even divorce from her first husband, who was named co-respondent in the divorce case of the woman he took to the drink with. But the darker experiences seem somehow unexperienced. It's as if the 93-year-old Dame Barbara is not a day older than the minimally experienced

25-year-old girl who, after the nastiness of the war and the General Strike, resumed her life at the Embassy Club and Deauville, dancing the nights away and collecting proposals ('After receiving 49 proposals of marriage I accepted the 50th). What is revealed, in both real life and the books, is a forever childish mind grabbing at the opinions of those she admires (men in general unless they're socialists, and Margaret Thatcher: 'Margaret was the only woman who understood money').

'Look what happens,' she says, summing up the damage done by 'Women's Lib'. 'We have got more children taking drugs than ever before. The women from the East bring them in, hidden in their clothes and then sell them.' Are you quite sure, Dame Barbara? Dame Barbara is quite, quite sure. Being sure is what Barbara Cartland excels at. But it's the certainty of a child mis-parroting the adults, who are always to be trusted.

'I make people happy,' she says over and over again. She makes them happy with her love stories without sex (though dripping with suppressed passion), and with vitamins, and advice about the failings of the modern world. She goes around the world and is received with smiles and awards for bringing health and happiness. In 1981 she was chosen as 'Achiever of the Year', by the National Home Furnishing Association of Colorado Springs, for her wallpaper and fabric designs, and all the women at the ceremony wore pink. The award is one of a score of achievements in 'How I Want to be Remembered'. Another was keeping Neil Kinnock out of government at the 1992 election with a letter to 962 newspapers and magazines. I don't believe this journal published it. It went as follows:

I am very surprised that the Church has not, in any way, pointed out to the people that Mr Kinnock is an avowed atheist, and his wife said the other day, 'I do not believe in

God, and when I get to No 10 I am going on teaching children.' If you vote for Kinnock, you are voting against Christ who said: 'Suffer little children to come unto me.'

Dame Barbara, for all her great age, must, I think, be very close to Christ.

Whatever Happened to Rosa?

Venus Envy
by Elizabeth Haiken
(JOHNS HOPKINS, LONDON, 1998)

The Royal Women of Amarna
by Dorothea Arnold
(METROPOLITAN MUSEUM OF ART, NEW YORK, 1996)

The English Face
by David Piper
(NATIONAL PORTRAIT GALLERY, LONDON, 1998)

Whatever happened to Rosa Travers after she was skinned (carbolic acid and phenol), had her nose snipped, received paraffin injections in her breasts and was irradiated to remove undesirable body hair? That would have been the first part of her prize. When all was done, she had an opera audition. Rosa Travers was a sweatshop worker who in 1924 had the distinction of winning the *New York Daily Mirror*'s competition to find the 'homeliest girl in New York':

A plastic surgeon has offered to take the homeliest girl in the biggest city in the country and to make a beauty of her. All you have to do is to send your photograph with name and address to Homeliest Girl Contest Editor. We will not print names, and the photographs will be 'masked'. Our art department will paint the masks on the photographs to obviate identification. Here is the chance for New York's homeliest girl. Her misfortune may make a fortune right away.

Somewhere, I suppose, in the archives of the *Mirror*, a masked Rosa Travers gazes out in muted triumph, and then, some time later, the new-model Rosa would have been unveiled. Unless the carbolic acid caused a third-degree burn, the scalpel slipped, the paraffin migrated or she developed paraffinoma or 'wax cancer'. There would then, we may imagine, have been no 'after' picture. Worryingly, in her history of cosmetic surgery, Elizabeth Haiken ends the paragraph on Rosa Travers with a parenthesis: 'what happened afterwards was not reported'. At the very least, it suggests that Rosa's misfortune did not turn out to make a fortune for her after all. Or shall we cheer ourselves up by assuming that the facelift did wonders for her vocal chords and she lived happily ever after under the name of Kirsten Flagstad?

We don't know whether it was homely Rosa herself or some concerned friend who sent in her picture and immortalised her as the phantom of the facelift. If it was Rosa then she wouldn't have been the only or the last woman to have been caught between the twin pressures of self-improvement and the puritan values of America. What's a girl without congenital wealth to do if she hasn't been blessed with some class-effacing talent or exceptional looks, when she knows that success in life is the result of an individual's effort? Grasp the opportunity; go for surgery – which, it would seem from the association of beauty with an opera audition, is likely to take care of both. And what's a girl to do if it all goes unpleasantly wrong on the operating table? Expect to be dropped like a burnt potato by her sponsors and informed that, then again, vanity reaps its own rewards.

If that strikes some as unfair, it probably wouldn't surprise Rosa and her sisters. What's fair about being born plain, flat-chested, or bandy-legged in a world where appearances are very nearly everything? Even talent in Rosa's day didn't quite compensate for an unsatisfactory face. Fanny Brice was the first famous woman to announce publicly in 1923 that she had had cosmetic surgery. She didn't lack ability or appreciation as a comic actress, but she had a large, irregular nose and felt that her hankering to play Nora in *The Doll's House* would never be fulfilled without recourse to surgery. Dorothy Parker sniffed that she had cut off her nose to spite her race, but Brice was just trying to enlarge her repertoire. Things may be thought different now; Barbra Streisand has climbed the heights of Hollywood stardom without a nose job. Her big movie break, however, was playing an unreconstructed Fanny Brice in *Funny Girl*.

We might blame Rosa and Fanny Brice's predicament on the advent of popular democracy and the mass media; go back to ancient Egypt and the assumed correlation of beauty with power would probably not have caused any young woman to lift an eyebrow, let alone dream of collagen implants. Monumental images were limited (no movie screens or giant billboards) and controlled (no nubile lovelies cavorting on the TV in the living room), allowing beauty to become one of the innate attributes, if not the prerogative, of members of the deified royal family. Their God-given royalty, indeed, defined beauty. No point in a common girl eating her heart out in the Nile delta if she didn't look like Nefertiti – she wasn't supposed to. Much as she might admire Princesses Meretaten and Meketaten their sloe eyes, full lips and massive, pathologically, elongated bald skulls, she

couldn't hope to look like them. And, though the chances are
she wouldn't know it, they didn't even look like themselves.
The depictions of the royal women of Amarna were concep-
tual rather than realistic, explains Dorothea Arnold, quoting
Edna R. Russmann, who dismisses the search by other scholars for a pathological explanation of the egg-headed
princesses. Such views are, she says, based on false premises.
'They arise from modern perceptions and preoccupations –
from scientifically oriented curiosity and from our irresistible
tendency to assume that distinctive features must, like a photograph, mirror an actual appearance. Akhenaten's concerns,
of course, were entirely different. In departing radically from
the styles of all earlier royal representations . . . the . . . representations of Akhenaten at Karnak are deliberately
unrealistic.' That is to say that the extraordinary features
were metaphors for the extraordinary, otherly nature of the
royal family. Not that this would be very different from the
way Hollywood depicted Gloria Swanson, Greta Garbo or
Clara Bow who were, in addition, called *stars* rather than
say *pebbles* to suggest that they were out of this world. It's
perfectly possible that Clara Bow's sweetheart lips would
have struck an ancient Egyptian scholar as pathological
rather than an image of other-worldly perfection, but our
common girl from the Nile delta would not be burdened
with Rosa Travers's democratically induced belief that it was
only sheer bad luck that she herself lacked such perfection,
nor with the scratchy feeling that if she could do something
about it, she ought. In 20th-century America anyone could
come from anywhere and turn out to be Greta Garbo,
indeed Fifties-pretty Elizabeth Taylor became Cleopatra and
married her Anthony a good few times, whereas in ancient
Egypt public beauty defined and was defined by the
ineluctable fact of breeding.

The early stages of European portraiture began, the late
David Piper suggests, with tomb-effigies in the 12th century.

Neither beauty nor individuality were the point in these monuments in death to rank, wealth and piety. None of these portraits in stone look like anyone I have ever met. In England, it was not until Chaucer's portrait in Occleve's manuscript (c 1412) that likeness began to matter. According to Occleve, 'in order to remind other men of his personal appearance I have had the likeness made here to the end, in truth, that those who have least thought and memory of him may recall him by this painting.' And, indeed, minus the smock and draped hat, he does look remarkably like my next-door neighbour. It becomes important that we have an image of what the individual looks like as well as what he or she has done, but it is not until Cromwell's notion of warts and all that veracity plays much of a part in portraiture. For those who wanted their quality – their power, their wealth, their talent – to shine through their face to posterity, the court painters functioned in much the same way as the 20th-century cosmetic surgeons. The images of Henry VIII and Elizabeth I were controlled by the sitters, Henry trusting Holbein to have the good sense, or sufficient self-preservation, to show him as awesome, though with a nicely turned ankle, rather than a fat, self-indulgent tyrant; Elizabeth did not trust anyone. In 1563 William Cecil drafted a decree demanding that she 'be content that some special cunning painter might be permitted by access to her Majesty to take the natural representation of her Majesty whereof she hath always been of her own will and disposition very unwilling, but also to prohibit all manner of other persons to draw paint grave or portrait her Majesty's personage or visage for a time until by some perfect pattern and example the same may be by others followed'. Elizabeth, for reasons of state, held back the years in her images, just as Cher, for reasons of occupation, goes under the knife; both being realistic working women. Vanity is in the eye of the beholder; women have always known the material value of looking good.

The scalpels used in cosmetic surgery, however, have largely been in the hands of men, and the profession was developed in the land of opportunity and private medicine. It began uncontroversially in Europe with reconstructive surgery on the faces of wounded soldiers in World War I. Maxillofacial treatment progressed not just for humanitarian reasons, but also because it was clear that severely disfigured ex-servicemen were less likely to get work in the post-war world. The urgency was to return the soldiers to economic independence: even then, it was agreed that looks counted when it came to applying for a job. But once the war was over, the plastic surgeons wishing to form a speciality of their own had fewer and fewer of what they thought of as legitimate customers, while they watched opportunists cashing in on their pioneering work to offer benefits to women who were neither disfigured, family breadwinners, nor in any obvious sense, ill. The quacks were raking it in. By 1939 the *Ladies Home Journal* was trilling about the surgical possibilities of 'widening the eyes, changing them from round to oval, shortening the eyelids, lengthening or shortening the mouth or varying the width of the lips'. The original surgeons, worried by their Hippocratic commitment, felt obliged to treat only those who were diseased, not those who were dissatisfied. The solution came with the popularisation in the Twenties of Adler's formulation of the inferiority complex. The now properly constituted organisation of plastic surgeons could justify performing the cosmetic operations they had previously sniffed at. Mental health became an issue, and to back it up, the economic effects of poor mental health could be cited if a patient could be deemed to be at risk. Market forces clearly had applied to movie stars who wanted to be more glamorous or appear younger for the sake of getting work; now middle-class housewives with noses that made them too self-conscious to be good hostesses for their husbands, or who risked losing their breadwinners to more youthful looking women could be helped. By 1941, the first diplomas in plastic surgery were awarded and plastic surgeons had incorporated cosmetic surgery into their practices.

There is a parallel here with the abortion on demand debate. Women had to present themselves as, and be deemed by their surgeon to be at risk of mental illness if their ageing process was to be remedied, rather than be free to make a personal choice about their appearance. Moreover, men did not just control the surgery, they also provided motivation as husbands or bosses: a woman who wanted to keep her looks to keep her man, or her job, was considered by the surgeons to have a good case. It looks as if the progressive popularity of cosmetic surgery had as much to do with what Haiken calls 'tyrannical reality' as it did with fantasies of perfection. According to Haiken, post-war American women found themselves middle-aged, ignored and invisible in an increasingly youth-biased culture. 'At this crucial juncture, plastic surgeons found that the social and psychological justification for cosmetic surgery . . . gave ageing a whole new look, while many middle-class Americans . . . found it easier to alter their own faces than to alter the cultural norms and expectations about ageing that confronted them. Together, surgeons and their patients forged a new image of the facelift as a sensible, practical and relatively simple solution to the social problem of ageing.'

Women with large noses and small breasts (and lately men with puny pecs and slim penises) wanted to be what was perceived as normal. The surgeons colluded mightily with this. They were performing a service in maintaining the status quo. In 1965 a surgeon gave *Esquire* an example of what he considered to be a bad outcome of cosmetic surgery:

I had a woman patient recently; a very smart, chic, well-dressed woman. Middle-aged. She wanted a facelift. She was married to a very responsible man in an upper-income bracket, and she wanted to look better for her husband. It sounded okay . . . Later on I heard she absolutely ran amok – divorced her husband, ran off to Mexico, took a 25-year-old boy as a lover – the whole route. It was dreadful.

If the cheering has died down, I'll continue: contrast this with an example of a case described by surgeon Donald Moynihan and quoted by Haiken: 'The prospective patient was a young black woman whose cornrowed hair and black studies major in college suggested to Moynihan that she was "really into the heritage thing," as did her request that he put a bone through her nose. "I respected the deep pride she had in her race," Moynihan recalled, "but the way I see it, no matter what, a bone through the nose is an unreasonable request. I turned her down."'

Difference became deformity. A dental surgeon explains how a child who was considered 'bucktoothed' in the Forties, would have had orthodontic braces in the Fifties and Sixties, but is now considered to have a 'dentofacial deformity, the treatment for which is maxillofacial surgery'. And the negative effects of racial difference from the accepted Caucasian norm were thoroughly understood by sympathetic surgeons. In 1926 a Japanese man called Shima Kito wishing to marry an all-American girl had his oriental eyes occidentalised and changed his name to William White. In the Fifties a Kansas woman called Gretchen Algren, who had always been teased about her large nose and learnt not to mind, finally had a nose job at 35 because she was lately being mistaken for a Jew and worried it would hold back her husband's career. In the Eighties, Michael Jackson wanted and rather tragically got a pert ski-jump of a nose rather than his own broad African-American one (to say nothing of whiter skin, thinner lips, carved cheekbones and permanent eyeliner).

The other side of all this is the pleasure we all take and have always and everywhere taken in artifice. Wander round the National Portrait Gallery and witness mile-high and drooping powered wigs, chalk-white cheeks, plucked eyebrows, whiskers, uplifted bouncy bosoms, hopefully huge codpieces – and that's just European artifice. For a decade or so, it has been common for men and women to sculpt their bodies, shaping discrete muscles in gyms with specialist machines. In France, performance artist Orlan takes herself to the operating theatre and films her surgeons reshaping her face into a facsimile of the *Mona Lisa*. The only change is that new techniques have permitted alterations to be carved out of or pumped into the flesh. Once women suffered the adverse effects of outlining their eyes with antimony, now silicone injections deform and disease. Pioneering plastic surgeon Jacques Maliniak understood this in 1933: 'If there is any striking difference between the old and the new ways [of enhancing beauty], it is that on the whole the old were safer.' But perhaps the enhancing of beauty is not just the self-mutilation by proxy of politically subjugated woman (and increasingly men), or merely a striving for social dominance, but is also a way of keeping us interested in ourselves. Growing old is also an interesting process, but it proceeds incrementally and without real drama. We should not underestimate the role of theatrical pleasure in the fast, thrilling transformations plastic surgery offers. Most of us know the gratification of seeing ourselves in a new outfit; perhaps it's not so different getting a new body or face.

It is true, however, that there is no record of women asking their cosmetic surgeons to transform their youthful faces into wrinkled age (though I once asked a hairdresser to dye my hair grey, before the Lord had done it for me, and was shown the door). On the contrary, recently an LA surgeon has offered injections of botulinum toxin to prevent wrinkles by causing localised paralysis, taking us back to the turn of the century when a practitioner advocated cutting facial muscles early in life as a preventative measure against wrinkled middle age. Smiling and animation is a real problem: 'The constantly enforced and exaggerated smile in vogue today [1968] is a major offender in causing wrinkles about the commissure of the mouth, the nasolabial fold and the eyes.' In 1977, serenity was advised: 'Profound, uncontrolled emotion leaves its imprint on our faces for all the world to see.' And I remember a worrying beauty hint from a contemporary beautician who explained that she kept a role of sellotape in the car and stuck a piece between her eyebrows to prevent dangerous frowning while driving. Our mothers put on clean knickers whenever they went out in case they happened to be in an accident; imagine the humiliation of being caught by paramedics with sellotape between the eyes.

To Germaine Greer's question 'If a woman never lets herself go, how will she ever know how far she might have gone?' the answer might be that she could make a pretty good guess and that there's no bus back from that terminus. And to the male surgeon who considered 'A woman of 40 years of age, or more, ought to be ashamed to have a face without wrinkles' we would now reply that *we* decide what to be ashamed of these days. Haiken rather disapproves of the fact that people try to take control of their bodies in a world that is uncontrollable. But reality *is* tyrannical, and we might see the refusal to conform to nature as some kind of guerrilla warfare, of the individual doing at least what can be done. Finally, it is death, of course, that is immutable, and cosmetic surgery is yet another brave though futile challenge to its visible advance.

Inflatable Dolly

> *Dolly: My Life and Other Unfinished Business*
> by Dolly Parton
> (HARPERCOLLINS, LONDON, 1994)

This may be the only book ever written that is dedicated to God, though He is not the sole dedicatee. Apart from God, it's also for Dolly's family, her friends and her fans. Which might mean that I'm the only person on or off the planet to whom the book isn't dedicated. This is reasonable. It wasn't until I started reading it that I realised I didn't really know who Dolly Parton was.

The song that came to mind was 'Stand By Your Man', and I understood when I saw the photos of Dolly, which looked oddly unfamiliar to me, that I'd had Barbara Windsor in my mind's eye, and Tammy Wynette in my mind's ear. They're all short, blonde, big-haired, big-breasted, so it's an easy mistake to make. But when you look closely, you see that Dolly's the one with the ice-cold glint in her eye.

I imagine God was very pleased to get his dedication (isn't it always the one who works hardest for you in the background who gets the least recognition?). They're very chummy, God and Dolly. She found him up in her hillbilly mountain home in a ruined chapel with used condoms on the floor and dirty pictures scrawled on the wall. 'I would sing hymns to God for a while and look at dirty pictures for a while, and pray for a while, and one day . . . I broke through some spirit wall and found God.' Or to put it another way, 'I had found God. I had found Dolly Parton. And I loved them both.' She doesn't say equally, but Dolly is big enough to give God a seat at her right hand.

She's also a bit of a philosopher. She doesn't just read the Bible, she interprets it. When she was at a low ebb – her family was jealous of her success, her best girl-friend Judy went off in a huff because she got too close to her musical director Gregg, and she got fat – she didn't just sit and mope, she wondered what the hell God meant by saying, 'Say that "I Am" hath sent me.' Well, haven't we all? But Dolly cracked it. It's the IAM, or Individual Awareness Method, and there's no one so individually aware as Dolly.

She rededicated herself to the service of mankind, made more movies, wrote more songs, had more plastic surgery and always counts her blessings before she counts her money. She is, you see, special. She has a mission. Every day she visualises 'God picking me up by the heels, holding me upside down until all of the bad, negative things fall out'. Don't try this at home, at least not unless you've got the Almighty hanging on to your ankles.

The poor kid from the Great Smoky Mountains of East Tennessee grew up fast. She wasn't popular at school. She had an early reputation for being a tramp, she says. Unearned, of course, but at 13, 'I couldn't get my hair big enough, or "yaller" enough. Couldn't get my skirt tight enough, my blouses low enough. Couldn't get my boobs to stand up high enough or squeeze them together close enough.'

She's very sure we're all dying to know who she did or didn't sleep with, while her ever loving, infinitely car-fixing husband waited patiently at home. She claims not have had affairs with Bob Hunka, Kenny Rogers and Burt Reynolds, among others, though I can't say I feel strongly one way or the other.

These were intensely close relationships with people who recognised Dolly's spirituality. Her body is a temple of course, and several surgeons are named who help build and maintain its edifice. Apparently, plastic surgery is also part of God's work. If He hadn't meant us to have big tits, He'd never have invented the D cup bra, would He? Soon Revlon will be bringing out The Dolly Parton Beauty Confidence Collection, and Dolly's Dailies and Nighties are on their way to the shops. There are plenty of charities for the homeless, she says, but isn't it time someone helped the homely? Dolly's a laugh a minute.

I have only one real complaint. I discovered that it was Dolly Parton who wrote the Whitney Houston hit 'I Will Always Love You'. I daresay God can forgive her this, being a big-hearted Almighty, but I haven't yet grown enough in spiritual stature. Maybe I should try listening to it hanging upside down.

Don't

Sex
by Madonna
(SECKER, LONDON, 1992)

Sex and Sensibility
by Julie Burchill
(GRAFTON, LONDON, 1992)

Too hot to handle
by Fiona Pitt-Kethley
(PETER OWEN, LONDON, 1992)

There are really only two things people want to keep from public scrutiny: their real, private self; or the fact that they have no private self of any particular interest. Now, my instinctive guess is that *everyone* is nursing the fear that the real them doesn't amount to very much worth knowing. The famous fear it most, but everyone, I think, suspects that they might not really exist in any interesting way beyond their public and superficial selves. Still, some part of me rebels at this thought, if only because it's so dull. Surely, there might be some individuals whose exterior and apparent love of themselves and all their works is genuine adoration for what they find in the privacy of their own self-regard. It's not my experience of how human beings are, but I might have missed something. I look, therefore, with great interest, at self-revelation and where its limits lie.

I had hopes of *Sex*. Wouldn't Madonna offer us her limitless confidence and dispel my nagging doubt that we all suffer from nagging doubts? Wouldn't she be saying: you've had the public stuff, now here's the raw material, the motherlode. All of it's worth having, and therefore all of it's available for public scrutiny. The private outer and inner self, which previously had been occluded by art and artifice, would now be displayed in its pure form, not needing the camouflage of false reticence. Here are the naked breasts, thighs, buttocks, pubis, as well as the equally naked inner thoughts, the secret fantasies, the *mind*. Madonna, I hoped, knowing her own value, would give herself like a stick of rock: every part of her could be sucked, and 'self-worth' found written right through her. Call me a romantic, but I want to find a righteous arrogance that has no need to protect the secret self with disclaimers.

Sadly, it's not between the aluminium covers of *Sex*. Before I'd laid eyes on the first nipple-ring, I read: 'by the way, any similarity between characters and events depicted in this book and real persons is not only purely coincidental, it's ridiculous. Nothing in this book is true.' I might as well have closed the book there and then, but I'd been allotted two hours alone with it in an executive's office in Michelin House. When again would I have the opportunity to sit at an eight-foot glass desk, in a room containing nothing but several sofas and a tree, with a view of a giant Michelin man waving at me through the glass wall? Also, I had signed a formidable piece of paper promising on pain of something so terrible it could not be stated, that I would not breathe a word of what I was about to see to anyone before publication day. How could I not tell of what I had not seen? So I turned the pages.

I've never gone along with the usual liberal response to pornography that it is *so* boring. If sex is exciting (and you won't find a liberal to deny that) then pornography must be exciting, at least if it's well done. This, however, wasn't. In words and pictures (the latter being as stilted as the former), Madonna displays the full range of sexual fantasy from anal to bestial. If *Still Life with Dog*, or *Portrait of Three Naked Girls on a Bed*, turns you on, then this is for you, but only if you are excited by those practices being no more than signified. The represented activities might as well have been replaced by labels planted where the actors stand, kneel or lie. The word 'blade' placed perpendicular to the phrase 'leather-covered labia' would, I think, stimulate the imagination more than the static pictorial version with Madonna and her chums. (It's a pity, really, that no one thought of a pop-up book: the tableaux might then have attained all the waxwork power of Charlotte Corday's knife arm moving mechanically up and down in Madame Tussaud's re-creation of Marat's murder.) But perhaps the posed disappointment is true of any soft-porn magazine you might buy (if you can reach) from the top shelf of the newsagent.

What you wouldn't have to put up with from *Spanking Monthly* (apart from a £25 price tag and cheap paper) are the regular warnings and denials Madonna sprinkles through the text. 'Everything you are about to see and read is a fantasy . . . But if I were to make my dreams real, I would certainly use condoms.' 'Ass fucking is the most pleasurable way . . . but if you're not doing it right things can really go wrong.' 'It's how you treat people in everyday life that counts . . . I wouldn't want to watch anyone get really hurt, male or female.' Go ahead, let rip, but be very careful, and incidentally, I don't mean any of this, is not the language of revelation, in any sense. At the end, everyone is thanked for their 'courage'. I saw none, nor, if it comes to that, any indication of style or desire.

Revelation beyond that of flesh unclothed was too much to demand, I supposed, but surely eroticism was not an unreasonable expectation? What's missing here is effectively simulated obsession, without which any attempt at the erotic might as well pack up and go home. No one told Madonna or her photographer that open thighs, peekaboo leather bras, a multi-gendered melée on a sofa, or a finger slid under a knickered crotch are only sexy if the camera lens, representing the voyeur's eye, is obsessed with seeing what it is not supposed to see. Of course, that's a fake, too, but good pornography knows how to tell a story. Only a single shot even begins to do this, and that's the one everyone has seen, with Madonna, back to camera, wearing boots and a Gap vest, looking out of a window, with one hand idly fiddling between the back of her thighs.

People keep joking, 'What's she looking at?' But that's the point. It comes near to giving the impression that she's been caught off guard, that what we are seeing is a private easy familiarity with herself. She's thinking about something else, and toying with herself lazily. We become peepers and she becomes, for the first time, an object of interest. It's almost a fine piece of porn. Then you turn the page, and there are half a dozen people pointing their private parts at the camera, giggling or trying to look very serious, and the Michelin man seems more enticing.

So, Madonna fails as the queen of self-revelation, but she's not the only girl in the game. Julie Burchill has a book out, too. Airing opinions in magazines and tabloids is another kind of stripping bare. Burchill, more than anybody, yells, 'This is *me*' as she tells you in 1500 words or less what she thinks about what's what. There's nothing that could be called false modesty lurking in her contempt for Hampstead intellectual wankers, patronising First World

Greens, and middle-class socio-psycho-babblers. It's a dangerous business collecting bits of journalism together in one place. A column of biting vituperation becomes an indeterminate fishwife shriek when multiplied by 250 pages. And a racy style loses its edge when someone has forgotten to edit out the repeated use of the same phrases ('fiscal not physical', 'powerless dressing', 'the difference between self-defence and suicide') which, at best, are only striking the first time you read them. I'm glad someone's out there pointing the finger at the Wankers, the Greens and the Babblers. She's right for the most part; the parade is pitiful, and the cultural establishment a great deal less thoughtful and less clever than it thinks itself to be. She might well rail against the insularity of Amis, Drabble, Mortimer and Rushdie, but it's a pity that all she can shame them with is Marilyn Monroe, Jim Morrison, Sylvia Plath and Marvin Gaye.

Being attracted to doomed and self-destructive talents, rather than trudging old plodders who don't have anything very startling to say, is understandable, but as with the Madonna book, when it comes to self-revelation time, there's nothing very original to be found. A kind of What Makes Burchill Run? piece at the end functions as self-explanation. Her main credentials are that she's a working-class girl from the sticks (like Madonna); an outsider who took the world of letters (or at any rate the *NME*) by storm, very young, very fast and ever so iconoclastic. And why? Not luck: enormous talent. She 'made it look effortless, like a skater, and you can only make it look effortless if you have a *lot* of talent. My greatest gift, apart from my talent itself and my big green eyes, has been this: an ability to combine the *modus operandi* of the simple person with the perceptions of the complex person.' I read this and long to think I have found the righteous arrogance I was looking for. But negating a bunch of half-baked fashion-bound political and social

theories by naming dead stars is not good enough. And the
bold, new, populist vision of culture she offers (drugs, drink,
fin de siècle desperation and contempt for all things Sixties
and Seventies) looks very like the quaint old-fashioned exis-
tentialism of the Fifties, with a dash of careful anarchy
thrown in. All the green eyes, talent and complexity in the
world can't make that much more than a repetition of a tale
already told.

When it comes to self-revelation, Fiona Pitt-Kethley's
volume makes Madonna's bared bits and bobs look like a
suburban room-setting in *House and Garden*. It is not,
however, quite the triumph of self-knowledge I was after.
There's a certain bravado in publishing a collection of
rejected articles. But even though there are none the world
couldn't live without, it was not the essays which made me
finally abandon, and deeply regret my search for the revealing self. The latter part of the book is taken up with a
series of letters written over a period of years by Pitt-
Kethley to Hugo Williams, in the hope that he would
finally come to requite her love for him. She offers these
letters to the world as evidence of her real self. They are
truer than her other writing, she says, because 'they reveal
all of myself – the tender side as well as the hard, cynical
outsider'. They are also, she tells us, witty, charming and
contain the full repertoire of her emotions. She decided to
publish them when, contrary to her view of them, Williams
described the letters as 'dreary and boring'. At last, I
thought. But beginning to read, I started to wish myself
away, back to the fabrication and self-concealment of fiction, where bad judgment and lack of self-knowledge have
somewhere to hide. Passing over the elementary, but essential truth that people who do not love you cannot be made
to do so, all I can say, now, to anyone who might be con-
templating self-revelation is: *don't*. You might be lucky and
merely fail to deliver the goods. But if you succeed, what

you risk revealing is how very little you know about yourself, and the great disparity between what you think you have shown, and what is seen. If you've got copies of letters you've written to an unwilling lover lying around, burn them. Do it now.

You Could Scream

Brando: Songs My Mother Taught Me
by Marlon Brando and Robert Lindsey
(CENTURY, LONDON, 1994)

Greta & Cecil
by Diana Souhami
(CAPE, LONDON, 1994)

The last thing that dreams should do is come true. It would end in futile tears if they did, much as it would for the autophagist who chomps away at himself from the legs up until he comes to his head and realises that he can never achieve the final consummation. Dreams are for dreaming about. The Hollywood dream-masters got it right when they had Judy Garland playing a star-struck teenager gazing at a pin-up of Clark Gable and singing 'If you were the only boy in the world'. It's *if*, not *when*. Mix them up and you remember the story of Gable resting on set minus his false teeth shouting gummily at another passing icon: 'Look here, Marilyn, America's sweetheart.' It adds enormously to Gable's individuality, but plays havoc for ever after with the moment when he's frank with Vivien Leigh.

You could argue that our tendency to demand *when* as

soon as we think *if* has been responsible for the development
of civilisation, and I daresay there are those who admire
the first hominid who looked at a rock and saw a tool in it,
but think of the unimagined marvels we might have achieved
if we'd settled for dreaming about things instead of chipping
the material world into the shape we first thought of. Very
likely we would have got around to dreaming up Brando
and Garbo at about the time of the woolly mammoths, and
what's more, they would still be with us in their perfect
form because, as knowing and committed dreamers, we
would have had the good sense not to ask them what they
thought about anything. As it is, we've only managed to
have them for a few decades in their ideal state as two-
dimensional light and shadow, before losing them to
biographical reality.

The true icon excites the curiosity without ever answering
the questions it demands you ask. Enigma depends on an
essential silence. The 20-foot image of Garbo might talk, or
even laugh, but the creature you see on the screen does not
speak her own words, tell her own story or even wear her
own clothes. We're given nothing of the real individual
except the endless opportunity for unsatisfied speculation.
Even names can get in the way. Garbo and Brando are suit-
ably iconic: the final empty vowel turning Garb and Brand
into every-and-no-woman and man, and offering, as a
bonus, a small gasp of astonishment. But once you start to
think of them as Greta and Marlon you're back with a bump
to the absurdity of real life. There's nothing more certain to
wreck a lazy daydream of being taken roughly into the arms
of your chosen idol than the moment when you have to
imagine yourself whispering, 'Oh, Clint . . . ', 'Oh,
Marlene . . . '.

Brando resisted writing his autobiography, unwilling to
satisfy the public's 'prurient curiosity', and his instincts,
which when he's on form are as good as instincts get, were

right. Everything you ever didn't want to know about Brando is available in this rambling, ghosted tale. Reading it is like waking up in the morning next to last night's dream lover and realising you brought the bar-room bore home with you. The trick is to go back to their place and leave before they wake. *Songs My Mother Taught Me* is the breakfast too far.

But Brando's fastidious reservations about his public were nevertheless overcome, and for the best of reasons – he needed the money. To wonder why someone who earned $14 million for two and a half weeks' work on *Superman* needs money is, I suppose, merely to display a failure of imagination. But there was, after all, a selfless, literary motive behind it all: Harry Evans of Random House told Brando 'that if this company published a book about a movie star, the profits would enable him to publish books by talented unpublished authors that might not make money'. Perhaps Harry Evans will oblige us with a list of the new writers who have Marlon to thank for their publication. How many literary novelists equal the profits of one Brando, do you suppose?

Brando does not want us to know about his wives or children, but he wants us very much to know about his own childhood and the traumas he suffered with a violent father he hates, and alcoholic mother he probably hates too. In spite of years of analysis, his anger and resentment as he speaks of his childhood is as fresh, at 70, as if he'd just left home, and there is a feeling that nothing very much in his inner life has been resolved, or even put to one side as no longer of very great importance. He is as sorry for himself and sulky about the way things were as an adolescent raging against his pimples. The degree of self-absorption is remarkable. But while it is what made him such a good actor, it also accounts for some central vacuum which requires him to trash his talent, his world and anyone he comes into contact with. If you stare too long at the reflection of your own eyes, you end up seeing undifferentiated emptiness.

Self-disgust spreads like sewage over his work. His ludicrous version of Kurtz in *Apocalypse Now* was every bit as self-serving as it appeared when it toppled the movie. After bending Coppola's ear for ten days on the errors of his script and the true meaning of *Heart of Darkness*, Brando rewrote the part and did it his way. 'I was good at bullshitting Francis and persuading him to think my way, but what I'd really wanted from the beginning was to find a way to make my part smaller so that I wouldn't have to work so hard.' Yet the nihilism is immediately undermined, the Hollywood soft-centre is never far away. A paragraph later he complains that a 45-minute-long monologue he wrote for Kurtz was one of the best scenes he ever played, but that Coppola hardly used any of it. Audiences can be grateful that Coppola was not as easily bullshitted as all that.

The same empty braggadocio tells us how lucky he has been with women. 'There have been many of them in my life, though I hardly ever spent more than a couple of minutes with any of them . . . I enjoy identifying and pushing the right emotional buttons . . . which usually means making them feel that they are of value to me and offering them security for themselves and their children.' You wonder why such a master of womankind should need to eat a quart of ice-cream before making a night visit to a woman whose husband was in hospital, and then, to make himself vomit, stick his finger down his throat so violently that he split his oesophagus and nearly died of internal bleeding. Well, you don't wonder much, because by then, you know what's coming. 'If you've never had warmth, love or affection, it is hard to give it, or if you've had it and it has been stolen from you, if you think you've been rejected and abandoned, you fear being hurt again. I always wanted several women in my life at the same time as an emotional insurance policy to protect myself from being hurt again.' It's going to take very many talented new authors being published to make up for all this slop.

Fired by the post-war revelations of the treatment of the Jews in Germany he became an active Zionist. However, 'I did not know then that Jewish terrorists were indiscriminately killing Arabs . . . Now I understand much more about the complexity of the situation than I did then.' So points gained all round. And although he believes that McCarthyite America 'missed the establishment of fascism . . . by a hair', he claims he did not realise when he agreed to do it that *On the Waterfront* was 'really a metaphorical argument' by Kazan and Budd Schulberg: 'they made the film to justify finking on their friends.' Then there was the unrequited flirtation with the Panthers, when, innocent that he was, he failed to twig that walking through the streets of Harlem with Mayor John Lindsay might be interpreted as supporting the political ambitions of a white politician in need of black votes. Rap Brown 'lambasted me as a shallow liberal poking his nose into a world he didn't know and in which he didn't belong'. Brando took Brown's point that, 'despite a lifetime of searching, curiosity and empathy, I would never understand what it was to be black.' And it is odd that so much searching, curiosity and empathy adds up to little more than the noisy self-publicity of this book. 'I was not Stanley Kowalski,' says Brando repeatedly of his early role in *A Streetcar Named Desire*, explaining that the Stanley Kowalskis he's met in his life were 'muscled, inarticulate, aggressive animals who go through life responding to nothing but their urges and never doubting themselves, men brawny in body and manner of speech who act only on instinct, with little awareness of themselves'. Mmm.

To her eternal credit Greta Garbo never made us suffer like this, though her disdain for what she did was just as deep as Brando's, and her narcissism, in its own way, quite as well-developed. Garbo maintained her public silence to the grave and Diana Souhami is not playing ghost to her shade. *Greta and Cecil* is not a biography of either Garbo or Beaton, but an account of their bizarre relationship, which, at its best, manages, improbably, to turn even the ineffably shallow Cecil Beaton into something of an enigma. We are presented with a world of wavering gender and identity, filled with reflection and reiteration, photographic images, mirrors and screens, where false façades conceal equally artificial foundations, and reality is just what you break your foot on as you stumble on it in the dark.

Biography is of course involved, and Garbo's silence is inevitably breached. What you always suspected, but didn't want to know, is explicitly stated in a quote from James Pope-Hennessy: 'then it gradually dawns on one that she is entirely uneducated, interested in theosophy, dieting and all other cranky subjects, has conversation so dull that you could scream.' There it is again, that waking-up-in-the-morning-feeling.

See her on the screen, however, and Barthes is right: she is the 'Platonic idea of a human creature', all the more so because of the uncertainty of gender she effortlessly displays. Never mind Queen Christina striding around in suede doublet and thigh-high boots, there is Camille frou-frou'ed from top to toe in layers of frothy net and ringlets, but what of those strong, bare shoulders rising out of the décolleté frills, as confident and mobile as a swaggering youth? She is sexual to the point of discomfort, but unanchored to any particular sexuality, so she's everyone's and no one's.

Even so, it's odd that Cecil Beaton should have decided that she might be his. Odd, until you read Souhami's description of the world Beaton created at his farmhouse, Ashcombe, in Wiltshire. 'He filled the place with life-sized cupids, silver and gilt candlesticks, silver bird cages, glass balls, engraved mirrors, shell pictures, crumbling Italian console tables, stone statues called Castor and Pollux and plaster casts of bits of his own anatomy.' Then he held parties, with 'lovely looking people, charades, impersonations and dressing-up games'. But apart from the theatricals, 'nothing much happened at Ashcombe,' and when everyone had gone home there was no ordinary, daily life going on.

Beaton languished for four years after the wealthy art patron Peter Watson, who was kind enough to him but emotionally committed to Beaton's rival, Oliver Messel. For a while Stephen Tennant looked like a possibility, but no one fell in love with Beaton, though he hankered and ached. When he turned his attentions to Garbo, she avoided him for 14 years, during which time she permitted Mercedes de Acosta (of whom Alice B. Toklas wrote: 'You can't dismiss Mercedes lightly. She has had the two most important women in the United States – Garbo and Dietrich') and Stokowski to run around after her, devoted but regularly dismissed from the presence.

Beaton's world was so unreal that he decided that Garbo should be his wife and make a home of Ashcombe. At which point the unreality has the quality of infinite regress, empty Garbo mirroring empty Beaton in their empty mansion filled with functionless stage props. Garbo's world, on the other hand, was strangely real. By 1941, at the age of 36, Garbo had made her last movie, since when she had lived in desolation, doing nothing, alone and in hiding from the press. Her days, she told Beaton in 1965, were spent lying 'in my bed looking at the wallpaper'. She toyed with Beaton, telling him that perhaps she would marry him, that he might 'make an honest boy' of her. Some kind of sexual relationship occurred, although we have to take Beaton's word for it. She went to his hotel room for tea and asked: 'Do you want to go to bed?' And Cecil's recollection? 'Sometimes photographs are more like people than people themselves. This afternoon there were many flashes of her in the Pilgrim hat as she was in *Queen Christina* and later in the half-light she was the living embodiment of her "stills". Later she said, "La nuit tombe" and outside there was only artificial light.' It seems he went to bed with a photograph.

His desire was always mixed with envy and the wish to deface his icon. He noted her ageing face with evident pleasure on a cruise in 1965. 'In this cruel harsh sunlight on board one sees every crinkle and crevice in the most cruel way. I have hawklike watched her in all lights, without mascara even.' In 1935, when he was still dreaming of a relationship with her, he was already writing: 'unused to putting herself out for anyone, she would be a trying companion, continually sighing, full of tragic regrets, without making any definite move to alter her general state of affairs.' He was right, she failed to make the decision to marry her beau, and when he finally published his diaries containing descriptions of his relationship with her, she dismissed him from her life.

What Garbo and Brando share is a loathing of what they did for a living. In some way, their refusal to over-value the business of making movies was admirable, beginning, perhaps, as a proper assessment of the relative value of things in the world. A little contempt for what you do is a useful tool in the inflated world of 'creativity', yet the balance Garbo and Brando might have been trying for tipped over into self-disgust, and the skills that each of them possessed became worthless. Tennessee Williams said of Garbo, as he might have said of Brando: 'How sad a thing for an artist to abandon his art. I think it's much sadder than death.' The autophagists eat themselves away and never satisfy their hunger.

Mrs Straus's Devotion

Last Dinner on the 'Titanic':
Menus and Recipes from the Great Liner
by Rick Archbold and Dana McCauley
(WEIDENFELD, LONDON, 1997)

The 'Titanic' Complex
by John Wilson Foster
(BELCOUVER, CANADA, 1997)

Down with the Old Canoe
by Steven Biel
(NORTON, LONDON, 1997)

We are moved but not overwrought at the fate of those who died at Pompeii, with the sinking of the *Mary Rose,* during the San Francisco earthquake and at the collapse of the Tay Bridge. We respond much more uneasily to the sinking of the *Herald of Free Enterprise,* the *Estonia* and the *Marchioness.* Lives cut short are less poignant once, to paraphrase Beckett, they would have died anyway. We are on the cusp of having the emotional load of the sinking of the *Titanic* lightened, but not quite there yet. As I write, there are at least two, and possibly seven, very elderly survivors of the disaster still alive, but late 20th-century impatience – with age, with taste, for trivia – has made us run a little ahead of ourselves. So it is with unconcealed regret that the authors of the *Titanic* cookbook point out that there is no way of knowing exactly what was on the menu at the super-first class A la Carte restaurant on the evening of 14 April 1912, because 'unfortunately, none of the surviving passengers who ate there on the last evening tucked a copy of the menu into the pocket of a dinner-jacket, so we can only surmise what the bill of fare included.' That would not be an insurmountable obstacle in itself: one of the less fortunate passengers might have provided the clue. A damaged but still partly legible menu from 12 April 'recovered from the body of a third-class passenger' is given a full-page reproduction (porridge, smoked herrings and jacket potatoes for breakfast), to prove the authenticity of the small steerage-class recipe section that follows.

The problem here is modern longevity. It is, after all, 85 years since the unsinkable liner sank; how long are we expected to wait before we can get down to building the *Titanic* theme park? Now, with this glossy volume, the *Titanic* experience can be yours – at least the dry part of it. Along with the recipes for the dishes served that night in first, second and steerage class, there are complete instructions for 'hosting a *Titanic* dinner party': 'The more you can choreograph the evening to create a period atmosphere, the more you and your guests will feel as though you've travelled back in time to the evening of 14 April 1912.' In order to get fully into the spirit of things, formal invitations and dress advice should be sent out weeks in advance on facsimiles of actual cabin tickets 'filled out with their names, the number of servants accompanying them, and the number of cubic feet of luggage to be taken'. Apparently, the compilers of *Last Dinner on the 'Titanic'* are not anticipating that many readers will re-enact the last meal in steerage, though a perfectly edible supper of vegetable soup, roasted pork with sage and pearl onions and plum pudding with sweet sauce is included for the down-market fantasists among us. This is perhaps the first of a series of last suppers, to include recipes and suggestions for staging a Hiroshima sashimi evening, a Dresden barbecue, the *Marchioness* cocktail party, and God knows what they munched with the Marquis during the 120 days of Sodom, but I dare say they rustled up something on day 119 that we could re-create in our own dining rooms.

Fantasy and cultural myth-making have been the main responses to the sinking of the *Titanic* almost from the moment the news was received in the wider world. *Titanic* has abounded in meaning, the actual event almost submerged by its multiple suitability as social metaphor. Analogy is irresistible when a vast floating city is scuppered in a glacially calm sea by the overlooked remnants of an off-the-beaten-track iceberg. The *Titanic* foundered because the sea was calm: no one expected trouble and the smoothness of the waves concealed the jagged lump of ice that would have been tossed and therefore made visible in a stormier ocean. The ship, hailed as the apotheosis of progress and modern engineering, sank so rapidly as a result of brittle fracture, the low-grade steel of the period breaking violently when chilled. The bald meteorological and technological facts are overwhelmed by the irony of calm waters and fragile steel scuttling the complacency of the very rich in the first class, and the hopes of the dispossessed in steerage. The *Titanic* was a ship of fools. As John Wilson Foster tells us, the grand staircase came in William and Mary style, though the balustrade was Louis XIV; the first-class dining saloon and reception rooms were Jacobean, the restaurant Louis XVI, the lounge Louis XV (Versailles), the reading and writing room late Georgian, the smoking room early Georgian. The women's clothes were newly purchased from Paris couture houses; and tucked into a pocket of whatever finely cut suit the bibliophile Harry Widener was wearing (for all we know, along with that elusive A la Carte menu) was a 1598 edition – possibly the only copy – of Bacon's essays. 'If he was lost at sea,' he had promised the London dealer, 'the Bacon would go down clasped to his heart.' In keeping with common ideas of the behaviour of the very rich, the *Titanic* cookbook explains that the A la Carte restaurant, whose food and service were superior even to the first-class dining room, was not part of the White Star liner's inclusive price. Passengers who took their meals there instead of the first-class saloon, paid at the time for what they ate, though they were entitled to apply for a rebate at the end of the voyage. After the sinking of the *Titanic*, several survivors put in their claims for a rebate, confirming, we are told by the cookbook's authors, who know how to extrapolate what is important from such details, 'that the restaurant had become an immediate hit'. One longs to know whether the applications were merely for their own extra expenditure on food, or if they included the bills of their lost loved ones' gourmet feasts.

Of all the emblematic themes that surrounded the sinking of the *Titanic*, the apparent obedience to the principle of 'women and children first' was the most engaging. It confirmed not just the idea of the difference between the sexes, but also the innate nobility of the upper classes, for a world on the brink of the Great War. The survivor statistics offered by Steven Biel tell something of the gender story: 94 per cent of first-cabin women and children survived compared to 31 per cent of first-cabin men; 81 per cent of second-cabin and 47 per cent of steerage women survived against 10 per cent and 14 per cent respectively of men in those two classes. As a story of social class rather than gender, the overall figures show that 60 per cent of first-cabin passengers, 44 per cent of second-cabin and 25 per cent of steerage passengers survived.

'Does not the heart of every true American woman go out in tender loyalty to those brave men of the *Titanic* who yielded their valuable lives that the weak and helpless might live?' asked a letter-writer in the *New York Times*. There is more here than a mere paean to old-world chivalry and one in the eye for the army of suffragists demanding equal rights: there is a note of regret that such financial and industrial eminences as John Jacob Astor, Benjamin Guggenheim, Isidor Straus and Harry Widener should have given up their lives not just to their own women, but to impoverished foreigners – the Guggenheims and Strauses apparently being accorded an honorary Aryanness for the occasion. The *San Francisco Examiner* eulogised the heroes whose place in the lifeboats and in the world was taken 'by some sabot-shod, shawl-enshrouded, illiterate and penniless woman of Europe'. The essential nobility of the rich and famous, indeed the natural rightness of their wealth and fame, was confirmed by the public image of these men standing on the deck in tuxedos, smoking elegant cigarettes while the *Titanic* slipped ineluctably under the water. For the virulently anti-suffragist and those especially alarmed by suffragist demands for more liberal divorce laws, Ida Straus, the wife of the Macy's executive, became a feminine icon as she refused her place in the lifeboat, choosing instead to stay and die with her husband. 'In this day of frequent and scandalous divorces,' declaimed one editorial, 'when the marriage tie once held so sacred to all is too lightly regarded, the wifely devotion and love of Mrs Straus for her partner of a lifetime stand out in noble contrast.'

The *Titanic* was known to be unsinkable, however. The slowness to react of everyone from the crew to the passengers testifies to the lack of alarm. It is entirely possible that the men who waited on the deck with such aplomb did not believe their lives to be in imminent danger. The ship sank astonishingly fast after what seemed a minor collision with a small iceberg. The visible evidence of damage was minimal. As Biel points out, 'the attitude of the first-cabin male passengers might just as well have been complacency as heroic

calm.' One surviving passenger remembered that at the time
he left the *Titanic* there was difficulty in filling all the
lifeboats, as the danger had not yet been fully realised by the
passengers. It might well have seemed that a place in the
lifeboat was no more than an extra safety precaution and
further, Biel suggests, the chances of the women surviving in
the freezing waters of the North Atlantic in an open lifeboat
were considerably less than those of the men waiting on
deck for the crisis to blow over. If we aren't happy at the suggestion that the heroes of the *Titanic* might have been doing
little more than paying lip-service to chivalry, and were in
fact in what they thought, until it was too late, was the opti-
mum situation, then perhaps our times are less transgressive
than they seem. But perhaps this interpretation makes a
dismal modern sense of apparently altruistic behaviour.
Moreover, the Straus's example of marital fidelity was balanced by several clandestine liaisons. The two sons of a
wealthy Frenchman from Nice were saved. Their father had
run off with their governess and, changing his name to
Hoffman, sailed from Cherbourg on the *Titanic*. Kate
Phillips was 19 and pregnant by her wealthy employer,
Henry Morley. He, too, had abandoned his wife and sailed
with his lover under the name of Mr and Mrs Marshall. He
died, she was saved, and the surviving daughter is cam-
paigning to have Henry Morley legally identified as her
father. The playboy, John Jacob Astor, reinstated as a hero
after the sinking, had been in poor public favour in the
States, having ditched his wife for a much younger woman,
with whom he had fled to France to avoid the scandal. He
was 'the world's greatest monument to unearned income';
Harry Widener, whose accumulation of priceless antiquarian
books kept him occupied and sailing the oceans in search of
further acquisitions, came a close second.

Biel is American and his admirable investigation of the
cultural history of the *Titanic* has a transatlantic skew – not

unreasonably since a large proportion of the passengers were either American or emigrants from Europe, heading for a new life there. The Americanness of his approach takes a bit of getting used to if, like me, all you had previously known about the *Titanic* had come from the 1958 film *A Night to Remember*. It's years since I saw it, but the overwhelming impression I have of it is the immaculate Britishness of the event, all black and white, clipped accents, Kenneth More and the evening-suited band on the sinking deck playing 'Nearer My God to Thee' (they didn't, it was actually something called 'Song d'Automne', just as elegiac but possibly not as catchy). The American film industry has only now appropriated the story with James Cameron's movie (a Broadway musical version had to be postponed when the stage *Titanic* refused to sink), but there are clear echoes of the *Titanic* in the very wonderful 1972 *Poseidon Adventure*, an upside-down version of nemesis at sea, and in the greatest disaster movie of them all, *The Towering Inferno*, which is clearly a vertical, dry-land trope for the engulfing of the *Titanic*. All the elements are there. Fire replaces water, but isolation and greed are the central themes: the design shortcuts of the skyscraper representing the lack of lifeboats, the idle rich at their unreachable penthouse party; death in fancy dress and with gourmet food, the sacrifice of male lives in favour of elegantly clad women and the occasional cad who gets his just deserts after attempting to save his own skin.

Although no blacks were on board, the *Titanic* has somehow managed to include racial tension among its meanings. The contemporary newspaper account of a white but grimy stoker attempting to steal the lifebelt of a radio operator who had heroically remained behind to continue calling for help, rapidly became a story of a murderous Negro stoker with a knife. But black Americans made their own contributions to *Titanic* mythology with bluesman Leadbelly composing a song that had the world heavyweight champion, Jack Johnson, bidding a gleeful farewell to the doomed ship from the dock, having tried to board, and been told by Captain Smith: 'I ain't hauling no coal.' Biel describes how the *Titanic* disaster became part of black urban folklore in the mythic person of 'Shine', the apocryphal stoker, who in numerous narrative poems is the only person on board capable of swimming to safety and refuses to help the whites who offer him all the treasures they have laid up on earth:

> when all them white folks went to heaven,
> Shine was in Sugar Ray's bar drinking
> Seagram's Seven

The *Titanic* belonged to everyone. Bob Dylan uses it in 'Desolation Row', which depicts 'a rock vision of contemporary apocalypse':

> Praise be to Nero's Neptune
> The *Titanic* sails at dawn
> Everybody's shouting
> Which side are you on?

It was, of course, a gift for those who saw disaster in modernity. The ship was supposed to be the slickest, fastest vessel ever. The maiden trip was an attempt to break the record for an Atlantic crossing, which is one reason so many notables were on board. Yet, as Biel points out, it was one of the last occasions when death on the move permitted a degree of gentility. For all the speed with which the ship sank, it still took two hours and 40 minutes to go down. It was precisely this time lapse that allowed decisions to be made about the manner of living and dying. Heroism, or even cowardice, is hardly possible under modern circumstances. *The Times* ended its review of *A Night to Remember*: 'This air age,

when death commonly comes too swiftly for heroism or
with no survivors to record it, can still turn with wonder to
an age before yesterday when a thousand deaths at sea
seemed the very worst the world must suffer.' By the late
Fifties the nuclear age had begun and death in fancy dress
looked like a luxury. And if the world hasn't become class-
less in the ensuing decades, no one can feel reassured that the
purchase of a first-class ticket on an airliner will give them a
statistical survival advantage over economy passengers.

Still, none of this quite accounts for the fervour which the
85-year-old disaster still produces. Collectors of memorabilia, amateur historians, curators of private museums,
writers of innumerable websites, regular visitors to conven-
tions form a kind of religious cult for which the *Titanic* is the
sacred text. There are passionate arguments about salvaging
the wreckage, now possible with our own leading-edge technology. There are those who simply hanker after
memorabilia, some who approve a memorial museum, yet
others who regard the sunken hulk and its contents as lying
in consecrated ground. There is even a schism: the *Titanic*
Historical Society, with headquarters in landlocked Indian
Orchard, Massachusetts, suffered a breakaway and the
founding of *Titanic* International, whose supporters claimed
that the election of THS officers was undemocratic and the
leadership of Ed Kamuda despotic. The *Titanic* buffs are in
the grip of an all-consuming, nostalgic, trainspotting passion
for the past. 'Today everything's tourist class,' moans
Kamuda, who along with the evils of classlessness, also cites
feminism as responsible for contemporary social turmoil and
decline. The *Titanic*, he says, represents the loss of 'a way of
life which I and others long for'. Like believers in reincarna-
tion who don't doubt that in previous lives they were
pharaohs and potentates rather than slaves and serfs, so the
dreamers of *Titanic* days assume their places would have

been in the first-class smoking room rather than the boiler-room. That's what the past, if not history, is for. If, ultimately, we are all passengers on the *Titanic* (the cosmic implications of a ship lost in the void of an empty sea are not easily resisted), at least we can go down with our dreams of exquisitely adorned heroism intact. Or as the authors of the *Titanic* cookbook put it, contrasting a criticism by Charles Dickens of the poor first-class fare aboard Cunard's *Britannia* in 1842, 'no such complaints are recorded from any of the *Titanic*'s survivors.'

Victim Victim

Why, an interviewer asked me recently in front of a couple of hundred people, do you condone rape? Once I'd got my breath back, I replied that while I could imagine possible justifications for almost any crime – murder, infanticide, arson, you name it, there might be mitigating circumstances – I couldn't think of a single condition in which an act of rape might be defended. 'But when a girl in one of your novels is raped, she doesn't react in the way we would expect a rape victim to behave. She seems to carry on.'

The fictional character in question is homeless, hungry and in the midst of a frightening psychotic episode when the rape occurs. Is it possible that those conditions might jostle for her attention and the rape be experienced as a secondary disaster? The answer, currently, is no. The idea of the victim has taken on a virtually fetishistic significance for the liberal conscience in the last couple of decades. We use the word so promiscuously that, like 'fascist' in the Seventies, it threatens to lose its value. We employ it for every shade of misadventure. What is the relationship between a fashion victim, an Aids victim and a child victim (no adults or soldiers, please) of the Bosnian war? There is, in fact, a connection; it is that they all must consider themselves impotent individuals helplessly at the mercy of forces – be they frock-makers, viruses or murderous human beings – beyond their control.

Once they have accepted this view of themselves we are ready with compassion and succour: counselling for the clotheshorses, charity performances for the terminally ill, mercy medical flights for a handful of children for whom it is essentially too late.

I suppose it could be argued that the negative self-image we encourage people to adopt doesn't matter too much as long as some people who need help of one kind or another are getting it. But there are sinister side effects of our attraction to the idea of the victim. When those we've designated as the bad guys in the current conflict in former Yugoslavia are suspected, as they have been, of harming their own people and then displaying them as atrocities committed by the other side, it is because they know that to redeem their reputation, and engage the support of the rest of the world, they need to supply us with victims.

Equally, there is something desperately disturbing to us about the fact that the Croats, our favoured victims until recently, have now taken up the role of oppressors. The concept of victims is a static one: they must remain the underdog as a group or forfeit our approval and risk our rage at having been 'fooled'.

What we lose is the understanding of what war really means, what it does to people whose values somersault in the face of chaos. Instead of recognising the disgusting effects of war, we take sides and collude in its dire consequences. If this is what is termed appeasement, it's no longer clear to me who or what is being appeased, apart from the idea of civil strife itself.

We have precise expectations of those we nominate victims: in a fearfully vicious cycle of compassion, our sympathy depends on their degree of suffering, and their degree of suffering must be seen to be what we say it is. To qualify, victims must be oppressed, wholly innocent and their lives in ruins. It is not enough that catastrophe happens to people, we insist that recovery is virtually impossible. We've been encouraged in this by the hold that popular psychology has gained over us this century. Beyond the wounding is the trauma and that, we're increasingly certain, will probably last a lifetime.

How do we balance the damage done by the perpetrator against the compassionately intended message to the victim that he or she has been emotionally scarred for life? A young girl was raped not long ago while doing her paper round. In the news report, the police officer in charge stated: 'This young woman's life has been ruined.' A rape crisis counsellor was quoted and used exactly the same words. A former rape victim described how, years after the event, she is unable to come to terms with her experience, and remains depressed and suicidal.

My thought is this: if the act of rape is an expression of a need for power, wouldn't that man – or any potential rapist – reading the report receive confirmation that he has succeeded in what he has set out to do? It is precisely the ruination of a life that he was after, and those most concerned for the victim seem, in a dreadful paradox, to be colluding in fulfilling his fantasies. And to what extent are we inadvertently disempowering the child (and the rest of the female population) when we tell her that what has befallen her is irreparable? Every act of physical violence will have traumatic effects but what do we mean when we tell a young woman that her sense of self-worth can be destroyed by an act of enforced penetration? Are we really meaning to say that a woman's central identity resides in her genitals?

In a society where depicting a rape victim reacting 'in a way we would not expect' is judged to be condoning rape, a disclaimer is needed. It shouldn't be; it ought to be obvious that none of this is to endorse disgracefully lenient sentences, or the kind of vilification women undergo during cross-questioning in rape cases. But if we contest those wrongs by sending each other messages about our special weakness we'll lose more than we can gain. We'll diminish what has been hard fought for, and end up once again in the special protection of those who historically have always offered people protection in return for an admission of weakness.

Something like that occurs when it is suggested that a woman who kills her violent husband should be acquitted by virtue of suffering from 'battered woman syndrome'. They should be acquitted on the grounds of provocation or self-defence, and if these statutes are too narrow in their comprehension of the behaviour of the long-term abused, they must be amended so that they do apply, and all ages, conditions and genders can receive justice.

The sidelining and making vulnerable of groups we seek to defend is a bizarre result of our need to pit the goodies against the baddies. We seem to have to consider the villains and depict them as overwhelmingly strong in order to fire our concern for people. The danger is that we end up enfeebling the very people who need above all else a solid sense of their own integrity and autonomy, while reinforcing a satisfying self-image of omnipotence in those most inclined to take advantage of the weak.

The Girl in the Attic

The Diary of a Young Girl
by Anne Frank, edited by Otto Frank and
Mirjam Pressler, translated by Susan Massotty
(VIKING, LONDON, 1997)

I wonder if to be Jewish is to be by definition lonely in the world – not as a result of the history, but on account of the theology. If ardent young men attending the *yeshiva* have traditionally engaged each other in intense arguments nagging at the nicer points of interpreting the Torah, it is surely because the Jewish God is notorious for evading questions directed at him. Was there ever such a one for sliding out of an argument as Yahweh? The last time he responded to a direct question must have been when the blameless Job, suffering a foreshadowing of the 20th century with the loss of his children, his worldly goods and afflicted with all manner of physical ills, demanded – quite politely under the circumstances – to know why of his maker. 'Where,' boomed the Lord, 'wast thou when I laid the foundations of the earth? . . . Hath the rain a father? . . . Out of whose womb came the ice? . . . Canst thou draw out leviathan with a hook?' All interesting questions, but not really to Job's point.

God does not seem to be a good communicator. Too busy
with the overall scheme of things, perhaps. He'll give out ten
blanket rules, but he won't tell you why your life seems to be
so bloody difficult lately. The problem of the senior executive
without the common touch. Catholicism seems to have
understood the Almighty's failing and provided its faithful
with a bevy of more approachable under-managers, each
with their own speciality, willing and able to intercede with
on high on behalf of the baffled individual. A Catholic knows
exactly who to apply to when hoping for better health, safe
travel, release from drudgery or persecution. There is a saint
for almost everything that ails you. For the Jews, however,
there is only a single very busy, self-important and fractious
God. So it seemed to me when I was young. I was troubled
by the unreliability of prayer, rather as one feels anxious
about sending important letters to large organisations.

Anne Frank is the only Jewish saint. I first read *The Diary
of Anne Frank* when I was about the same age as she was
when she began to write it. She seemed to me perfectly to fit
the bill as a possible intercessor. Perhaps, in the years after
the war, young Jewish girls all over Europe discovered her as
a saint all their own: someone to share the miseries of pre-
adolescence, someone to turn to in times of aching
solitariness within their raucous families, who would without doubt understand. She sounded so like oneself, and yet
she was dead, which gave her a necessary gravitas. She may
have personified the Holocaust for millions of adults – the
diary is the most widely read non-fiction book after the
Bible – but for me, aged 12 or 13, she simply told the story
of what it is like to be 12 or 13 in a world where no one
seems to be listening to you. Read the diary without hindsight (impossible for any adult, of course, but not so difficult
when you are a child looking for a literary friend) and it is a
masterly description of the sorrows and turmoil of any
bright, raging, self-dramatising young girl. Read in this way,

in the way I first read it, the sequestration becomes peripheral, the fear of capture secondary. 'I don't fit in with them'
is an early and continuous complaint that for me, at the
time, quite overrode Anne Frank's particular circumstances.
Being locked in an attic in fear of one's life was, to my mind,
just another version of being trapped with the family. What
counted was someone who looked not very different from
me, saying precisely what was on my mind. Anne Frank,
wanting to be a writer, precocious, isolated, furiously adolescent and angry with her family, was the point:

Last night I went downstairs in the dark, all by myself . . . I
stood at the top of the stairs while German planes flew back
and forth, and I knew I was on my own, that I couldn't
count on others for support. My fear vanished. I looked up
at the sky and trusted in God. I have an intense need to be
alone. Father noticed I'm not my usual self, but I can't tell
him what's bothering me. All I want to do is scream: 'Let me
be, leave me alone!'

I knew that the war, the Holocaust and the tragedy of a
young and pointless death was what I was supposed to be
reading the diary for, but I was far too engaged with her
inner story to pay much attention to the other stuff. Now, of
course, reading it from the other end of the age telescope the
story looks a little ambiguous. Quite a good family, as families go: liberal, affectionate, willing to tolerate the moods of
a difficult adolescent, and under an unimaginable pressure.
There's a new sympathy for Mrs Frank as she turns away
from her daughter, who has refused to allow her to listen to
her prayers instead of her father: '"I don't want to be angry
with you. I can't make you love me!" A few tears slid down
her cheeks as she went out of the door.' Anne's main complaint against Mrs Frank is that she doesn't take her
seriously. 'The truth is that she has rejected me,' she writes

after this incident. 'She's the one whose tactless comments and cruel jokes about matters I don't think are funny have made me insensitive to any sign of love on her part.' Everybody behaving just how they are supposed to, I think now. A good enough family under any circumstances, let alone theirs.

But imagine the liberation of reading at the age of 12 or 13:

> I simply can't stand Mother . . . I don't know why I've taken such a terrible dislike to her. Daddy says that if Mother isn't feeling well or has a headache, I should volunteer to help her, but I'm not going to because I don't love her and don't enjoy doing it. I can imagine Mother dying someday, but Daddy's death seems inconceivable. It's very mean of me, but that's how I feel. I hope Mother will *never* read this or anything else I've written.

In fact, I didn't read that the first time. That passage from the entry of 3 October 1942 was heavily edited by her father, Otto Frank. The entry I read concluded: 'Daddy would like me to offer to help Mummy sometimes, when she doesn't feel well or has a headache, but I won't. I am working hard at my French and am now reading *La Belle Nivernaise*.' This is not just a new translation, but The Definitive Edition of *The Diary of a Young Girl*. That 'but I won't' was quite thrilling, it suggested a fervent obstinacy which was very attractive, but 'because I don't love her and don't enjoy doing it' would have offered more than a stubborn young girl, would have given me and the world an Anne Frank who had the horrible honesty of a writer who says what there is to be said, even if it is unspeakable. Niceness was not her project; describing how things were was what she was doing, at first for herself and later with the idea of publication. There are three versions of the diary: Version A is the first unedited diary; Version B is her own edited variant, worked on when, in 1944, Gerrit Bolkestein, a member of the Dutch government in exile, broadcast from London his wish to collect eyewitness accounts of the Dutch Occupation and publish them after the war; Version C is the one Otto Frank cut and culled from Versions A and B and what we have read. There is a Critical Edition which lays out all three versions side by side, so the Definitive Edition is not new, but culled itself, adding about a third more material, but also dropping some of the text. This is the kind of publishing history you might expect of the testimony of a saint; authorised, unauthorised and apocrypha.

It was perfectly reasonable for Otto Frank to censor his daughter's diaries. Of the eight people in hiding he was the only survivor and Anne's pent-up peevishness about her mother, sister and the van Daans – who shared the secret Annexe with the Frank family – did not serve the purpose he intended in publishing his dead daughter's diary. In a schools' version (Otto Frank's version, edited by Christopher Martin) published by Longman's to commemorate the first national Anne Frank Day on 12 June 1996, the inside front cover states: 'By thinking about Anne Frank and her message to the world, it is hoped that the day will enhance young people's spiritual, moral, social and cultural development.' This is not exactly the personal saint I envisaged, but a Jewish version of St Thérèse of Lisieux, the Little White Flower, who was canonised in spite of a complete absence of the usual mandatory miracles, for dying an early death and struggling with her dislike of some of the Sisters in her Carmelite convent. St Anne, like St Thérèse, was offered to the world as an example. Each put up with their respective lots: the Nazis and tuberculosis. What father, and what champion of martyrdom, is going to include his daughter's detailed description of her vulva ('In the upper part, between the outer labia, there's a fold of skin that, on second thought, looks like a kind of blister. That's the clitoris'), or her haughty dismissal of her mother (' I need my mother to set a good example and be a person I can respect, but in most matters she's an example of what not to do') or her irritation at her father ('Father's fondness for talking about farting and going to the lavatory is disgusting')? There are moments of saintlike repentance, but they rarely come without a sting in the tale :

> I was offended, took it far too much to heart and was insolent and beastly to her, which, in turn, made her unhappy . . . The period of tearfully passing judgment on Mother is over. I've grown wiser and Mother's nerves are a bit steadier. Most of the time I manage to hold my tongue when I'm annoyed, and she does too . . . but there's one thing I can't do, and that's to love Mother with the devotion of a child.

Right from the start, the diary was personified. 'To enhance the image of the long-awaited friend in my imagination, I don't want to jot down the facts in this diary the way most people would do, but I want the diary to be my friend, and I'm going to call this friend *Kitty*.' 'Dearest Kitty' is how all the entries begin, and they end, 'Yours Anne', or later, 'Yours Anne M. Frank'. It enables her not just to grumble about her parents and the other members of the Annexe, but also to practise a heroic jauntiness, a public voice: 'I look upon our life in hiding as an interesting adventure, full of danger and romance, and every privation as an amusing addition to my diary.' She apologises and tries for distance when a previous entry has sounded depressed, and makes sure that Kitty gets a thorough and up-to-date picture of everyday life in hiding. The beginning of the entry for 13 December 1942 is disturbingly vivid, but also literary, reminiscent of young Jane Eyre reading alone behind the curtains in the window-seat: 'I'm sitting here nice and cosy in the front office, peering out through a chink in the heavy curtains. It's dark, but there's just enough light to write by.' Making the diary her reader allows Anne Frank to be a writer, to get a sense of the overall work, to balance it, to convey a mood, to reach for an effect:

> To Father, peeling potatoes is not a chore, but precision work. When he reads, he has a deep wrinkle in the back of his head. But when he's preparing potatoes, beans or vegetables, he seems to be totally absorbed in his task. He puts on his potato-peeling face, and when it's set in that particular way, it would be impossible for him to turn out anything less than a perfectly peeled potato.

This is Anne with her public-writing face on, and there's pleasure and great sadness in witnessing her working like this. 'I've made up my mind to lead a different life from other girls, and not to become an ordinary housewife later on.'

Her burgeoning love for Peter van Daan is also part of the work. She creates a romance out of poor material, but all there is to hand. Peter, whose name is the same as that of a boy she had a crush on before they went into hiding, serves to practise on. At first he seems to lack qualities of mind and personality she would prefer, but Anne is undaunted and begins to perceive all manner of gentleness and shyness that she can use to transform him into a suitable first love. They sit close and alone watching the stars. The first kiss is breathlessly described to Kitty: 'How I suddenly made the right movement, I don't know, but before we went downstairs, he gave me a kiss, through my hair, half on my left cheek and half on my ear. I tore downstairs without looking back, and I long so much for today.' And then, just a few pages later, the falling away of a passion she couldn't, and under normal circumstances wouldn't, be expected to sustain: 'I forced Peter, more than he realises, to get close to me, and now he's holding on for dear life. I honestly don't see any effective way of shaking him off . . . I soon realised he would never be a kindred spirit.'

The diary ends with an entry for Tuesday, 1 August 1944, in which she describes herself as a bundle of contradictions, wondering who she would be if she could be truly herself: 'if only there were no other people in the world'. Two days later the SS arrive and we are briefly informed in an Afterword of the final fate of the members of the Annexe. There's a curious hiatus here. We have witnessed Anne Frank's life and development over a period of two years, then we hear how, seven months later, she died of typhus in Bergen-Belsen just a few days after her sister Margot, and a month before the camp was liberated. But from the moment of discovery in the attic, to her final illness, Anne, who has been so vividly herself, disappears into the mass. We've followed her fears, first love, anger and joy, but it is impossible to follow her imaginatively as she is transported across Europe, when the irritations of family, the hormonal ups and downs, the dreams all disappear in a fearful reality that she refused to imagine in her letters to Kitty. Later, thanks to one of her Dutch protectors finding and saving the diary, she was to become the most famous victim of the Holocaust, and does achieve her ambition: 'I can't imagine having to live like Mother, Mrs van Daan and all the women who go about their work and are then forgotten . . . I don't want to have lived in vain like most people. I want to be useful or bring enjoyment to all people, even those I've never met. I want to go on living even after my death.' But there is something haunting about her absence during those first weeks after she was discovered and the diary was silenced. She disappears into a fog of cattle trucks too full of humanity to see any one individual clearly. She becomes part of a mass disaster, and as alone as it is possible to be. It is in her sudden anonymity that Anne Frank becomes most emblematic of all the individuals caught up in the midst of an immense tragedy.

Queuing for Pearl

There are some questions that are so urgent that they have to be asked repeatedly, even though there has never been, nor ever will be an answer. They may be addressed to another person, but it is just as likely that they are spoken aloud to an empty chair when no one else is present. Certain questions have to be articulated, made real and sent off pulsing into the ether. When another person is present they behave as if they were expected to answer and focus their attention on the question, even perhaps, attempt some form of words, knowing all the while that the only proper response is a bewildered shake of the head. There is some ineffable Zen Buddhist koan to which the correct reply is to take off a shoe and place it on one's head. It's a response which is as absurd as the question that has no answer, but which also respects the necessity of the question by engaging with it.

Pearl Jacubowicz asked me her question a good half-dozen times during our conversation in her flat in West Hampstead. Sometimes it came out of what she had been saying, sometimes it seemed simply to arrive, a small explosion bracketed by a brief silence, as if the thought perpetually rolled around in her mind and from time to time had to be spoken as a form of release. Each time she paused and looked at me and each time the silence was prolonged while I failed to come up with an answer. Then, with a slight shrug of her shoulders, she would continue with her story.

'Why am I alive?' she asked. 'Why do I deserve to be alive? Can you tell me that?'

The simple answer is that everybody deserves to be alive, though that's simple indeed and perhaps not even true. But the context of the question is that Pearl, now nearly 70 years of age, lost 65 members of her family during the Nazi catastrophe. All of them: uncles, aunts and cousins, her parents, her eight brothers and sisters, her favourite sister's five children of whom the oldest was six. In that context, the simple answer merely reiterates the question.

'Have you read Primo Levi?' I ask her. 'He wrote about that. The feelings the survivors were left with.'

'Yes, yes. Someone gave me a book. I read it over and over. He was a very clever man. He killed himself, you know?'

Primo Levi also could only ask the question. But Pearl's mother had an answer of sorts.

'My mother always used to say to me: "If you have years to live, nobody can kill you." And she was right. I don't know why I lived when everyone else died. In Belsen I didn't care any more. I didn't care if I lived or not, I was all alone, but I didn't think of dying. I wasn't sure I was going to live but I just didn't think I was going to die. There was a girl in the bunk opposite me, she was eating the whole time – she had a friend in the kitchen – while I was starving and had typhus. You know, two days after Sunday the 15th of April, the liberation, she died. And I was alive. What do you make of that?'

Pearl always gives the date whenever she mentions the liberation of Belsen.

Pearl also has an answer of a kind to her question, though

she thinks of it as the same answer her mother gave her, which it may not be.

'Just before the liberation I had a dream; I was crossing the water and got to a place where there were wooden bungalows. I looked through a window and I saw my oldest brother. I said to him: where is everybody? He said, if you go round the corner there are other windows. Behind the green curtains, ask the woman there and she will tell you. I went there and I said to her: "I want to see my parents." She told me: "You can only see them if you die." I said: "But I haven't lived yet." She looked at a list and said: "You're right, go back, you're right at the bottom, you've got a long time to live." When I woke up, I was crying my eyes out.'

She says she dreamed of her mother a lot in the camp, but every time, her mother turned her away. 'She didn't want me to be with her.' Later in England she dreamed of her repeatedly. 'She was so small. She was smaller than me. I was holding her in my arms and suddenly she fell. She died in my hands.'

Pearl doesn't mention her father much, though in fact she was closer to him than to her mother. 'I can't think about him very well,' she says. It's the loss of her mother that she dwells on most, perhaps because the relationship was far from easy. 'I used to think: if we ever go home, I'll tell my mother what happened to me. But she went before me, so there was no one to tell.'

When she was little she ran home during a family outing. Her mother, she says, lived for her sons and this used to hurt her. 'She felt everything was for the boys.' None of the other sisters seemed to mind, but she did, and that day, when her mother found her back at home, Pearl told her that she'd run away because she loved the boys better. 'I have ten fingers,' her mother told her. 'Whichever I cut, bleeds.' 'So what could I say?' Pearl asks me.

Her parents quarrelled incessantly, about business and money, and, it seems, about her mother's disappointment. 'She used to tell me never to get married unless I really loved a man. Not to be like her.' It made Pearl unhappy, running between the two arguing parents, trying to be the peacemaker of the family. She was 18 when her family were taken away and she began a journey from the Budapest ghetto to a labour camp, and then to Dachau where Doctor Mengele ('a blonde giant, so handsome') selected the younger women who would march to Belsen, leaving the older ones behind. One night during that march, another handsome man in a leather coat came to the place where they were resting and took all the young children away. Pearl supposed the children were killed until a few months ago, when she saw a documentary on television about Raoul Wallenberg and recognised him as the man in the leather coat. 'I screamed when I saw a picture of him. Those children were saved. They were sent all over the world. Some of them spoke on the programme.'

Pearl details her experience willingly, knowing herself to be a witness to a monstrous piece of history ('I was in the same barracks as Anne Frank. Of course, I didn't know who she was then. There were just some Dutch girls. They cried all the time.') Watching the VJ Day commemorations brought it back. 'I saw those old men, Japanese prisoners of war, and I thought: you shouldn't forget. Nobody should forget. I have to talk about it. Sometimes it has to come out.'

But talking about it is not personally therapeutic for Pearl. Recently she lost her best friend, Barney, who she had known for 25 years. They had a loving relationship, though she refused to marry him, and would never consider having children in case they might one day have to go through what she experienced. Barney's stroke brought all the other losses back, and someone suggested she see a therapist. She went for 12 weeks. 'Barney was still alive when I started going. The therapist said to me: "Do you want bereavement counselling?" "Already?" I said, "He's not dead yet."'

At home, alone after Barney's death, 'I shed tears, you wouldn't believe it.' She has to attend hospitals, she tells me, because her eyes are dry. 'I ask them, "How can I shed tears when my eyes are dry?" but they tell me it has nothing to do with it.' She speaks of being lonely, of never having had time for friends because she was always busy with work. She has one woman friend, but is reluctant to ring her up when she's feeling like company or to talk about how much she misses Barney. 'I wouldn't want her to think I'm running after her.'

What Pearl has to say about the conditions and treatment in the camps will be familiar to anyone who has read survivor accounts and seen the grim newsreels taken by the shattered Allied troops when they arrived. What is so disturbing about hearing the facts from Pearl at first hand is not the details, which are dreadful and necessary repetitions of what is already known, but the familiar way she uses certain words which most of us utter carefully, as if they were our tribal fetishes, because they contain unspeakable and unimaginable meanings. Pearl pronounces 'Dachau' and 'Belsen' with no more emphasis in her sentences than we would if we were talking about a university we had once attended, or a district we lived in when we first left home. At one point she describes, to elaborate some event, the barracks she was in. 'The bunks were that wide.' She waves her hand to indicate the distance between the window beside my chair and the sofa on which she sits. 'The passage between them was about the width of this table,' she says, touching her fingertips on a coffee table between us. For Pearl, Belsen is a real place with a memorised landscape, one that she can relate to her present surroundings, not a generalised geography of horror. 'Are you cold?' she asks me, noticing during the wave of her hand that a breeze is coming in through the open window. I'm not, but she gets up and closes the window anyway in case I'm just being polite.

She makes me coffee. 'I only drink fresh coffee,' she says smiling, and seems to wait for me to join her in some joke.

Pearl, like everyone else, was weak and sick when liberation came, but she noticed one day that the German guards had white cloth around their sleeves and she remembered how her brothers used to play soldiers as children and that when they lost whatever war they were fighting they wore white armbands. She said to the other women in her barracks: 'You know what? I think it's over, the guards have got white armbands on.' Naturally, they didn't believe her.

Pearl spent two and a half years in Belsen after the liberation. The British turned it into a Displaced Persons' camp for those who, like Pearl, had no family anywhere in the world and therefore no other place to go. The ex-internees had to be sponsored to emigrate to England or the US (where Pearl dreamed of living), but though she thought there were some distant relatives somewhere in Cleveland, Ohio, she had no names. Belsen, the DP camp, was not so bad when the British were in charge. But Pearl is not very romantic about her liberators. When a German was murdered, the British exercised their sense of justice by locking all the inmates in their barracks until they found out who had committed the crime. The camp survivors rebelled, broke down the doors and demonstrated in front of the British, angry at being treated in this way. 'They were holding guns at us,' Pearl remembers. 'They were standing there with their guns pointed at us. Can you believe it?' It turned out to be a non-Jewish Pole who had done the killing. The soldiers held dances every night and took the young women out. Best of all were the Italian prisoners of war, when they arrived. They serenaded the girls and one day, while looking into a shop window, she saw an Italian passing by with a huge rat on a lead. 'He was walking so proudly, as if he had some wonderful pedigree dog. That's the first time I laughed. They helped us to survive, they gave us a lot of life, the Italians.'

Marriages were made and children born in Belsen after the liberation while the survivors waited for somewhere to go and begin their lives. But food was short, and became shorter once the British left the camp to the Polish Army to administer. 'There was food coming in,' says Pearl with a shrug. 'But we didn't see much of it after the British left.'

Finally, one of the girls who had left got a Jewish family in Birmingham to sponsor Pearl to come to England for a year as their domestic servant. She left Belsen on 21 September 1947. 'I came out of Belsen and went into a kitchen. It hit me so hard. Mrs Short would put a spoonful of food on the plate and ask: "Is that enough?" I was too embarrassed to ask for more, so I always said yes. She could have said, help yourself, but she always asked: "Is that enough?"' Pearl made up her mind that if she ever had a home she was 'going to put everything on the table'. When no one was around, she ate packaged soups Mrs Short got from America to fill herself up. One day she mentioned that the biscuits she had for her tea were dry. 'Did you have it better in the camp?' asked Mrs Short's mother. This is why Pearl stops and smiles when she tells me she only drinks fresh coffee. When my coffee arrives, there's also a plate piled with fancy Belgian biscuits and a slab of dark Dutch chocolate, and I'm exhorted to eat. Even then, I'm not allowed to leave until she has successfully pushed a full packet of biscuits and another bar of chocolate into my bag.

After six months there was the offer of work in another family in London through contacts she had made in the Hungarian Club. She hadn't fulfilled her contract with Mrs Short, but she went to the authorities and told them that if they didn't let her go to London she wanted to go back to Belsen. They gave her the necessary papers. She spent eight years caring for three small children whose mother was 'in

Jenny Diski

an asylum'. Their father was the love of Pearl's life, but when his wife had an operation that returned her to the outside world, Pearl clearly couldn't stay. Though she kept in touch with the children until they were grown up, their father did not want to continue a relationship of any kind. Some years later she phoned him. 'This is Pearl,' she said. 'Pearl who?' he answered. 'I know many Pearls.' She didn't call again. After leaving the family she got a job in Waitrose, in the basement of John Barnes in Finchley Road. She worked there for 31 years on the check-out, and they were, Pearl says, unhappiness notwithstanding, 'the best years of my life'.

This is how I met her. She had the longest queues, but still people lined up to have their goods taken by Pearl. She chatted, was never brisk or bad-tempered and didn't mind your fractious toddler whining with boredom. It's the only time in my life when I've actually chosen to stand in a longer queue than necessary. It was a slow business, because everyone paused for conversation. People told her their troubles ('If you knew what I know about so many people') or swapped recipes, or got tips on what was best and cheapest in Waitrose that week, but still it seemed worth the wait. She had to retire three years ago and badly misses her old life.

Pearl, in her brown Waitrose uniform, made friends with everyone over the check-out, but it was friendship on her terms, with a barrier between her and others. She enjoyed the talking and loved all the kids, but the limits were set, as she set them with Barney. 'Even when he was ill, I would stay with him most of the night, but I always came back to my own flat to sleep.' She could see Barney's window from her flat and would check to see his light was out before she went to sleep. She still looks across at the window, though the house has been sold now. 'It's just a habit,' she says. Sometimes, looking out of her window during the summer afternoons, now that she is no longer working, she sees Bernard Kops in his garden with his children and grandchildren. He also knows Pearl, and when she meets him in the street, she tells him: 'You've got such a wonderful family. So close-knit, so loving. I love to watch you.'

Ever Thus
in England

Let Nothing
You Dismay

Christmas is like the end of a love affair. Months before it's arrived, I sort of know it's coming, though I keep the information locked away as long as possible in the Scarlett O'Hara Think About It Tomorrow Memorial compartment of my mind (it has its own sector, sandwiched between What's the Next Novel Going To Be and My Car Tax Has Run Out). The anxiety scraping away at my insides remains undesignated, but eventually (analogy continued), the truth of the event is an inescapable reality – the evidence is everywhere and it becomes clear that friends and family have known about it all along. When the actual day comes it is, of course, a relief, and generally not nearly as distressing as I'd feared (analogy crumbles). Christmas Day distresses like no other, and it's 168 hours long: it doesn't stop until 2 January, 'The horror. The horror.' Where's the mystery about Kurtz's final cry? Clearly Christmas was just around the corner.

Of course, I describe only what goes on in here, behind my eyes. Out there, all the cleverness and deviousness of the human mind conspires to warm the cockles of my heart (it's only my brain, liver, lights, stomach, pancreas, intestines and reproductive organs that are subject to spasms of Christmas gloom). In spite of myself, there are things I like. Christmas morning, when it's clear and icy, and London's been deserted by half its inhabitants going home for the annual rise in domestic murder rates; lit up trees in windows, their multi-coloured blinking making a change from the usual blue flickering of TV sets; New York, where everything's covered with white, starry lights, becoming a mugger's fairyland (muggers have dreams, too); Christmas truces (after Christmas bombing campaigns) making the chest fairly burst with pride at a humanity which once a year chooses not to kill other people. Then there are the carols, bringing the good news that two thousand years ago we were redeemed for all time – tidings of comfort and joy – which certainly makes me feel better . . . Grumpy? Me? Nah, it's just that I suffer from a terror of disappointment. Christmas is like death. What's disturbing about the idea of death is not oblivion (certainly not that), or hell, but the chance – high chance – that when we get there we'll have to face the fact that life has not lived up to expectations: 'Was that it, then?'

Expectation, like neurosis, is taken in from the world outside while very young, and internalised. Good Christmas/ Bad Christmas lives in us like Good Parent/Bad Parent, and is just as much a misbegotten fantasy. So somewhere along the way from the birth canal to the dawning of long-term memory, the world imposed on me, and I took in, an ideal set of parents and an ideal Christmas, which pair of disjunctions with real life have ever since come together on 25 December to make me a shivering jelly of apprehension. For a small, constantly exploding nuclear family which had trouble being civil to each other on any day of the week, Christmas was a catastrophe. The problem with expectation is that it grows exponentially. I have an expectation, she has an expectation, he has an expectation, but she also has an expectation about my expectation, and I certainly have an expectation about her expectation. And he'd just like to avoid any trouble.

Aged eight, it was the Petite Typewriter Disaster. By then, I was fully initiated into the high hopes and low realities of Christmas, but I loved the disruptive two weeks at the end of the winter term in my primary school in Kentish Town. A red cardboard letter box appeared in the hall, teachers arrived back after lunch the worse for seasonal celebrations, and each year we watched Laurence Olivier whipping up enthusiasm for beating the French at Agincourt. ' . . . Cry God for Harry, England and St George . . .' – though the film projector always went wrong and it was only a clip, so we never found out who won. Lessons were given over to making endless paper chains that ran several times round the classroom, and interrupted by messages for me to go to rehearsals for my scene in the school play. It was not a big part: Squire Trelawney in *Treasure Island*. I only had one line, but it was dramatic. I had to stagger on stage and gasp 'I couldn't stop him, he ran right under the horse's feet.' Unfortunately, I was too small for Squire Trelawney's breeches, and as I lurched on stage they slipped down to my knees. Trouper that I was, I said my line through the audience's laughter and my tears, but that was it with the theatre for me. Then it was Christmas morning and I had got what I yearned for: a typewriter. The three of us, her, him and me, were a picture of Christmas as it should be, for about an hour.

She went off to the kitchen to try to make the turkey taste of something, he sat in the armchair to dream about his mistress dreaming of him, and I settled down on the floor next to him to begin my autobiography.

Dangerously, I began to relax. Maybe, this Christmas would be all right all day. Then the Petite typewriter didn't work. I can't remember why, but it was something fatal.

Nothing appeared on the page. The horror of Christmases past came back to me, and I did some hefty bargaining with God to make the damn thing do what it was supposed to do. My soul was nothing to what I offered to give away that morning. No use. I stopped.

'What's up?' my father asked, coming out of his reverie.

'It doesn't work,' I whispered.

He dropped his voice to match mine, and I could see by the look of alarm on his face that he'd been gripped by Christmas terror, too. 'Don't tell Mummy.'

'But she'll ask to see what I've written.'

'Don't tell Mummy!' he hissed in desperation. I knew what he meant.

I took the Petite typewriter into the bedroom and sat with it on the bed, disconsolately, not just alarmed for the immediate future, but wondering if this would be a fatal setback to my plans to be the world's greatest writer. From time to time, to allay suspicion, I clattered the keys, but I knew we were doomed.

Of course, we were doomed anyway. Even if the wretched machine had worked and I'd started Vol 1, my mother would have asked the same question over lunch: 'Let me see what you've written', and when she saw my version of Life in Tottenham Court Road, all hell would have broken loose. But that, at least, would have been a proper disaster for an author.

When the question came, I was silent.

What could I say? If I'd said I hadn't written anything, it would have started the trouble: 'So it's not good enough for you? Ungrateful . . . the trouble I went to . . . no one cares about me . . .' If I'd said I had written something but wasn't going to show it to her, it would have been worse: 'You think I don't know what you've written about me . . . incapable of love . . . one day you'll realise . . . I might as well be dead . . .'

So, I kept schtum, which is a natural response to a fight or flight conflict, and one my father endorsed.

Of course, it wasn't my fault, or her fault, or anyone's fault that the typewriter didn't work, but, as I knew it would, it turned to be symptomatic of everything that was wrong with her life. Basically, it was God's fault, and she railed at him for a while before getting on to his agents on earth – my father and me, sent specifically to make her life a misery, and to punish her, although she was guilty of nothing but spending her life skivvying for the ungrateful likes of us, and one day we'd be sorry, we'd know the hell we'd made of her existence and she'd be better off dead. The turkey went cold, the brussels sprouts ended up greening the wallpaper and on the floor, the gravy lubricated the typewriter, and my mother retreated into the bedroom for the rest of the day, screaming, moaning and clutching her big white box of Codis. Let nothing you dismay.

The problem was my mother's addiction to expectation: she knew how things ought to be, and yet perversely, for her they never were. Even at Christmas, the world conspired to spoil her life. Especially at Christmas. But I've long ago put away childish typewriters, so what's the problem now?

Expectation, of course. I've advanced a little – for the past 16 years I've checked very Christmas Eve, to make sure the daughter's present works, but equally, for every moment of those same 16 Christmases, I've lived in terror of something going wrong, of the dread possibility of failing her Christmas fantasies. But it goes without saying that my fear is precisely what created the expectation. As it was in the beginning, now and ever shall be, world without end. I do have a perfect Christmas stored up for one of these years. It begins when I wake to a silent house. I make a cup of tea, and maybe hum a chorus or two of 'We Three Kings' before getting into bed with the book I can hardly bear to put down. In the fridge, quantities of over-spiced salami, cucumbers and radishes await my appetite. All's well with the world. The Christmas truces are holding, once again humanity's reborn, my word processor is in working order and, with any luck, there'll be a decent movie on the box in the evening. God rest ye, merry gentlemen.

It's Mummie

The Little Princesses
by Marion Crawford, introduced by A.N. Wilson
(DUCKWORTH, LONDON, 1993)

'It was not ever thus in England,' says A.N. Wilson, stilting his prose in deference to the text he's introducing. He's speaking of the deluge of intimacies we can expect these days in the press about the Royal Family. The 'mystique of kingship', Wilson explains, was restored in the late Thirties by George VI and Elizabeth, who, even before they moved into Buckingham Palace, erected a wall of silence around the House of Windsor, as soundproof as the walls of all those castles they processed around. Who knew of David Windsor's dereliction of duty in favour of love (or whatever it was) until a week before the Abdication? Well, quite a lot of people actually, but not the readers of the popular (as in lower orders) press. Marion Crawford, governess to Lilibet and Margaret Rose, started the rot by ratting on her employers in 1950. Which means that, like liberated and consequence-free sex, the period of royal mystery was brief, helped by the fact that a large war was going on for much of the time, when the intimate doings of the royal family may not have been uppermost in people's minds.

Reading the reissue of *The Little Princesses*, a simpler explanation for what Wilson calls the 'cocoon of unknowability' comes to mind. The life of the House of Windsor in the days when it wasn't ever thus, was like the soup of the day, so appropriately named after them, ladled out by truculent landladies and waiters in chilly boarding houses and cavernous hotels right through the Fifties and into the early Sixties: watery, dun-coloured and without the slightest hint of spice. If it's interesting you're after, you could see the waiters thinking as you stared glumly into the brownian motion, you'd better live Abroad.

Once disgraceful Uncle David was shipped off into exile and never spoken of again (are the palace walls imprinted with his anguished whispers: 'Wallace, I long to be your tampax'?), royalty and impeccability became synonymous, at least for a while. So says Crawfie, and she should know. She spent 25 years governessing her charges, beginning when Lilibet was five and her mother, 'the little Duchess of York'.

Read Crawfie and you have to adjust to diminutives. Margaret is still described as a little girl when she's 17. On the other hand, she's very helpful on history, explaining about Glamis Castle: 'Here dwelt Macbeth, who is reputed to be by no means the entirely vicious character Shakespeare makes him out to be in his play. The real Macbeth, though said to have murdered Duncan, was otherwise a good enough king, as kings went in those days . . . and he gained the respect of his people.' Respect and respectability are what counts. Crawfie, for all the scandal of the publication of her book, was no scandalmonger, and wouldn't hear a word said against royalty, not even the 11th-century variety. A bit of a Shakespearean tragedy herself, she devoted her youth to the Windsors, flung herself over her young charges at the sound of a doodle-bug, and put off her own marriage to a bank manager beau until she was 38 in order to see

Princess Elizabeth through her wedding and Margaret beyond it:

> The Queen kissed me and wished me great happiness, but asked: 'I do hope you won't think of leaving just yet. It is going to be such a busy time.' Once again I made my promise that I would remain as long as I was needed, though I realised this meant postponing still further the real start of my married life or making a home of my own. We then had tea.

There's no mention of Crawfie having any children of her own when she did finally get permission to marry, and you wince as a pregnant Princess Elizabeth waltzes into Crawfie's room with the heirloom pram, cooing, 'Look, Crawfie, I'm getting my hand in.' Well-behaved the Windsors might have been, thoughtful they were not. Still, best not shed too many tears for the childless governess, she was where she wanted to be, and George the banker, invited to the Abbey for Elizabeth's wedding, had to kick his heels outside Buck House while Crawfie attended the wedding supper.

She didn't start at the top, however. She trained to be a teacher in Edinburgh in what she describes as the poorer part of the city, where she saw, she says, a great deal of poverty and children who were not very bright because they were undernourished. Fired with 'the crusading spirit', she developed a sense of vocation and the 'feeling I had a job to do in life'. This misbegotten vocation was quickly sorted out and she went to work, first for the Countess of Elgin, and then the little Duchess of York. Poverty is never mentioned again, and the undernourished children of Edinburgh were left to manage as best they might. Destiny beats powerfully in Crawfie's breast, and her prose is littered with 'Little did I know then's and 'Fate was marching up on me's.

Once she enters the employ of the Duke and Duchess of York, you are pitched into a world of ineffable middle-class vapidity that reminds you of cloud fluff. Mr and Mr Darling lived there before Peter Pan came and troubled things, and later Celia Johnson and Cyril Raymond lived there before Trevor Howard chuffed along and briefly encountered them. It's a mauve sort of world, and worn to this day by the Queen Mother like a flag of remembrance.

To Crawfie, at their first meeting, it was obvious that the Duke and Duchess 'were devoted to each other and very much in love, and I remember thinking they looked just as a Duke and Duchess ought to look, but often don't'. Crawfie knew how things ought to be. Things like English nursery tradition, whose death in the Fifties she so regrets – a world in miniature with Nanny as the head of state – and then the princelings' banishment to boarding school before returning to take up their rightful place as masters of the universe.

The Duke and Duchess, before being kicked upstairs to monarchy, were a pair of stay-at-home lovebirds, sitting on either side of the fireplace, the Duke at his *petit point* (Crawfie obliged by filling in the background while he got on with the more amusing part of the design) and the Duchess apparently just gazing devotedly at her needleworking spouse. Everything was nice. Little Lilibet stabled her toy horses and Margaret Rose enchanted everyone with her singing and dancing.

Oh, very well, if you must know, Little Lilibet was a compulsive obsessive, Margaret Rose was a screaming creative talent who was crushed by the demands of respectability and the mauve mother and father floated around in some other ether, incapable of making decisions on behalf of their children. And what of Old Queen Mary, who wore gloves when toasting muffins on the fire with a silver toasting-fork, because she never allowed food to touch her bare hands? They are the modern royals in the making, and much as Crawfie paints sunshine over the canvas, the clouds are discernible. When Margaret sees her mother go by in a car, she shrieks, 'It's Mummie,' and waves wildly even though the car has sped past. 'I really don't know what we're going to do with Margaret, Crawfie,' says Lilibet. And, says Crawfie, full of pride for her maturer charge: 'How often . . . have I heard her cry in real anguish, "Stop her, Mummie. Oh, please stop her," when Margaret was being more than usually preposterous, and amusing and outrageous.' Oh dear.

Even Crawfie admits anxiety about Lilibet's fads, however, describing her behaviour as 'almost' too methodical and tidy. At 13 the Princess was given to jumping out of bed several times a night to get her shoes arranged quite straight, and her clothes precisely laid out. The Princess is mother to the Queen. At her marriage Crawfie lyricises about her childhood in 'a home in which no door banged, and voices were never raised in anger, and a little girl had grown to womanhood with natural good manners and a charm peculiarly her own'. Perhaps a little too peculiarly her own. Our dutiful monarch's charm seems frequently to have been subsumed by a rigid sense of obligation and propriety, as Princess Margaret was to find out.

It's little Margaret Rose who is the most poignant. Crawfie obviously adored her and suggests repeatedly that she had remarkable musical and dramatic talents. Even if that's putting it too strong, Margaret was clearly her own person, with energy and ability that had no real outlet. 'Highly strung', she's called, and in all the photos has a heart-stopping beauty with eyes that are focused and alert, too focused perhaps for the Windsors' world of misty mauves. If Laing and Co were right, there's no doubt who was the scapegoat of the House of Windsor. She hit the headlines, of course, a tentative Fergie of her day, too outspoken,

seen about town, and berated by the press for being out
seven nights in a row. Austerity-conscious Britain wasn't
going to stand for that – she was ordered to stay home at
least two or three nights a week. But she was the only one of
all of them who showed the slightest interest in anything
other than horses and dogs, and could been seen actually
enjoying herself at the theatre and taking an interest in the
arts. She was always in Lilibet's severe shadow, and was
livid not to be allowed to join the ATS when her sister did. 'I
was born too late,' she fumed. Wrong. She was born too
early.

Lilibet remained obedient, waiting for months while her
parents failed to attend to the fact that she was in love with
Philip, being whisked off to South Africa while she really
wanted to stay home and moon to the sound of 'People will
say we're in love' on the gramophone. 'Poor Lil,' says
Margaret. 'Nothing of your own. Not even your love affair!'
Later, Lil was to display less understanding of her younger
sister.

Finally, of course, the marriage was allowed, to the young
Greek who Crawfie persists in referring to as 'the Viking',
and the governess was at last allowed to buy her curtains
and crockery and marry, though she was still living in and
taking care of Margaret, while hubby George lodged in a
hotel in South Kensington. There are those (the Queen
Mother, apparently) who say Marion Crawford went public
because she was given a paltry honour – nothing more than
Commander of the Royal Victorian Order – and felt she
deserved better. A.N. Wilson rejects this, claiming Crawfie's
only motive was that she was a 'compulsive blabbermouth'.
But beside the sycophancy and the desire to tell the world
whose shoulders she rubbed, there is an undertone of resentment. With the wedding over, the King and Queen went
about their royal duties, and Crawfie still had not got the
Queen to agree to her retirement. She succoured the solitary

Princess Margaret, left behind while Princess Elizabeth sent happy postcards of the honeymoon. 'It was nice to know that somebody's married life was beginning full of peace and sunshine. My own was not.'

It's OK, Crawfie, it didn't last. It's ever thus in England.

Sweetie Pies

> *Below the Parapet:*
> *The Biography of Denis Thatcher*
> by Carol Thatcher
> (HARPERCOLLINS, LONDON, 1996)

Denis Thatcher is entirely inventable – as John Wells understood: he comes in a flat pack with easy-to-follow
instructions, all the components familiar general shapes, all
parts from stock, no odd angles, no imagination required.
When they came up with the idea for Ikea, they used Denis
Thatcher as the prototype. You can make him up in the time
it would take to boil an egg.

Whether you see Denis Thatcher as a national treasure or
as dismal confirmation that stereotypes live and breathe, and
it is only our arrogant fantasy that the planet is inhabited by
three-dimensional complex life forms, depends, I suppose, on
how phlegmatic your temperament is. You can roll with reality and settle down to write the entirely documentary 'Dear
Bill' letters, or you can despair, gnash your teeth and rail
against the Lord for culpable laziness when he got round to
inventing humankind. He was, perhaps, boiling an egg at
the time. I'm inclined towards teeth-gnashing, but aspire to
being a more balanced person, so I alternated reading the

Denis Thatcher story with a rereading of *Moby Dick*. A dozen pages of Denis ('He was happy in his own skin and had played with a straight bat since the day he was born') over a cup of tea, and then back to Ishmael ('whenever it is a damp, drizzly November in my soul; whenever I find myself involuntarily pausing before coffin warehouses') to cheer myself up.

There may have been a touch of the Ahabs in Denis's genealogy. Thomas Thatcher, grandfather of the present baronet, was a bit of an adventurer, sailing to New Zealand in the 1870s to seek his fortune rather than following his father and grandfather into farming near Swindon. He made his mark, and initiated the Thatcher family business by producing an arsenic-based sheep dip for the Wanganui farmers which turned out to be a very useful wood and leather preservative as well. More interesting, according to his great-granddaughter, Thomas Thatcher, after returning to England a wealthy man, suffered a nervous breakdown and died in Croydon Mental Hospital aged 63, with the cause of death given as 'melancholia, dilation and fatty degeneration of the heart and circulatory system'. We are told he had a 'bullying, despotic nature' and my spirits quite rose with the possibility of a convergence between the Denis Thatcher story and *Moby Dick*, but Thomas is as near as the Thatcher dynasty got to Captain Ahab. Though Thomas's son, Jack, was a bit of a gambler, the dubious genes had exhausted themselves by the time they reached Denis.

Denis is clearly a great believer in genetic destiny: 'If you're born shy, you're born shy, aren't you?' and 'I think you're either born with a gambling instinct or you're not.' According to his sister, Joy, Denis was 'born grown up', and at 18 he joined the family business, now called Atlas and to become eventually 'the largest de-greasing and de-scaling service of its kind in the world'. His father's secretary remembers that at 18 Denis 'was already the man he was to become'. Common sense, says Carol, has always been his most valuable asset, along with 'pragmatism and homespun logic'. Two of his favourite sayings – 'Any fool can make it: we've got to sell it' and 'If all else fails, read the instructions' – provide a flavour of the Thatcher thrust of mind.

In fact, if one was a serious student of human nature and not a thrill-seeking dilettante, it would be books about Middle England's businessmen and their wives one would read avidly, rather than turning for succour to folderols about high emotions on the high seas. Though the temptation is great, we skip Denis Thatcher's unremarkable life and sayings at our peril, for they are what gave us ten years of radical nastiness while we weren't looking. It is by no coincidence called 'Thatcherism' and not 'Robertsism', for Denis is fully representative of the culture which allowed it to flourish. He married her, the rest of them voted for her, and some of us, foolishly, with our noses in the wrong books and not paying attention to reality didn't even dream that such a thing could happen.

If there is a quirk, it is Denis's tendency to marry Margarets. At any rate, he married the wrong Margaret to start with, though what with there being a war on and his being a bit lacking in experience, it is an understandable error. Certainly, both the first and second Mrs Thatchers have done their best to keep it from preying on his mind. The first Mrs T considerately changed her first name to Margot, while the second and correct Margaret warned her daughter (who until the *Daily Mail* published the story in 1976 had known nothing of her father's first marriage): 'Don't mention it to your father . . . He won't talk about it. It was a wartime thing.' Although, according to Lady Hickman, formerly Mrs Thatcher, 'Friends do say we look rather alike,' Carol explains that her mother detests the comparison, wishing to consign the entire affair to history. Denis's memory, however, is quite sharp about that period of his life. When

Carol tells her father that she has been to see Margot he gets 'rather misty-eyed' and asks: 'Is she still incredibly beautiful?' 'Yes,' replies Carol and they sit in silence. The awkward moment is retrieved, however, by another of Denis's timeless observations: 'God guided us both. Neither can one, nor would one want to rewrite history.' The guidance that God gave Margaret the First was to have an affair with someone else, while Denis was keeping his staff officer's desk tidy in Sicily. 'It was entirely my fault, and I regret it a lot,' says Margot now. 'The war was a strange time. You never knew what was going to happen. You grabbed happiness while you could.' Even the redoubtable Denis could not entirely avoid the unorthodox events of war, but his fatalism is surely sound: the loss of the initial Margaret must be seen as returning him to the right Margaret and his true destiny.

The romance between Denis Thatcher and the young Margaret Roberts, she of the Tory hats, the unreconstructed hairdo and piping voice, was no rushed affair. They met in February 1949, when Margaret was trying and failing to get into Parliament, and married in December 1951. Having been told by her political mentor Lord Bossom ('What sort of a name is that?' grumbled Winston Churchill. 'It's neither one thing nor the other') that she needed a husband and children to get on in politics, marriage was on Margaret's agenda. Though neither of them can recollect the proposal when asked by their daughter, the honeymoon was, Denis remembers, 'quite pleasant' and they settled into a marriage which their daughter describes as a tacit agreement to get on with their own interests. He was by now wealthy, and spent from early morning to late at night at the office and his winter weekends refereeing rugby. His wife, still lacking a secure constituency, decided to read for the Bar. 'Do what you like, love' was Denis's response, as it would be to all her future plans: it would indeed be the response of all God's Englishmen for some time to come.

If daughters are to be believed on this subject, the Thatchers did not have a close marriage even at the beginning, nor was he deeply moved by the birth of his twins. 'My God, they look like rabbits. Put them back.' As to the impression Margaret gave her daughter about maternity, Carol comments: 'Margaret, who had felt unwell during much of her pregnancy, was relieved that we had arrived safely. As she now had one of each sex, that was the end of it as far as she was concerned.' She'd bagged the full set, as Bossom had instructed, and it was back to work and ambition. Denis would travel abroad for whole months, selling his wares; he rarely wrote a postcard home and never phoned so he only found out that his wife had finally become an MP from the *Evening Standard* provided on the plane as he returned from a South African trip. Emotional neglect clearly kept the family together, though it isn't something which has seeped down to the next generation, apparently. Mark's then wife, Diane, complained that her husband never phoned during the long periods he was away. 'Well, when I was away, I never rang up,' Denis told her.

The young people were so demanding. When Carol foolishly asked her mother, 'Why can't you be home more?' she was told: 'Darling, you have to understand that you have a lot of benefits that other children don't have: you can come to the Opening of Parliament and have supper at the House of Commons.' When Carol expressed anxiety on the morning of her Bar finals, as it happened the same day as the Tory leadership election, her mother snapped: 'Well, you can't be as nervous as me.' The children grew up learning to put their problems in perspective: that of their parents. It's hardly surprising that Mark got lost in the desert, the only direction he knew was the direction in which his mother was going. There's been loose talk around on publication of this book, suggesting that the Thatchers were a dysfunctional family, but in fact the family was a microcosm of the Thatcher view

of how a nation should comport itself. No such thing as
society, each individual an emotionally independent capsule
getting on with his or her best interests, and no namby
pamby caring. Say what you like about the Thatcher
woman, she wasn't all talk.

Once Margaret was elected Prime Minister however,
Denis stood by her. He was, by then, very wealthy indeed
and retired, so he had time on his hands for common sense
and a kind of stand-offish devotion. He snuck off at weekends to play golf and drink copiously with his male pals, but
when his woman needed him, by God he was there.
Canniest of all, he never gave interviews. This was just as
well, since his opinions were precisely what you would
expect them to be. Mistaking a cast member of *Anyone for
Denis* for a real policeman, he praised him: 'You get fuzzy
wuzzies going on the rampage down in Brixton, you people
sort it out in no time at all.' To critics of the South African
regime speaking on TV, he could be heard in the privacy of
the drawing-room of No 10, to mutter like any retired
English gent: 'Bet you don't even know whether Simon's
Town [*sic*] is east or west of Cape Town!' A pretty definitive
argument against sanctions, you will admit. He wasn't that
keen on the Commonwealth, either, and sidled up to his
wife after a scathing attack on Thatcherite Britain by a
Commonwealth leader, to give advice: 'I'll tell you exactly
how to deal with this, Sweetie Pie: cancel all their aid and he
can work out how much each minute of that bloody speech
cost his country.'

He only let rip in public a handful of times. Once in Delhi
at the Heads of Government meeting he failed to take a
liking to Indira Gandhi, who he believed had 'chips on both
shoulders' and finally let her have it: 'Well, Ma'am, we did
build the railways for you and without them India wouldn't
be what it is today.' And he was overheard at a cocktail
party asking: 'Who do you think is worse, Sonny bloody

Ramphal or Ma sodding Gandhi?' Then there was the moment after the Harrods bombing when, seen carrying one of their bags, he shouted across to the press in Downing Street: 'No murdering Irishman is going to stop me doing my Christmas shopping at Harrods.' There's no question that Denis is made of the stuff which made the Empire what it is today. At Mrs Gandhi's funeral, Denis the practical Englishman came to the fore. They had trouble getting the fire under the bier started. 'The bloody fire wouldn't go. And then they started to throw ghee on it – melted butter to you and me . . . I thought to myself: Why doesn't someone go and get some paraffin and get the bloody thing going? The poor old girl wouldn't burn.'

Unfortunately, we are not given any fly-on-the-wall after-work conversations between the tender-minded Mr Thatcher and his right-minded Prime Minister wife, though Carol is clearly her father's daughter: Africa is still 'the dark continent' and she berates Zambia for providing a 'rather amateur motorcade' and accommodating the VIPs in 'rather pokey prefabs hastily erected to host some previous summit of African leaders'.

Robert Morley consoled Denis when he complained about 'those buggers at *Private Eye*': 'You should be grateful, my darling; they have given you a personality.' The only unusual thing about Denis and his opinions is that he happened to have the ear of a prime minister, though to be fair, according to Carol, he never attempted to sway her to his way of thinking – though to be fairer still, he probably never needed to. Margaret would surely have fully approved his letter wondering what 'the great Churchill would have said of those who wish to "sell" the House of Commons to Brussels; and what he would have said of Heath, the latter-day appeaser of a latter-day Hitler'.

He was there for Margaret during the tough times; applauding the sinking of the *Belgrano* and backing her

during what Carol calls the 'gutless treachery' of the leadership election of 1990. 'Congratulations, Sweetie Pie, you've
won; it's just the rules,' he told her with tears trickling down
his face as Sweetie Pie failed to win enough votes in the first
ballot. And you do begin to warm to his devotion: after all,
everybody needs someone they can rely on. Except that once
she was out of office, and a suburban housewife at a loss for
something to do in Dulwich, Denis made himself scarce. She
sat at home eating TV dinners, while he visited his club every
evening. Without the No 10 staff, she was helpless. When
Carol asked why her mother never rang, she answered:
'Because I haven't got your number, dear.' Margaret's diary
was blank at first, while Denis's cronies kept his social life at
full swing. 'My father's friends stayed with him, rain, hail or
shine; Margaret's stopped with politics.'

Happily, she pulled herself together after a while, and
now they both go their separate ways, just as they did at the
beginning of their marriage. Margaret was unable to attend
the launch of her daughter's biography of Denis, being off
somewhere on a lecture tour. Carol, who lives in Klosters
with a ski instructor, is quoted as saying that she had been to
a launch of both her mother's books. Nobody mentioned
whether Mark was there, but then it seems that the family is
not inclined to mention Mark if at all possible. Thankfully,
Denis made it, and the free gin flowed like gin. I wonder if he
made his standard speech, the one that ends: 'When the real
battle comes we will all up and fight and like the soldiers at
Agincourt cry, "God for Margaret, England and St George".'

Unnecessary Fortitude

> *I May Be Some Time:*
> *Ice and the English Imagination*
> by Francis Spufford
> (FABER, LONDON, 1996)

Snow is cold. Some more information I am prepared to accept as plain fact: near 90° South if you take your gloves off for more than a few moments, your fingers die; at its edge, the 5.5 million square mile ice-cap (twice that size in winter) calves bergs, some as big as London, the largest recorded 60 miles long, which drift through the most turbulent seas in the world; no land-based vertebrate inhabits the southern-most continent, because nothing can live on it apart from breeding penguins and seals; the seas freeze into great shifting platelets of ice which can crush to toothpicks a ship caught in their grip.

Yet as the unadorned details emerge, so too do images and memories, and before you know where you are, meaning (isolation, desolation, hardship, challenge) has sidled into your transparent pile of data and thickened it into a story. Though scientists, in dogmatic mode, might shake their heads in disapproval, it's another plain fact that we explore ideas as readily as we do the physical geography of the planet, and neither kind of exploration is untainted by the other. Francis Spufford describes the history of this interaction and examines its consequences. He makes the claim with his title (*I May Be Some Time*) and subtitle ('Ice and the English Imagination') that the mythic status of Captain Oates's fruitless self-sacrifice is the direct result of the accretion of meaning around the idea of the snowy wastes.

To the cultural historian, just to call Oates's walk into the snow 'fruitless' is to declare oneself a member of the post-war generation. Until the Fifties or Sixties, this view states, Oates was regarded as having made a great death, a model death to be, as it were, lived up to. Three of the four other Edwardians who made up the doomed Polar party died with equal public aplomb. In his farewell letter to his mother, Bowers apologises for his 'short scribble', but assures her that 'it will be splendid . . . to pass with such companions as I have'. Dr Wilson, according to his obituary in *The Times*, 'beautifully lit up the wastes', and Scott, in his last message, found in the tent with the three bodies, declared: 'We are weak, writing is difficult, but for my own sake, I do not regret this journey, which has shown that Englishmen can endure hardships, help one another, and meet death with as great a fortitude as ever in the past.' Only Edgar Evans died a rather commonplace death – at the foot of the Beardmore Glacier, of concussion after a fall. 'He died a natural death,' was all Scott could manage by way of an epitaph for him in the last message, but then Evans was only a petty officer, not a gentleman like the rest, and had slept on the wrong side of the packing-case wall dividing the officers from the men in the over-wintering hut.

The England of 1912 indulged in an orgy of admiration for the manner of these deaths, seeing, as Scott intended them to see, the spirit triumphant rising out of mere physical annihilation. According to Spufford, it could not have been otherwise. He traces the history of English responses to men's attempts at overcoming wild nature, as well as the developing nature of the English over time, in order to account for the Edwardian reaction to what we understand to be a débâcle. For Spufford, attitudes to the barren world of ice and to the meaning of exploration had built up since the mid-18th century, when the schoolboy Edmund Burke, watching the Liffey overflow its banks into the streets of Dublin, began to define the feelings it evoked as the Sublime: the terrible but inspiring otherness of nature out of control, the voice of this otherness calling to the soul and making men like Cook pit themselves against an inhuman landscape. By the time of Scott, both to conquer the elements and to be conquered by them had nobility and moral worth. To die with beautiful resignation in a place inimical to life itself, to be able to say as Scott did, 'We took risks, we knew we took them; things have come out against us, and therefore we have no cause for complaint, but bow to the will of Providence, determined still to do our best to the last,' was quite as much to be applauded as an arrival and safe return.

The Romantics took up Burke's notion and endorsed it. Spufford focuses on *Frankenstein*, in which Mary Shelley made the Antarctic, the white empty space where no one had been, the setting for the struggle between what was and was not human, a battle between flesh and ice. Cook's crossing of the Antarctic Circle in 1773 and his exploration of Alaska in 1778 would enable the writing of *The Ancient Mariner*, but the later Arctic voyages of Ross and Parry in 1818–19 caused Coleridge to contemplate the making of a poem in which 'I would *allegorise* myself, as a Rock with its summit just raised above the surface of some bay or strait in the Arctic Sea . . . all around me fixed and firm, methought as my own Substance, and near me lofty Masses, that might have seemed to "hold the Moon and Stars in fee"'. The Romantic imagination took up the Far North and South, its impossibilities, its auroras, its uncanny stillness, its palatial icebergs, and turned them into dreamstuff. When Ishmael, in a kind of homage to *The Ancient Mariner*, looks into the 'inexpressible, strange' eyes of an albatross caught on the deck of the *Pequod*, he believes, 'I peeped to secrets which took hold of God.'

The actual Arctic experience of Parry's men was in fact excessively cold and tedious despite the morale-building activities – theatrical performances, newspapers, dances, lectures, grog – but this did not deter those back home from romancing the wonderful indifference of nature and its heroic explorers. Indeed, the loss of Sir John Franklin and his party during his search for the Northwest Passage in the 1840s only further fuelled the imaginative drama of the ice. Lady Jane Franklin, reminding the nation of her husband's heroism with her own heroic bearing, whipped up sympathy and money for years of searching which finally located the bodies of the party – though not the remains of Franklin himself. But the drama of reality had its limits. Lady Jane and the rest of England, ably assisted by an enraged Charles Dickens, were having none of the suggestion that the party might have been nibbling on itself in the throes of starvation. It implied that in extremis Englishmen might lose the very treasure they took with them to plant in the wilderness: their moral fortitude. Without that, the deaths by cold and starvation became just an unhappy event, and the expedition the failure which, in fact, it was.

By then, the struggle to reach the North and South Poles had become completely gratuitous: it was clear that if a Northwest Passage existed it would lie too far north to provide any trading advantage, while in the South there was no rich territory to be claimed. Nothing practical was to be gained by reaching either Pole – as far as the English could see there was nothing there. In fact, things were different in the North and the South. The North was teeming with animal life, as it was with Inuit, who were skilled in living off it. But to the English explorers the North was as vacant as the South. The Inuit considered themselves to be surrounded by abundance, but what the English saw was the challenge of empty landscape. By then, Spufford believes, the very unnecessariness of the project of getting to the Poles was what gave it the purity of a perfect quest. It was soul food, good for the men who made the journeys, bracing for those who watched from the comfort of their drawing rooms, and inspirational for the younger generation.

It is this conflation over time of the imaginary and the actual meanings of the world of ice that, Spufford suggests, accounts for the disaster that was Scott's bid for the Pole. The folk memory of a buccaneering Elizabethan past; a love of boyish wildness (J.M. Barrie was a close friend of Scott) and amateur adventure; the belief voiced by Sir Clements Markham and endorsed by Scott, that real Englishmen walked to the Pole rather than slid on effete Norwegian skis; that real Englishmen loved animals and to take dogs was cruel when the man-hauling of sledges 'has been handed down for all time as the pattern to be followed in Polar exploration' – all had their place in the fiasco. Markham, President of the sponsoring Royal Geographical Society, insisted that 'the fatal mistake in selecting Commanders for former Polar expeditions, has been to seek for experience instead of youth . . . The inexperience and haste in decision of young leaders are disadvantages which sometimes accompany their youthful energy, but they alone have the qualities which ensure success.'

The youthful and inexperienced naval officer Robert Scott was taken up by Markham and eventually given the job of reaching the Pole ahead of the suspiciously efficient Norwegian, Amundsen. There was talk of science to seal the legitimacy of the enterprise – meteorology, geomagnetism and mapping – but for Markham science was just a way of attracting funds for the expedition. The main thing, as the

Marquis of Lothian explained, was that 'the work of
Antarctic research should be done by Englishmen.' Pour a
wash of empire imagination over the already fevered brows
of the Edwardian English, and the placing of the Union Jack
at the South Pole becomes the quintessence of birthright and
civilisation's struggle to overcome the alien.

But still, in 1911, the world was old. The cultural assumptions and imaginings of the English had not yet been tested
by the cataclysm of the First World War, which in Spufford's
view was to usher in the modern era and disillusion. Apsley
Cherry-Garrard was one of the babies of the expedition, an
eager, hero-worshipping boy with no call to go to the South
Pole other than his longing for adventure. After the war and
in middle and old age, Cherry-Garrard declined into disappointment, guilt and recurrent despair. Yet of all the accounts
of that expedition, his, *The Worst Journey in the World*,
most clearly spans the two universes of pre- and post-war
England. It was written seven years after the event, when he
had returned and recuperated from soldiering in Flanders.
He freely voices the boyish derring-do, the camaraderie, the
testing nature of the expedition, and his remorse for the lost
age of just seven years before: 'an age in geological time, so
many hundreds of years ago, when we were artistic
Christians'. He never felt so happy as when he, Wilson and
Bowers nearly died on their astonishing five-week winter
journey to collect Emperor Penguin eggs. In temperatures of
70 below, with their tent blown away, in the pitch dark, and
buried in the snow, they sang songs, remembered to say
'please' and 'thank you' and no one uttered a single profan-
ity. Even so, this romantic traveller and unquestioning
participant in the expedition remembers, and puts on record
that Scott 'cried more easily than any man I have ever
known'. And if he comes to a respectably Edwardian positive final assessment of his dead leader, he does so in a most
roundabout and remarkably clear-eyed way: 'he had moods

and depressions which might last for weeks . . . he had . . . little sense of humour, and he was a bad judge of men . . . Naturally so peevish, highly strung, irritable, depressed and moody. Practically such a conquest of himself.'

His final judgment on the death of his comrades comes directly from the remade post-war world which he was to inhabit as a near-solitary and depressive. 'I now see very plainly that though we achieved a first-rate tragedy, which will never be forgotten just because it was a tragedy, tragedy was not our business.' This sounds so modern that you can practically see a new sensibility arriving, taken up later by the reassessments from both the New Right (Roland Huntford) and the Left (Trevor Griffiths), which finally replaced the old reverence with repugnance for the ineptitude and waste of life. Or perhaps it is something else, something more interesting than people just being of their times. Cherry-Garrard understands the wasteful tragedy in 1919; but in 1938, long after the disillusioning watershed of the First World War, though with the next one looming, Lieutenant Teddy Evans (by then Admiral Sir), a member of that last expedition, wrote an account of it, *South with Scott*: 'the object of this book is to keep alive the interest of English-speaking people in the story of Scott and his little band of sailor-adventurers, scientific explorers and companions. It is written more particularly for Britain's younger generation.'

Cherry-Garrard represents the gradual transition from one cultural moment to another. Spufford gives a nod to the idea that all times are transitional ('Scott seems to inhabit 1911 only forty years on from the 1870s, Amundsen's 1911 seems only forty years in advance of the Fifties'), but he allows very little intellectual autonomy to the individuals who inhabited the past and is unable to concede that originality of thought or a distinctive perception of reality might exist, not comfortably, but in a complex way, in the most attuned man of his time. This is discouraging. It makes it difficult to see how we can trust ourselves, locked in our own time, to investigate and gain any understanding of the past. We must ourselves be looking through a skewed lens. It is also slightly ugly in its supposition that our skewed lens is better skewed than those of the past.

Look more closely at the revered Oates and you discover that he himself was not a party to reverential thinking on the subject of inexperience and worthwhile death in the snow. He did not want to go to the Pole, knowing the ponies he was in charge of were not suitable for the environment, and believing that Scott's idea of man-hauling the sledges through the final stages was wrong-headed: Scott 'should buy a shilling book about transport'. In his diary he wrote that Scott had direct responsibility for the imminent deaths of the Polar party through his incompetence and bad leadership. Earlier he had written, 'Scott has always been very civil to me . . . but the fact of the matter is he is not straight, it is himself first and the rest nowhere and when he has got all he can out of you it is shift for yourself.' Even this was a guarded criticism. When Oates's mother tried to find out the truth about her son's death, she wrote of her meeting with Dr Atkinson, one of the surviving members of the expedition, that she had discovered that her son Laurie 'was a good deal worried about the way things were done . . . Neither Dr Atkinson nor Laurie had ever been accustomed to such treatment from their superior officers . . . I asked Dr Atkinson point blank if he thought Laurie had ever regretted going on the expedition. He hesitated before answering and said that there were times when Laurie did.' Another member of the party, Meares, told her there was 'great trouble and unhappiness. Captain Scott would swear all day at Evans and others. Laurie said it was shocking – and the worst was it was not possible to get away from the rows.' Though Mrs Oates wanted to publicise this, it was hushed up so that the heroic version of the deaths could serve as grand propaganda for the forthcoming war. So was the fact that Oates left his final walk too late to be of any use to the Polar party. Had he acknowledged that his hopelessly frost-bitten feet were incurable just two days earlier and taken his leave then, there is a chance that the others could have sat out the blizzard with sufficient food to get to the depot just 11 miles away from their final camp. Scott – who incomprehensibly had taken an extra fifth man to share a four-man tent and rations – had been complaining to Wilson for days that it was time Oates made the final gesture. Oates, apparently not feeling all that Edwardian about it, was by no means keen to give up his life while there was even the remotest possibility that he might survive. By the time he took a walk, he was pretty sure that none of the others would try very vigorously to stop him. Somehow, once you know this, 'I am just going outside and may be some time' begins to take on an ironic note. You can hear in your mind's ear more than one tone of voice in which the resonating phrase might be said. Oates was a man of his times, but also of ours, it seems – inevitably since the changes the times have undergone do not account for everything.

Equally, it is not impossible, even with Scott thoroughly debunked in the way we do best, to find something in his thinking that accords with our own. The first men walking on the moon was still an event the most cynical paid attention to. Had the South Pole never been reached, we would not find it odd that someone should attempt it. Yet it is very hard to get excited about Ranulph Fiennes crossing the great white continent with atomic sledges, Internet and satellite communications and a computerised mobile igloo with facilities. The idea of testing the physical and mental boundaries of endurance in very difficult circumstances has not gone away. People still wonder how they would cope with adversity. There is a moral, interior component to exploration.

And even without the Romantics flinging themselves about, there are still people who imagine themselves as rocks in the Arctic Sea. At least, I hope there are.

Shackleton gets rather little attention in Spufford's book, but he makes an interesting parallel to Scott. His *Endurance* expedition, at the start of the First World War, failed hopelessly in the attempt to make a trans-Antarctic crossing. They never made landfall; the ship was crushed after over-wintering in the ice. The 26-man party was marooned for eight months on a series of diminishing ice-floes and finally took refuge on Elephant Island in the South Shetlands. No one knew where they were and there was no chance of rescue, so Shackleton and five men made an 850-mile journey through the worst sea in the world in a 20-foot open boat to the whaling station of South Georgia. Improbably, they made it, more dead than alive, though to the wrong, uninhabited side: so Shackleton and two others crossed the uncharted mountains and glaciers of South Georgia without even a sleeping-bag, to reach Stromness and find help for the stranded men on Elephant Island. Since the Falklands War, the Army, fully equipped for mountaineering, has tried three times to repeat the crossing of the island, and failed. Not one man died on the *Endurance* expedition. The failure of the aims of the expedition and of Shackleton's previous attempt on the Pole, were largely down to a lack of know-how similar to Scott's. But Shackleton, Edwardian though he was, did not think that dying in the confrontation between individuals and nature was *de rigueur*. 'Better a live donkey than a dead lion,' he announced when he turned back just 97 miles from the Pole, realising that to go on would jeopardise their food supplies, even though there was just a chance they might make it. Shackleton and Scott were contemporaries, yet the imaginative value of life and death to each could hardly have been more different.

Spufford's elegant narrative builds like layers of snow on

the ice-cap, yet the expectation it incites doesn't finally lead to somewhere new. The ice, as ever, has the power to excite richly imagined visions: 'the ship sometimes floated at the centre of a depthless white globe of mist, was sometimes reflected upside down in the air off the bow, was assailed by phantom shapes of all descriptions, refractions of the already peculiar ice and peaks and horizons.' These images and the feelings they evoke must, as Spufford suggests, be subject to the accumulation of past imaginings, but it's very likely that such extreme landscape would provoke wonder and terror – those emotions we've always allowed to thrill us whatever the era – in anyone, then, now or in ten thousand years to come.

Porter for Leader

London: A Social History
by Roy Porter
(HAMISH HAMILTON, LONDON, 1994)

A City Full of People:
Men and Women of London, 1650–1750
by Peter Earle
(METHUEN, LONDON, 1994)

Rose was my next-door-neighbour-but-one when I lived in the furthermost reaches of Camden – three steps and one foot off the pavement and I was alienated in Islington. Rose was in her eighties and her husband had just died. I popped round to have a cup of tea and found her sitting in her darkened front room as glum as an old wife and new widow might be expected to be. 'It's terrible,' she said. I nodded silently; even when tragedy isn't surprising, it's a bugger. 'The bulb's gone,' she said, looking up at the ceiling. 'Just like that. Bang! I haven't got a new one, and anyway I get dizzy if I don't have both feet on the ground. First him, now this. They say things go in threes. Gawd knows what's going to happen next.' Rose was a real Londoner. She'd lived in the same place since she was a child and told me once when we were chatting outside the corner shop, how she remembered the herds of cattle thundering up York Way from King's Cross to the slaughterhouses in Market Road. 'You could feel the ground shake under your feet well before you could see them. It was always dangerous crossing that road,' she'd say, standing on the kerb, eyeing the cars and lorries as they streamed past.

There's a grizzly, grumbling note in Londoners' recollections of London. It's not devoid of affection or sentiment or even delight of a kind, but there's always a steady patter of complaint which matches the drizzle that bathes the city in its dirty yellow light. The authentic Londoner's lament can be heard throughout Roy Porter's history of London, which has, in addition, the other great metropolitan quality of cunning built into its very structure. What looks for all the world like yet another coffee-table picture book is in reality fat-full of angry words building to a lucid, polemical aggregation of all the tongue-clucking and head-shaking we get up to. Londoners are voluble experts on what's wrong with their city; Roy Porter, in this incarnation, is a Londoner's Londoner who relishes the chance to mix rage with historical research.

The woes of contemporary London, according to Porter, have their roots in the very beginnings of settlement. Uncontrolled and unplanned since the haphazard Saxons ousted the fetishistically orderly Romans, London has ever been the opportunist's paradise. Centuries ago, its wall decayed and the neatly laid-out Roman streets went to potholes. The present sprawling chaos is just an echo of the past: 'Today's antipathy to planners may reflect Anglo-Saxon attitudes!' But Porter does not settle for historical fatalism. From Tudor times, the refusal of the Corporation of the City of London to widen its area of responsibility to the growing suburbs around the Square Mile, and its determined protection of its privileges, helped create a climate

where self-interested commerce could do virtually what it
liked to boost its profits. The speculators and get-rich-quick
merchants date from long before Peter Rachman's Sixties
and the Yuppie Eighties. In the history of London, Porter
suggests, greed had *carte blanche*. The free-for-all continued, with neither local nor Parliamentary government
overseeing London's growth, until the setting up of the
London County Council in 1888, by which time the metrop-
olis was what it was and is, a monster that had grown by
spreading its suckers in the dark. The City became a money-
making machine, and suburbs – ever widening as industry
moved out of the depopulated centre – places of escape for
those who could.

London thrived, Porter explains, even while Londoners
died: 'the city was a killer, for burials far exceeded baptisms,
at least till around 1780. Had not newcomers congregated
there from all parts of the island, from Flanders and from
every other place, filling the shoes of those felled by pesti-
lence, London would certainly have proved self-destructive.'
There may not have been gold cobbling the streets, but there
was the promise of apprenticeships in the enterprises of
shopkeepers and merchants, and it was enough to override
the depleting effects of plague and other epidemics.

London took Protestantism to its heart. The 'massacre and
mayhem' the Reformation inflicted in the Netherlands and
France by-passed London, where the City fathers, looking for
stability, moderation and a suitable creed for businessmen,
gentled in the new religion. 'For many citizens the spread of
the gospel, the progress of trade, and England's deliverance
from popish Spain's Armada were all manifestations of divine
Providence.' Tudor confiscations of Church property
amounted to a privatisation of land and buildings, creating 'a
hectic property market . . . encouraging opportunistic rede-
velopment comparable perhaps to the speculative fever
following the Second World War'. The economic expansion

of London might have been God's voice unmediated in the believing Protestant ear.

Without planning controls, London just grew. By the mid-18th century, Defoe was feeling it had all got out of hand. 'When I speak of London, now in the modern acceptation, you expect I shall take in all that vast mass of buildings, reaching from Black-Wall in the east, to Tot-Hill Fields in the west . . . to Islington north . . . to Cavendish Square . . . and beyond to Hide Park Corner in the Brentford Road, and almost to Marylebone in the Acton Road; and how much farther it may spread, who knows?' London was 'straggling, confus'd . . . out of all shape'. Already, he complained, 'Westminster is in a fair way to shake hands with Chelsea, as St Gyles's is with Marylebone; and Great Russell Street by Montague House, with Tottenham-Court. Whither will this monstrous city then extend?' The solution, as it ever would be, was to find a place to escape to. The Rev. Dr Stukeley spent nine years searching until he finally found 'a most agreeable rural retreat at Kentish Town . . . an half-hour's walk over sweet fields. 'Tis absolutely and clearly out of the influence of the London smoak, the dry gravelly soil and air remarkably wholesome.'

Nobody lives in London – any inhabitant of the city will tell you that. Whatever 'Maybe it's because I'm a Londoner' meant, it wasn't intended to imply that the consciousness of a Pearly Queen of Brick Lane was as one with an accountant who gets off the Tube at Morden. Morden, the stop at the southernmost end of the Northern Line, exists purely in the imagination of most Londoners. I did once go there, and discovered that it was a place, but only just, and imagination had nothing to do with it. Prejudice and parochialism is everything in London. It's too big to exist as a unity, so we carve it up into discrete and manageable areas of familiarity. We live north or south of the river, as in right side and wrong side, depending on which side is yours. Cross a bridge and you're somewhere else, no matter that an outsider might not be able to tell the difference between Camden High Street and the Walworth Road. More specifically, we live in boroughs: Hornsey, Hackney, Brixton, Bermondsey, and even then, we feel restricted to certain areas within the borough. When I buy food I invariably turn right and head towards the shops in that direction, not to the shops in the other direction, although the two are equidistant. I would feel a nameless but distinct unease if I went the other way.

London, always something of an abstraction, seems conceptually to have burst like a bubble. But only those who are especially community-minded will find this an entirely negative quality. the medical model of London as a monstrous growth, a cancer within the harmonious cells of rural English life, is only one side of the story. There have always been those who rejoice in the urban dynamism and who flee to it, not just for its energy but also for its freedom. In *A City Full of People*, Peter Earle quotes Fielding's Tom Jones on the positive side of urban living:

I hastened therefore back to London, the best retirement of either grief or shame, unless for persons of a very public character; for here you have the advantage of solitude without its disadvantage, since you may be alone and in company at the same time; and while you walk or sit unobserved, noise, hurry and a constant succession of objects entertain the mind.

Those of us brought up in London, nodding amiably but briefly at our neighbours before shutting our front doors firmly behind us, shudder at the prospect of life in a close-knit village community, and not without reason. Around 1968 I spent some time in a perfect and untouched village in the middle of Dartmoor. I was there during the revelation of a great scandal: it had been discovered that the couple – Major and Mrs Smith, as it were – who owned the local stables were not actually married.

Recently, thinking I'd like to return for a few days, I phoned the nearby hotel, but mysteriously got the local post office instead. The hotel had long closed, the post-mistress told me, had I been there before? I said I had, that a friend of mine had owned a cottage just outside the village 25 years ago. Impressively, or scarily, she remembered. 'Well,' she said helpfully, 'Major and Mrs Smith do bed and breakfast as well as run the stables.' Her voice dropped to a confidential whisper. 'Of course, they're not *really* Major and Mrs. She changed her name. They aren't married. They *live* together.' The unscrupulous Major and Mrs No Better Than She Ought To Be were, I calculated, pushing 70 by now. I let the unforgiving countryside go hang and stayed put in London.

Even two hundred years ago, things were allowed to pass in the big city more easily than in 20th-century Devon. 'There came a man and a woman to the inn and asked me whether they could not have a lodging in the inn for that night . . . and I imagining by their calling each other My Dear and My Love and such like kind of expressions, that they were man and wife, did prepare a bed for them.' It was live and let live-in-sin in Bishopsgate Street, at least until the ecclesiastical courts interfered.

Peter Earle, having made in the first half of his book a respectable enough analysis of the social patterns of London life from the mid-17th to the mid-18th century, gives over a more vivid second half to the voice of historical Londoners themselves. Mostly taken from the ecclesiastical court records, as above, and the Ordinary of Newgate Prison's accounts of the lives of those about to be executed, they represent, as E.P. Thompson said, 'the lives of unremarkable people, distinguished from their fellows by little else except the fact that by bad luck or worse judgment they got caught up in the toils of the law'.

It's hard not to read the accounts without a sense of recognition:

We have bin soe disturbed with theifs that we have not bin suffer'd to lay in our bedd after 1 a clock this three nights. They have attempted Mr Slaughters house twice and one Mrs Bells but have not carried aney thing away with them as yet. Though they can't be taken, I wish it don't prove some of our neighbours when taken.

The current sense of alarm, not just about the amount of crime in the city, but the feeling that the nature of it – perhaps even the human nature of it – has changed, is not new either. Roy Porter quotes William Shenstone in the mid-18th century: 'London is really dangerous at this time, the pickpockets, formerly contented with mere filching, make no scruple to knock people down with bludgeons in Fleet Street and the Strand, and that at no later hour than eight o'clock.'

Even then, Porter suggests, the apparent surge in violence had to do with the desperation of the increasing numbers of urban poor, unemployed and hungry as a result of the 'ambiguities of capitalism itself'. But it's possible that London has always been an alarmed city, its citizens working up each others' anxieties with their whispered fears. Present police figures suggest that more people are frightened of violent crime than its actual incidence warrants. There seems to be a continuous sense of crisis and foreboding in the historical record. Though we cannot be sure that our present feeling of doom and disaster is not *this time* accurate, it may be something of a comfort to know that every generation of Londoners before us felt much the same.

Some aspects of London life, however, seem more cyclical

than continuous. It is not doom-mongering for Roy Porter to make the point that by the beginning of the 20th century destitution was on the way to being eradicated, but that during 'the Thatcher years the number of homeless shot up from eight thousand to 80,000'. It's not a matter of figures, but of experience for anyone who grew up in the London of the Fifties. When I spent time in Paris in 1970 I saw people living, sleeping and begging on the streets for the first time in my life. It seemed to me to be as extraordinary and dreadful as the fact that the French police wore guns. There were drunks and tramps in London, of course, but not that many, and I have no recollection of seeing anyone shivering the nights away on the pavements. With the Government's refusal to support local councils' attempts to provide for their most needy residents, with the infrastructure of the city falling into decay, the sewers collapsing and public transport grinding to a halt, the disintegration of the inner city has been alarmingly fast and is probably irreparable.

But as Roy Porter reminds us, we did have some passing fun with the GLC. Livingstone and friends may have annoyed the tabloids and ultimately ensured their own demise, but for a while County Hall added greatly to the gaiety of the capital and its inhabitants. One policy after another was designed to enrage No-Society-Thatcher. Fares Fair gave us a taste of what it would be like to have decent and usable transport services, funding was given to ethnic and other minority projects. County Hall under Red Ken (voted runner-up to the Pope in the BBC's 1982 Man of the Year competition) was London's last cheer and its irritation value, if not its ultimate usefulness to the citizens, made it a memorable adventure. Roy Porter's volume does the splendid trick of coming close to rabble-rousing without skimping on the underlying historical analysis. If we ever get the GLC back again, he is assured of my vote for leadership.

How Old is Rupert Bear?

> *Hippie Hippie Shake: The Dreams, the Trips, the Trials, the Love-ins, the Screw Ups . . .*
> *The Sixties*
> by Richard Neville
> (BLOOMSBURY, LONDON, 1995)

'Time! It's passing. Oh, God. Time!' mourned the legal adviser to *Oz*, transfixed by his wristwatch after his first and last joint. Who said nothing profound ever came of smoking the weed? Time was passing. It has passed. Twenty-five years after the dope, the hair, the music and the flowery rhetoric flowed free, those of us who were young enough to inhabit the land of spiked milk and honeyed hash fudge are in our forties and fifties. Which is only to be expected, although, of course, it was the last thing that anyone did, in fact, expect. There's nothing more difficult to get a solid grip on (except perhaps the Anthropic Principle in quantum physics) than the passage of time between being young, and the discovery that, at best, you're halfway through your allocation. It feels as if an error has been made – a decade skipped by some careless calendar designer. Try and make sense of it: 25 years ago I was 23. All right, that's not so difficult. Twenty-five years before that the date was 1945: the war had just ended, and I was two years short of being born. Twenty-five years from now it will be 2020 and I'll be 73 (maybe). Which is ridiculous – these are altogether different sorts of 25 years, surely? Why didn't anyone tell us about time passing, the way it accelerates, how it skitters along without so much as a pardon-me-do-you-know-you're-in-the-way? It would be a simple enough statement: you get three lots of 25 years and then you die. It's possible, of course, that someone might have mentioned it, but we had the music ('The Times They Are a-Changing'; 'I Can't Get No Satisfaction'; My g-g-Generation') turned up too high to hear.

It probably wouldn't have made any difference. Unless you were listening to Cliff Richard or attending Billy Graham's hallelujah meetings, the Sixties (not the decade, but that period from 1965 to 1972ish) were irresistible. They have been the good fortune and the curse of my generation ('May you live through interesting times'): we thank our lucky stars that our time for being young was then and not the Eighties or Nineties, but found – or find – ourselves a little slow to get on with the getting on, hypnotised as we are by the brief period of excitement in our past.

Hippie Hippie Shake (what a title, for goodness sake) includes a multitude of photographs of Richard Neville in his twenties, but none of him in middle age; the writing, too, tells of his adventures then, even his hesitations, but there's no sense of having moved on intellectually or emotionally, of the man reassessing the boy. The present is barely referred to beyond the fact that he lives back in Australia and has a wife and two children. Of course, what he's up to and thinking now isn't necessarily any of our business, and he may have actually intended to write a book that merely described the events that brought him to the dock of the Old Bailey rather than a thorough analysis of the period, but the time-warped effect contributes to the slightness of the enterprise. A lot of grand thoughts were rolling around – counter-culture, revolution, alternative reality – but when all is said and done in Neville's recollection, it appears it was little more than a hiatus, an over-extended gap year between school and real life.

Certainly, it was all said and done pretty rapidly. In the already darkening days of 1970, Birgitta Bjerke wrote a heart-breaking epitaph from Ibiza, which was published in the fatal *Schoolkids Oz*. 'LOVE was a wonderful word we all believed in. Where is Love now? Where is all the fantastic exuberant joy and optimism from the Flower Power times?' Birgitte had been 'living and learning on this beautiful island for nearly eight months. Writing, drawing and crocheting.' Writing, drawing *and* crocheting. Was a life ever so idyllic? Yet it seemed to slip away before it was fully in our grasp. As early as 1967 the Underground paper *IT* was writing: 'If our ideas are quashed in the future we can look back on the ball we had now.' Joy and optimism? Or the sneaking suspicion that the game was always and already up; that we might, after all, grow old and grey and hear ourselves sounding alarmingly like those class and style enemies, our parents? Hey, let's have ourselves a past.

In *Schoolkids Oz*, one of the teenage guest editors, Charles Shaar Murray (now a revered, middle-aged rock music critic), issued an interesting warning. Talking about the popularity of straight, commercial pop music ('Sugar, Sugar, Honey Honey'), and the often dire pretensions of progressive, underground music ('You're Two Thousand Light Years from Home'), he noticed that the mumsy commercial stuff 'is crap, but the people are honest. With us, half the music is good, but half the people are dishonest.' The fractions might, in retrospect, be underestimated (the music more than half good, and the people more than half dishonest), but it's an accurate enough analysis that applies beyond just the music of the time. Unless, that is, dishonesty is too harsh a word. According to Richard Neville all most people were trying to do was get 'in tune with the times, wanting to make waves, to make a buck, to make a difference'. The usual mixed agenda which even Norman Normal, *Oz*'s straw straight man, could live with.

So how did they manage, after all, the nabobs of the underground? They did make waves for a while, though perhaps not the kind you surf to paradise on. I suppose some bucks were made (think Felix Dennis: distribution manager of *Oz* and now higher than Her Majesty on the richest people list; and Ed Victor – ex-editor of *Ink* and currently mega-agent), but only a few, and generally not until life had got more sensible again. Some made writing careers for themselves which developed smoothly enough from their media involvement at the time – Richard Neville himself, Germaine Greer, Robert Hughes, Charles Shaar Murray. Some people died, but only the famously talented (Hendrix, Joplin, Morrison) stick in the public memory. Most of the freaks, hippies and radicals recognised that youth was just a holiday, and come the end of the summer of love they bought suits, cut their hair and dropped back into regular lives, keeping only a small warm memory of the ball they had then. What was crucial was that you could drop out of school or university and know for certain that education and work would be waiting for you when you'd had enough of fun. If 'dishonesty' turns out to be the right word, it was only the ordinary dishonesty that afflicts all human psyches. A venal not a mortal mendacity like that of the liars who were running the Vietnam War.

Mostly, for Neville, it seemed to be about sex – lots of it with plenty of people, while his live-in lover Louise put up with it, or didn't from time to time. Germaine Greer hadn't yet written *The Female Eunuch*, so for women sexual libera-tion meant sleeping with as many famous rock stars or radical magazine editors as possible. According to Neville (Greer was offered the manuscript but sent it back: 'I shall not read it. Ever'), the soon-to-be seminal feminist discovered groupiedom as a radical activity. 'Every girl should try it at least once. Groupies will be a significant element in the revolution . . . You know, I even find Engelbert Humperdinck horny-making. Those high-fronted shiny mohair trousers . . .' You would think it would be for revealing this (with who knows what degree of accuracy), and not anything Neville wrote in passing about her reproductive organs, that Greer was suing him.

Felix Dennis is also suing, though not Richard Neville, but Michael Argyle, judge in the *Schoolkids Oz* trial, for appearing to say in a recent *Spectator* that Dennis used *Oz* as a cover to sell drugs to schoolchildren. It must have slipped the now retired judge's mind that he told Dennis, 'You are very much less intelligent than your two co-defendants,' when he sent him down for nine months. Dennis clearly hasn't forgotten. I imagine the courts will be kept very busy, as the middle-aged publish recollections of a time, by definition, hazy with mind-muddling smoke and half-arsed philosophy, and other sober citizens attempt to defend their past from the prying eyes of their children, business associates and students.

But what about making a difference? The atmosphere had changed by the time the word 'hippie' made you giggle with embarrassment, though it's hard to say whether the difference wasn't already happening and wasn't itself the original cause of the behaviour. The times were a-changing, but times do: it's moot whether they were changed by those who jumped in and perhaps only swam with the tide. The beginnings of change were not stimulated by the Sixties' kids growing their hair or dropping LSD but are found somewhere further back, in the period belonging to the insupportable greyness of the post-war Fifties, with the harder types who did radically alter the course of their whole lives and who provided a space in which those to come could breathe. Kerouac, Genet, Burroughs and John Coltrane were there before Timothy

Leary, Marcuse, Germaine Greer and the Beatles. I remember feeling wretched in the early Sixties that I had been born too late, the Beats had already happened, the parade, the great time had passed before I was old enough to join in: just as later generations felt deprived of the excitement of the Sixties counter-culture. And it must have been a pain to find you'd just missed out on the French Revolution. It's not so much what a drag it is growing old, as what a drag it is finding you're too young to have joined in the fun. The young wake up from childhood and want to be there when something's happening, and time and history being what they are, it always seems as if it's already happened. The world was made just before you arrived and there's nothing left to do but live in it. It was pure serendipity that the economy had picked up enough to allow the post-Fifties kids time to play, and that those earlier loners had given the play some direction. There were no wars over here to sacrifice ourselves for, so we had the space to go to war with the grown-ups in the name of freedom and personal liberation. The battalions of the young, armed with LSD, cannabis and Little Red Books, their long hair and liberated genitals swinging in the wind, sang 'We Want the World and We Want it Now', as they marched on the old, who, behaving impeccably, threw up their hands in dismay and were duly shocked.

But there is a limit to how patronising I can be about our youthful self-deceit. When Richard Neville's book starts to tell the story of the *Oz* trial, it is hard not to become engaged, or re-engaged. All the old astonishment and enragement at the idiocy, time-wasting and viciousness of the law and its officers comes back as strong as ever. The absurdity that put young people in prison for possessing enough cannabis to make a joint, the self-righteous hatred for anyone who chose to grow their hair or wear unrespectable clothes; the establishment terror of social and political dissent: all this still makes you shake your head in disbelief.

Schoolkids Oz was edited by self-chosen sixth-formers and mostly complained about restrictive rules and regulations in school, forthcoming ecological catastrophe and the sexual concerns of rampant adolescents. It was at worst naughty, but it was prosecuted for obscenity and corruption of minors, focusing especially on a Robert Crumb-like cartoon strip of a baffled Rupert Bear, massively erect, battling to break the hymen of the monumental Gipsy Granny. It's actually a quite funny piece of iconoclasm, though not as funny as the prosecutor's exchange with social psychologist Michael Schofield: 'Yes, but what age do you think Rupert is?' 'I'm very sorry. I'm not up to date with bears.' 'He's a young bear, isn't he? He goes to school.' Evidently, the charge of corrupting minors must have included underage bears. The pottiness of this has a certain charm until you remember that the trial went on for weeks and the physical freedom of three people was at stake. The real objections were put by Detective Luff, Neville's nemesis and England's moral protector. 'Do you think that the underground press has a right to exist?' asked Neville, defending himself and examining Luff. 'As far as *Oz* is concerned, I think it's undesirable from a family point of view. And when they attack society and try and change it, then – yes! I do have an objection.' For this reason, before the trial, a 16-year-old Vivian Berger, creator of the Rupert Bear unpleasantness, was regularly stopped and searched on his way to school by Luff and his colleagues, and at least once beaten up.

So fearful was society of the disruption to conformity that having being found guilty of obscenity (though not of corruption), the three first offenders were sentenced to 15 months, 12 months and nine months' imprisonment. And so incensed were the forces of law and order that while still on remand Neville, Jim Anderson and Felix Dennis had their hair shorn so that their next court appearance became a public shaming. They were not, of course, Samsons, and they did not bring the pillars of society down with them as they were shipped off to the Scrubs, but even the tabloids, who had been calling for blood, were shocked at their treatment and the excessive sentences. Justice was seen not to be done but to be revelling in revenge. It certainly wasn't preventing anything from happening. The counter-culture's time was already up. Neville was tired of *Oz*, people were putting away their beads and wondering what they were going to do with the rest of their lives. Richard Neville had already written in the *End of an Era Oz*: 'The flower child that *Oz* urged readers to plant back in '67 has grown up into a Weatherwoman; for Timothy Leary, happiness has become a warm gun. Charles Manson soars to the top of the pops and everyone hip is making war and loving it.'

Perhaps we do not hate our young people so much now, but then two decades have passed and the present generation are too busy wondering whether they'll ever get a job or a place to live independently to go in for any threatening alternative lifestyles. They are troubled, but they play the game within existing parameters: they break rules which are already set, and behave in a way society can understand and deal with. They commit robbery, steal cars, do violence to themselves and others, and sink into spirals of apathy and despair: all these things diminish them by limiting their possibilities, and comfort their elders by confirming the old virtues. The Sixties generation challenged social mores, but failed finally to make a lasting case for the destruction of the old virtues. It may be that those virtues have a lot to be said for them, but, these days, no one seems to be checking.

Madness and its Uses

Moving Day

Moving day. My ex-Live-in-Lover will come this afternoon to move his things out, 18 months after moving in. First thing, I wave the daughter off to Ireland with her dad, for an Easter holiday of dosing sheep and castrating lambs on a friend's farm. Apparently, they use elastic bands. Father and child might be having me on. What do I know, born and raised in the Tottenham Court Road?

I will have three whole weeks alone in my flat. It hasn't happened since L-i-L moved in. I have a scratchy feeling of excitement in my head as I anticipate the next 21 days. Is this true? There must be sadness at the break-up; am I telling myself lies? No. The sadness is there, all right, but in a different compartment from the excitement. I put both on hold until the clearing out is done.

In the event, it's a very jovial affair, with all the brittleness and pretence that joviality implies. So, 18 months after the beginning of the Great Experiment, I do all I can to be amiable and assist. He says he's pleased to see me smile at him. I smile away as we pack things into boxes, disconnect machines, fill black plastic bags with socks and underpants. We wind leads and flexes into manageable coils, joking about missed sexual opportunities and how it's too late to be inventive now. Like a fast cut between forward and reverse in an old silent comedy, with suits over one arm, and bits of stereo equipment in the other, we put things back into the car from which they emerged something very like a geological age ago.

Two cars were needed, in fact, since by now too much has accumulated to fit into his car alone. Still smiling, I volunteer to help. We drive in convoy to his office, cornering carefully because we don't want anything to break, decant the worldly goods, and settle down in the pub next door for a well-earned gin and tonic or two. I express surprise, as I sip, at how much extra stuff there is after only 18 months. 'Imagine if it had been 18 years,' he says ruefully.

Such a time-span is beyond my imagination; in much the same way, I cannot grasp the size of the universe. The brain is not equipped for the understanding of mythic quantities. Of space: such as the universe. Or time: such as more than 18 months of living with someone. My brain goes into spasm. 'They say the universe is set to implode in 20 million (or is it billion?) years,' I reply.

There was only one moment of open disharmony in the whole event. It echoed the tension there had been all along. There was always an inequality of certainty about the project of us living together. He spoke easily about *forever*. I did not consider the week after next a safe bet. In recognition of our different styles I bought him an ironic bottle of wine when he moved in, chosen to be ready to drink in 1997, on my 50th birthday. It was partly a small gesture of risk, but mostly I expected to be doing exactly what I was doing with it today: popping it into one of the cardboard boxes of his belongings, well before 1997. We stood in the doorway looking at the bottle in the box on the floor. He said he didn't want it. I said it wasn't mine, and neither did I. The stalemate was broken when I took the bottle by its neck from the box, and swung it (I like to think with some elegance) against the stone step by the drain in the front yard. A storm cloud accompanied the crash of breaking glass, and darkened the day with the threat of sudden, electric rage from each of us. It took a dangerous moment to pass over: but it did, and the milder breeziness returned. 'Nice one,' he said. 'Thank you,' I smiled, with a warm inner glow of satisfaction at the unlaunching of *us*. No sense crying over spilt claret.

Altogether, a rather civil end to the affair. Refreshments over, I return home, nicely balanced by the gin between a proper sadness and the anticipation of the next three weeks entirely to myself. As I drive, I sing along to The Evs's 'All I have to do is dream' on the radio. It feels as if the car has acquired power steering, so light and easy is the journey back.

Sunday. I wake to the sound of the kitten being sick on the carpet at the foot of my bed. I hadn't planned for this. It was to be a morning spent repossessing my space. Still, cats are often sick. I get on with my plan.

Taking back one's space is something of a technical operation. It involves moving through the flat, doing what one does, but in a particularly alert frame of mind that follows the activities slightly up to and to the left of one's physical body. This watchfulness, this observation of the minutiae of your use of contained space, calls for concentration. Everything is deliberate: breathing, movement, the set of the head. After a little while something else occurs: the splitting-off of a protoplasmic self that insinuates itself into every part of the flat. Like smoke, it wisps into corners and under sofas, investigating places that are too awkward for the body to go, and which never get dusted. It's almost like a dance, a floating self that breathes its way around the place while you only seem to brush your teeth and make a cup of tea. It's a celebration of solitude that won't be broken by people coming in from the outside world with their own stories and their own internal speed. Without that kind of solitude

I get lost. It's as if someone is vacuuming the air out of my lungs. Impossible to live with another person all the time and not begin to scream that they are stopping your breath. For some reason, the other person thinks you're mad, when you're really only being practical and trying to save your life. Then it's time to collect empty cardboard boxes from the off-licence.

All of which is all very well, but the kitten keeps on being sick, and protoplasm won't flow naturally under these conditions. *Worry* sets in. I have a special place devoted to worry that has an insatiable hunger to be filled. When it's empty, it worries anyway about what it's going to worry about. A sick kitten is ideal worry-material.

To the vet. It is every bit the medical emergency I'd been trying to tell myself it wasn't. Darwin's gut has turned inside out. Christ. An unhappy accident. Major abdominal surgery is needed. Now. I don't ask the price. I think of the worst number I can and try very hard not to imagine how many stomachs could be filled by such a sum in far-off places (or nearer by). What am I going to say? Too expensive, kill it, please? Actually, yes. But I can't. So I leave Darwin to the vet and his fate (he might die anyway). I feel wretched; he's been in pain all day, while I've been wafting. What am I going to tell the daughter, whose kitten Darwin is?

I'm furious. I didn't want another cat. Although, perhaps I did. I allowed the daughter to persuade me that three cats aren't any more trouble than two. Now look. God is very strict.

In bed, I cry, which isn't unpleasant, but it is unusual. Is it for Darwin, or ex-L-i-L? Or is it just an interstitial sort of crying that lives between night and the following morning, between sleeping and waking? It feels like sadness, but not mine; or rather, not a personal sadness, but one of great immensity, and slightly up and to the left of me, where I lie saturating the pillow.

Monday. I call the vet first thing. Darwin has survived the operation and the night. It will be two days before he's out of the woods, but his chances are better. I am hugely relieved, but livid at having to mind so much about a cat, or anything at all, come to that.

As luck would have it, today's the day a man comes from Bristol to talk to me about depression. I giggle maniacally to myself when I remember. He's making a documentary on the subject.

What about being alone? Where did that go? I consider phoning and telling him he can't come. I spend 20 minutes inventing stories about why. An imaginary aunt has just died. I've had my first ever epileptic attack. I have to do an emergency reading in Aberdeen. What about a kitten whose gut has turned inside out? What about I'm too depressed to talk about depression? I give up. Anyway, if he's coming from Bristol he won't be home answering his phone.

He turns out to be a perfectly nice man and pleasantly acerbic with it. His only obvious fault is that he drives up in an Alfa. We drink coffee and talk. He thinks there's a distinction between depression and melancholia – he's right, there is. He thinks there's a connection between melancholia and writing (or any of that creative stuff) – he's right, there is. But I'm wary of making much of that, because a real bone-deep depression is as painful as cancer, and that's a fact, too. I worry about romanticising it. On the other hand, last night's howling was precisely what he is talking about. Melancholia *is* a curiously different condition from clinical depression, or, at least, a place you can get to if you go through the clinical depression and wait. And it isn't negative. It's more like being in the part of my head that I write from. So, we bat this about a bit, but I still hear myself hissing aggressively about not wanting to make depression or writing seem mystical or magical. They are, of course, in a way. But they're also not. Long may confusion reign. Things are difficult; why shouldn't they be? The nice man nods. It seems we aren't having a disagreement.

Tuesday. Wednesday. Thursday. Nothing. Nothing. Nothing. These are the days. Don't speak to anyone (except the vet on Darwin's progress: all is well). Leave the answering machine on. Don't answer the doorbell (luckily, no one rings it). This is it, then. Me in my space. Me and my melancholy.

I do nothing. I get on with the new novel. Smoke. Drink coffee. Smoke. Write. Stare at ceiling. Smoke. Write. Lie on the sofa. Drink coffee. Write.

It is a kind of heaven. This is what I was made for. It *is* doing nothing. A fraud is being perpetrated: writing is not work, it's doing nothing. It's not a fraud: doing nothing is what I have to do to live. Or: doing writing is what I have to do to do nothing. Or: doing nothing is what I have to do to write. Or: writing is what I have to do to be my melancholy self. And be alone.

Moreover, I don't have to think about food. No one here now finds eating an essential part of their life. In addition to smoking, drinking coffee and writing, I make regular trips to the fridge to gaze on its cosmic emptiness. I adore its lit-up vacancy. No L-i-L, no daughter, needing the fridge full of possible feasts. I haven't been shopping for ten days now. There's a bit of inedible cheese, a jar of jalapeno chillies which I nibble at when I'm peckish. Every 36 hours or so I call in an emergency pizza. Another nice man on a bike brings it round. I do not die of starvation. I continue to drink coffee (sometimes tea), smoke, write and stare at the ceiling.

Pages pile up. I feel guilty. Someone else must have written them. Anyway, even if I did write them it was too easy. They won't be any good. Uh huh, there's the worry centre activating again. Because Friday I have to go out.

Friday. A trip to the Zoo. I want to know about orang-utans for the novel. Mr Carman, the head keeper of the

primates, has agreed to talk to me. He's wearing green
wellies with khaki trousers tucked into them. He's been at
the Zoo for 26 years. Again, I feel a fraud. I'm planning to
write about a talking orang called Jenny. He'll think me friv-
olous. Cautiously, I tell him I'm just a fiction writer. I need
some facts, but I make things up, too. Do I know, he asks
without prompting, that the Malays believe orangs can talk,
really, but they don't because they think they'll be made to
work if the humans find out? I didn't know. Thank you,
God, and I love you, too.

We discuss the daily routine. Mick Carman reckons that
orangs are closer to humans than gorillas or chimps; he does-
n't care what anyone says. I'm delighted to hear this, more
grist for my fiction mill. Buy why? Because they're lazy,
sullen and devious, if I see what he means. Oh, yes, I do see.
They're by far the most difficult animal to keep in captivity
because of this, *and* because they're basically solitary animals, not social like the other apes. They each live in their
own territory, defending it vigorously from all comers,
except for sexual encounters. It's every orang for himself or
herself. Speaking of which, I tell Mick, I read a paper written
by a Scandinavian woman anthropologist demanding that
'orangutan' (meaning 'man of the forest') be amended to
whatever is the Malay for 'person of the forest'.

Quite right. Quite right. We must defend the personhood
of the solitary, female whatevershe'scalled-utan with all our
might. For she is me and I am her, and soon I'm staring
through reinforced glass at Suka (meaning The Delightful),
who will be Jenny in the novel. She sits in her cage, solitary
and morose, as melancholic as you please, dropping handfuls
of straw onto her head. And I wouldn't mind betting that
some protoplasmic wisp is nuzzling into the corners of her
cage, aching for the curious eyes of the likes of me to piss off
and leave her on her own.

Having Half
the Fun

An Unquiet Mind:
A Memoir of Moods and Madness
by Kay Redfield Jamison
(PICADOR, LONDON, 1996)

Touched with Fire
by Kay Redfield Jamison
(FREE PRESS, LONDON, 1994)

Welcome to My Country:
A Therapist's Memoir of Madness
by Lauren Slater
(HAMISH HAMILTON, LONDON, 1996)

Once, the mad were exhibited at Bedlam for the fascination of Sunday tourists; ooh'ed and ahh'ed at as examples of how the human mind can distort the civilised and rational behaviour which was supposed to be its very particular accomplishment. Lately, they are more freely available between the covers of books, described and philosophised over by neurologists, psychiatrists and therapists who, besides seeking to cure them, wish to illuminate the meaning of their mad patients for the general – as in normal – public. We are offered the chance to marvel at the way minds warp, and to feel that there is some telling connection between the warped mind and its supposed original state of sanity. There is anxiety, too, mixed with a little excitement, at the indistinct boundaries between madness and sanity, and perhaps a degree of envy, with the suspicion that the mad, agonised though they may be, are having a more interesting, or at least more significant, time of it.

It's not hard to imagine a near-future when the neurobiologists will have identified the physiological bases for all the major mental disorders, but I doubt that, even then, we will think of them in the same way we think of physical illness. Afflictions like multiple sclerosis or osteo-arthritis do not carry the same weight of apparent meaning as manic depression and schizophrenia, for all that discrepant genes may turn out to be equally implicated in all of them. People don't read case-studies of diabetes in the hope of gaining some insight into the nature of man's relationship with the world, even though extreme physical illness and pain may be quite as tumultuous and alienating to the individual as mental disturbance.

Madness has always been modish: Shakespeare dramatised it; the Romantics romanticised it; the Surrealists painted it; the Existentialists philosophised with it. It is, as Lévi-Strauss said of totemic animals, good to think with – unless you are mad, of course. Then you are thought *about*, and so far as treatment goes, at the mercy of whatever school of belief or current trend you happen to fall in with. In the past, you might have been hosed down with icy water, had parts of your brain excised or been cut loose and sent off to the margins of society. Now, you might be given drugs, electro-convulsive therapy, paint, drama, group conversation, a strict one-on-one analysis – or be cut loose and sent off to the margins of society. You might also, if Kay Redfield Jamison and Lauren Slater's books are any indication of present trends, choose either to become a creative artist or, if the muse doesn't speak, train as a clinical psychologist. Nowadays, it seems, you can be a success or failure as a mad person. As if mental disarray wasn't enough to cope with, there are career decisions to think about.

Neither Jamison nor Slater is writing about mild neuroses: their books concern major debilitating, life-destroying mental afflictions – manic depression in Jamison's case, schizophrenia and severe personality disorders in Slater's. And both write about their specialties in the context of their own experience of mental illness. Jamison's is the most overtly autobiographical, being a straightforward description of her manic depression and its management throughout her student and working life. She is a professor of psychiatry at Johns Hopkins School of Medicine and clinical director for the Dana Consortium of the Genetic Basis of Manic-Depressive Illness. She subscribes to the current view of bipolar illness: that there is almost certainly a genetic predisposition, and that it must be managed throughout the course of the patient's life with drugs, preferably lithium.

Mood swings are something everyone is familiar with. Most people wake up on some mornings filled with an unreasonable optimism and confidence, on others with their unreasonable opposites. Unaccountable feelings of well-being are bright spots in most of our lives, gratefully received. For Marie, one of Slater's patients, they were all that kept her from committing suicide. Marie would probably be diagnosed as manic depressive on Jamison's criteria, though Slater sees her as a chronic depressive with sporadic remissions. She was depressed almost all the time: there were episodes often lasting only days, but sometimes longer, when she was energetic and filled with the light of the world. This is the kind of mild mania that makes unipolars mutter grimly that bipolars have all the fun. And from the outside, at least for a while, it is a most beguiling state to witness. As Jamison describes it, 'my manias, at least in their early and mild forms, were absolutely intoxicating states that gave rise to great personal pleasure, an incomparable flow of thoughts, and ceaseless energy.' When you see it in someone else it is hard not to want to join the party. For Marie, the mania never really gets out of control before depression intervenes. For Jamison the mania ran riot, sliding from a sense of well-being into catastrophe. Manic depression forms a continuum from surprising intermittent pleasure to cyclical disaster: where you stand on it depends on whether you have the chemistry to stop feeling good before it's too late. Watching someone you know to have severe manic-depressive illness reach a condition of vitality and euphoria after months, or even years, of feeling low and utterly flattened by their chemistry, you are both delighted and filled with alarm. Responsibly, you must say to them, as they display real pleasure: 'You are getting ill.'

Jamison's delicious highs turned into classic manias, running out of control, keeping her on a 24-hour schedule, emptying her bank account on wild spending sprees, allowing her uncontrolled thoughts to spill out into the world in the form of abuse to friends and lovers, eventually wrecking her system, bringing terrifying hallucinations and a suicide attempt. She was given lithium along with supportive therapy, and the mood swings stopped, but here is the catch that all manic depressives know about and the nub of her book: the effect of lithium is to colour the world grey. It can impair memory, concentration and attention span, and make reading almost impossible. It flattens the emotions, causes you to feel physically heavy and lethargic and often makes people seem mere shadows of themselves. Jamison, like many others, found it intolerable, stopped taking it once she started to feel better – and had another manic episode.

Her experience gives her the authority to take a tough line

with her patients: if you have manic depression you have it for life and there is no alternative but to take lithium. Although it is possible for some people to manage on a low enough dose for the effects to be less debilitating, the consequence is an increase in the degree of mood swing. Jamison herself opted for this solution, deciding to live with a certain amount of cyclical emotional upheaval. But it doesn't work for everyone. Some people simply have to live with the disability that seems to be an unavoidable part of the cure. Most people are not so fortunate as Jamison in having the kind of professional and family support that enabled her, remarkably, to maintain her career as both an academic and a clinician. Her colleagues, her lovers and her professional superiors all, by her account, accept her condition, and do everything they can to enable her to continue her career and social life. Very few people with her severity of illness can have been so lucky. Those I know with the condition find their lives repeatedly in tatters, long periods in hospital and the debilitating effect of lithium making an uninterrupted career no more than a passing dream, their friends and family often alienated, frightened and simply exhausted.

It is not just the unpleasant physical effects of lithium that incline people not to comply with treatment. 'People say, when I complain of being less lively, less energetic, less high-spirited: "Well, now you're just like the rest of us" . . . But I compare myself with my former self, not with others. I am far removed from when I have been my liveliest, most productive, most intense, most outgoing and effervescent.' To be in the early stages of mania is intoxicating: to be 'just like the rest of us' is to be reduced and domesticated. Even someone like Slater's patient, Marie, concussed by depression most of her life, subsists on the memory and hope of the brief highs when she feels 'unbelievably alive'. Jamison, knowing how hard it is to give up the chance of euphoria, is all the more

adamant that bipolar illness is a strictly physical disease
which must be treated pharmacologically. She rails against
'clinicians who somehow draw a distinction between the
suffering and treatability of "medical illness" such as
Hodgkin's disease or breast cancer, and psychiatric illness
such as depression, manic depression or schizophrenia. I
believe, without doubt, that manic depression is a medical
illness; I also believe that, with rare exception, it is malprac-
tice to treat it without medication.' It's a good practical
argument, and there is masses of corroborating evidence for
her insistence that manic depression is a neurophysiological
disease, but it is a medical illness that makes people feel at
times that they are the inheritors of the universe, and the
pain of knowing and having to lose that sensation is very
great, while the side effects of lithium make it a desperate (if
necessary) remedy.

An earlier book, *Touched with Fire*, written by Jamison a
couple of years before *An Unquiet Mind*, sits uneasily
though not incomprehensibly with her rigorous medical
approach to manic depression. It is a study of the relationship between manic depression and what she is pleased to
call the artistic temperament. She is not the first to locate
the wellsprings of poetry in a diseased mind, and though she
insists that talent, as well as manic depression, is necessary
for great art, she nonetheless equates the 'possession' poets
speak of with manic states. Byron, Blake, Coleridge, the
Jameses, Melville, Van Gogh and, of course, Virginia Woolf,
are all tested, by their works and their known heredities, for
bipolar illness and the findings are positive. While Jamison
acknowledges that 'there are many artists, writers and composers who are perfectly normal from a psychiatric point of
view', she focuses on those in whom she divines mental illness because 'the fact that there is only a partial correlation
does not mean there is no correlation at all.' So I suppose
you could turn the whole thing on its head, and using the

partial correlation of mental health with writers, artists and composers, write a study showing sanity to be a remarkable trait in creative types.

While on sabbatical in England, Jamison conducted a survey of 47 modern British writers (using the receipt of literary prizes as the criterion, and the self-selection of those who responded to her questionnaire) and found that 38 per cent had been treated for a mood disorder, of whom three-quarters had been given anti-depressants or lithium, or been hospitalised. Further historical research shows many of the writers Jamison deems to be manic depressive to have relatives also suffering from mental illness. A genetic theory emerges which suggests that the downside of the mutation in other family members is offset by the benefits conferred on society by the positive achievements of those suffering relatives who are driven towards creativity. 'Such a compensatory advantage . . . would be roughly analogous to the resistance to malaria found among unaffected carriers of the gene for sickle-cell anaemia.' It would be nice to think that nature regarded great art as an essential benefit in species survival, but Jamison, accepting that a genetic push for poetry is a little unlikely, explains that manic depression must also be the spur for many industrial and scientific innovators.

Even so, underlying her thesis is the irritable question that is asked of all writers and artists: where do you get your ideas from? For Freud it was unresolved, sublimated neurosis; for Jamison it is the over-excited, speedy state of mania. 'Hypomania and mania often generate ideas and associations, propel contact with life and other people, induce frenzied energies and enthusiasms, and cast an ecstatic, rather cosmic hue over life.' So much for where ideas come from. The other ubiquitous question is: 'How do you discipline yourself to work?' That's where the depression side of the equation comes in. 'Depression prunes and sculpts: it also ruminates and ponders and, ultimately, subdues and focuses thought. It allows structuring, at a detailed level, of the more expansive patterns woven during hypomania.' First you soar into the realm of ideas, then you come down for the editing process.

This is not, Jamison insists, a reductive view of the artist, but an enhancement of our understanding. She is not, she says, merely reiterating the stereotypical tormented artist with statistical and diagnostic knobs. 'Seeing Blake as someone who suffered from an occasionally problematic illness . . . may not explain all or even most of who he was. But, surely, it does explain some.' This supposes that who Blake was needs to be explained. The diagnosis is of no use to Blake, because he is dead. Is it of some help to his readers? Only if, like Jamison, you feel that a diagnosed Blake gives us more than the texts he left. You can carry the diagnosis to the text, but whether that enhances our understanding of it is moot. Of course, if Blake were not dead, he could be treated with lithium, which would doubtless make it less likely that we should find him sitting naked up a tree in his garden. Would Blake on lithium have been Blake? This doesn't strike me as an urgent question. I would sooner know in what way we think we benefit from pathologising the extraordinary. Is it because, like Jamison's friends, we like the idea that, properly medicated, the extraordinary becomes 'just like the rest of us'; and that medicalised and unmedicated they are simply sick? I do wonder what dismal effect books like *Touched with Fire* have on those sufferers of manic depression who do not find themselves compensated with artistic greatness, but only scuppered by a dreadfully debilitating illness.

Lauren Slater has a more flowery approach to her patients. 'My patients – borderline personalities, sociopaths, bulimics, schizophrenics of every type – are foreign, tropical, green roses and striped plants that are hard to understand. I seek their scents and sounds, to enter deeply into their cupped, closed worlds because that is the struggle lying at the core of me.' Beneath the barrage of very distressing prose, Slater's 'me' lies at the core of all these essays purporting to describe her work with the mentally unwell. Each individual, no matter how catatonic and remote from the world, is eventually understood via an insight about Slater herself. Her own emotional experiences and psychiatric history shed comprehension on all mental disturbance. Peter's violent leather-clad misogynist is interpreted in terms of her own bout of adolescent anorexia. 'I made my body a whitened bone, a pale blade. Like any real man, for years I lived with my fist and not my flesh. I was so hungry, but I could not risk the softness of surrender.' They are, it seems, one and the same. So things look up for her relationship with Peter when he is shaken by the desertion of his masochistic woman. 'And I, well, I grew to love him and love the strength of his slow surrender.'

Marie, the depressive with momentary flashes of happiness, provokes an ecstatic emotional decline in Slater: 'I closed my eyes and dropped down. At the bottom of the hole, past the push of scalpels, lies that unalterable stone of suffering. I could see the stone now, in half-sleep – deep blue, raw coral.' In the meantime, having tried every antidepressant in the book, including Prozac, Marie is still trying to cope with two children and deep depression. Looking out of the consulting-room window, Slater still wonders 'if I was taking on some of Marie's heightened moments, some of her occasional spasms of joy. I wondered if, in travelling with me into the wound, she had, inadvertently, shown me a place of clear colour and exceptional angles.'

Joseph, a middle-aged schizophrenic, once an academic, suffers from writing mania, penning his every cluttered thought. Eventually, Slater takes his writings and edits them into what she considers to be their proper order. She creates a community of 'me and him together . . . He put his hand on my mouth as a lover or a mother might, and I let myself breathe into him.' She is aware that she is making *her* sense of Joseph's hypergraphia but 'perhaps narratives are the one realm that cannot ever . . . be confidently claimed by any individual'. Still, Joseph is pleased to have his words typed up. 'My words', he weeps, stroking the 'streamlined sentences'.

None of the patients described here seems to benefit over the long term from this rampant counter-transference. Marie, told that after all she must just learn to live with her depression, is justifiably pissed off. Peter is deemed to be on the road to recovery when he finds himself a fat woman, and Slater has seen enough of him 'to imagine how his body would be within a fat woman's arms . . . I could not help but see her spread legs on a bed, and he, a little cowed by the sight of so much, trying to touch her, first with his fingers, then with penis, allowing himself entry into the many layers of her life.' Watching Joseph weeping over her typescript, Slater concludes: 'there is only so much you can do for a patient, only so much hurt you can heal. This is what is hard about my work, knowing when to exit, knowing there are times you must take a soft touch, fingers formed into a strainer, and bring them back to your own body.' Everything is brought back to Slater, and her patients fade from the page, managing as best they may.

Her actual task at the clinic where Joseph was one of the patients was to help them master 'low-level self-care skills'. To get them washing, eating, able to go to the shops, budget, make a meal. To give them a modicum of practical self-sufficiency. She detected, however, a passionate desire for intimacy within their psychotic terrors that she considers more interesting than the provision of day-to-day independence: 'I sometimes catch glimpses of continuous themes, diced-up apples of desire, green leaves of love. I want to go there, tread through those gardens.' And this is a pretty accurate description of what she is; a tourist in the gardens of the mad where the hard graft of actual gardening is somebody else's task.

Rhythm Method

> R.D. *Laing: A Biography*
> by Adrian Laing
> (PETER OWEN, LONDON, 1994)

Not long ago a friend of mine was walking back to her car
after the cinema when, not unusually for the time and the
place, a distraught man placed himself in her way. She was
not frightened; he was easily identified as mad, not bad. A
shuffling walk, a drooping, defeated posture which required
a special effort to raise his head so he could address her, and
eyes, when they lifted, which were more distressed than
aggressive. He put out a hand, as if the fact of his body being
in her path would not be enough to gain her attention. 'Can
I talk to you?' he asked. My friend felt around in her hand-
bag and came up with some money which she pressed into
his hand. It was a normal inner city exchange. Except that
the man shook his head, put the money back into my friend's
open bag, took some more from his own pocket and dropped
that in too. 'No, I've got money. It's not money. I want to talk
to you,' he said, and launched into a rambling tale of woe
about being evicted from his hostel and how it felt to have
nowhere to go and no one to tell. He was not asking for anything except what is most difficult to give: time and attention.

At it simplest, at least in the early days, what the existential psychiatrists were advocating was careful listening. Their point, though, was never that simple: they were advocating listening *for*, not just listening *to*. Apart from the fact that psychotics, like everyone else, would benefit from being heard, there was the bold suggestion that they were actually saying something which their doctors needed to be told in order to do their job. The mad monologue contained real information, and psychiatrists would have to listen to their patients in the way medical doctors had to take into account what physically distressed patients said about the nature of the symptoms.

In the early Sixties, R.D. Laing and others began to define psychosis in terms of its relation to society, and psychotics as individuals who in their own way were making sense of their social circumstances. The mad might be alienated, but they were not aliens, and therefore their doctors must be, not alienists, but interpreters of the language of the alienated. If that seems obvious now, we have Laing and his fellow theorists to thank for it. At the time it came as something of a revelation, not least because there was an audience beyond the psychiatric community primed by the zeitgeist of the late Fifties and early Sixties to fall on their ideas and make much – too much, perhaps – of them.

I was a member of that wider audience. When Volume One of *Sanity, Madness and the Family* by R.D. Laing and his colleague Aaron Esterson, was published in 1964, I was 17 and living in the house of a woman who had rescued me a couple of years before, both from my disordered family and from the psychiatric hospital I was stuck in. The book took the form of case-histories of diagnosed schizophrenics, but what made it different from the usual run of psychiatric textbooks was that the views and voices of the patients and their families were presented side by side.

It was the case of the 'Abbotts' that made an impact on

me. 'Maya Abbott' believed that her parents were trying to influence her by telepathy and thought-control, and showed clinical signs of 'catatonia . . . affective impoverishment and autistic withdrawal'. Laing and Esterson discovered on speaking to the parents of the girl who now experienced herself as a machine, that for many years they had indeed been trying to influence her thoughts, believing her to be telepathic; that for some time before she became 'ill' they'd been experimenting with their daughter – sending each other signals which 'Maya' was not supposed to perceive – in order to test their hypothesis and alter her attitudes and behaviour.

For Laing and Esterson, the 'Abbotts' confirmed their thesis that madness could have a socially intelligible basis. For me, there was a starburst of recognition. At 13, I fled my emotionally erratic mother and went to stay with my father, with whom I'd had no contact for three years, and Pam, the woman he lived with. It wouldn't be anyone's idea of fun to have an angry adolescent arrive out of the blue, but the way Pam responded to me was, from the moment I arrived, mystifyingly aggressive. Nothing I did was right; everything was criticised or scorned. She ignored me when I tried to initiate or join in conversations, but called me idle and useless when she found me reading. She objected to me spending too much time in my room, but if I walked into the living room she'd go silent and turn her back on me. She complained that I didn't help out with the chores, but when, after that, I made a cup of tea after a meal, she poured it away and made a new pot. I wasted money by taking too many and too deep baths, but I was also 'dirty'. It seemed to me that she was viciously unkind even before I'd had a proper chance to make a nuisance of myself. I withdrew into a sullen silence and relations became impossible. Gradually, I began to believe that Pam was trying to poison me.

My social worker was disbelieving, even though I left out

my poisoning theory. Obviously I was having Oedipal (or Electral) difficulties and suffering delusions of persecution. In all honesty, it seemed a bit improbable even to me. But things were so bad in the house that the social worker got the council to send me away to boarding school. It was when the long summer holidays were imminent that I got a letter from Pam confessing that before I'd gone to live there, she had had a secret meeting with my mother whom she'd never met before, and together they had made a plan. Since (not unreasonably) Pam didn't fancy having a difficult adolescent around, and (very dubiously) my mother wanted me back, the pair of them decided that Pam was to treat me in such a way as to ensure I'd be miserable enough to want to return to my mother. Now that the plan had plainly failed, and alarmed, I suppose, at the prospect of six weeks' togetherness, Pam wrote to me at school to explain and apologise, and suggested we make a fresh start.

Sanity, Madness and the Family showed me how fortunate I was to get that letter which made it clear that it wasn't me who was behaving madly, and how fortunate, too, I had been to get away from them. What was extraordinary about the book to me then wasn't just the news that my family might have driven me mad – I already had an inkling of that – but that my family was not a unique quirk in a universe of normality. To have been a party to a cosmic irregularity left the answer to the 'Why me?' question wide open – I might still, in some way I didn't understand, have deserved it – but if normality itself was under suspicion there was something wider and less personally reprehensible to be investigated.

What I – and I think quite a lot of other people who fell on this material – failed to notice was the word 'sanity' in the title *Sanity, Madness and the Family*, and the fact that it was planned as the first of two projected volumes. The second book was to complement the first by studying the interaction

of families in which no one had been diagnosed as schizophrenic, and was intended to investigate the theory that,
while mad-making behaviour was always present in the families of schizophrenics, it was only sometimes present in
families with no pathological members. Volume Two was
never written, with the result that the key (and still unan-
swered) question which would explicitly have arisen as to
why potentially mad-making behaviour only caused madness
in some people was never addressed. The unwritten second
volume on 'normal' families allowed both Laing and his
admirers to skip the question and to suggest instead that
there were no normal families, no normal society, and that
the highest form of existential sanity was to be found in the
individual who refused to conform to the madness of a
demented civilisation. The autism of the mad became a
heroic, hyper-sane response to an inauthentic world.

Well, it made sense to me, and I launched myself into the
world of mental ill-health with all the fervour of a career
move. I had a problem, though: I didn't have the right symptoms, the sort which might allow me (and the radical
shrinks) to think of myself as a channel for social prophecy
and higher truth. I was only a dull, inoperative depressive of
the kind Laing showed not the slightest interest in. So far
from liberating myself from the shackles of society's false
diagnosis, I found, in my enthusiasm for existential psychiatry, a new logical framework in which to house and develop
my free-flowing guilt: if I wasn't mad (properly mad, cor-
rectly mad, Laingian mad) then I was a miserable existential
failure and as insubstantial as my depression insisted I must
be. Laing, the clarifier of the concept of the double-bind, had
invented a brand new version of his own. Exciting times?
You bet.

Of course, I was young and flying without any background to keep me from floating away on the wings of
misunderstanding, but judging by the practical results of

Laing's theory and his own life's progress, my reasoning on the basis of what I read may not have been too far off the mark. It may even have been that Ronnie Laing, romancer of madness, suffered from the same problem as me. According to Charles Rycroft, who was his training analyst, he had 'an extremely effective schizoid defence mechanism against exhibiting signs of depression'. Laing was a depressive who needed drugs and drink to achieve what came naturally to his patients. He was more than capable of behaving badly, but perhaps behaving madly was beyond him. A tragedy of a kind, but, in retrospect, a massive irresponsibility towards those who were his concern. Like many at the time, he chose to overlook what is clear to anyone who has spent time with the mentally ill – the extraordinary pain involved. To find authenticity in the signs of madness is like finding a desirable simplicity in poverty; only those not obliged to experience either can afford such intellectual slackness.

Considering their relationship, Adrian Laing's account of his father's life and work is an astonishingly disciplined effort, which only occasionally betrays his private feelings ('Ronnie's nauseating desire to rationalise external events began at a very early age'). If anything, the controlled attempt not to allow personal judgment to colour his narrative results in a book that often reads more like a curriculum vitae than a biography. But you can see why. Laing was the kind of father that would have given Papa Kronos indigestion. He made babies by the tribe (ten altogether) and deserted them in pursuit of his destiny with barely a glance back in their direction. He didn't see the five children of his first family for two years, and by the time he made a visit Adrian had forgotten what he looked like. When his daughter, Susie, was terminally ill in her early twenties, he made a special and exceedingly rare trip to Scotland to tell her, against the wishes of the rest of the family, her doctor and her fiancé, that she would be dead in six months. Then he returned to London almost immediately, leaving others to cope with the emotional aftermath of his searing honesty. Subsequently, his oldest child, Fiona, had a breakdown, and Laing failed to provide support. 'It would not be fair to say that Fiona was callously abandoned,' says his son, but it sounds as if some wording very close to that *would* be fair.

Perhaps none of that is our business. There are no end of families badly treated by self-obsessed individuals who have made great and lasting contributions to the wider world. The personal failures ought not to detract from an assessment of the work. But there is a question to be asked of a purveyor of wisdom who displays none in his dealings with the individuals in his life.

There was wisdom, or at least great intelligence and originality, in the early days. *The Divided Self* still comes across as a serious new attempt to describe the dynamics of schizophrenia. It was written before the collaboration with Esterson, while Laing was still a working psychiatrist in Gartnavel Hospital. He has no difficulty in acknowledging the reality of 'insanity', and describes a plausible decline from 'normal' schizoid thinking into psychotic insanity. If it isn't a final description of the aetiology of mental illness, at least it's an interesting view of it. On the other hand, his unquestioning belief in the existence of an authentic, absolute self which is subverted by society looks carelessly romantic, and no thought is given to the possibility of a predisposing biochemical component in mental illness (or its symptoms).

Fame struck. Laing went to a lot of dinner parties. He began his training analysis with Rycroft, and in spite of grave doubts on the part of the Institute's training committee ('Dr Laing is apparently a very disturbed and ill person'), he qualified as a psychoanalyst. Things started going strange once Kingsley Hall was up and running. Laing had founded a group known as the Philadelphia Association along with

Esterson, David Cooper, Clancy Sigal and Sid Briskin, and
these men formed the core group of loving brothers. The
idea had been to find a house in which people could live
while in the throes of a psychotic episode, where the process
of madness could run its course without intervention.
Kingsley Hall in the East End had been formerly used as a
settlement house. Gandhi had once lived there – and the
brothers obtained it in 1965 for a peppercorn rent. It was a
place to go crazy in and going crazy had already been
defined as a counter-cultural necessity, so no one held back.
'David Cooper was beginning to crack up . . . There was
concern that Clancy Sigal was cracking up. Aaron Esterson
and many others thought Ronnie was cracking up. Ronnie
thought Aaron's problem was that he was unable to crack
up.' Adrian Laing doesn't mention whether there were any
patients waiting their turn, but psychiatric nurse Mary
Barnes had already settled in for her lengthy non-symbolic
regression and was demanding full-time nappy-changing and
bottle-feeding: who would have taken care of the lay crazies?

It was also the case that Laing panicked when faced by
intractable madness. He was not a good practitioner. When
Clancy Sigal's 'true' self failed to emerge despite LSD sessions
and non-interventionist therapy, and he flipped out too
alarmingly even for Laing's tastes, he was forcibly sedated
and handed over to the regular mad-doctors for sectioning.
Sigal never forgave Laing, and when he later wrote a
scabrously funny novel on the whole existential psychiatry
scene, Laing threatened to sue if it was published in Britain.

Adrian Laing suggests that it was his father's excess of
fame, too soon, and the slide into guru-in-chief of the
counter-culture which was responsible for his decline. By
1967, in *The Politics of Experience*, he was writing, 'We are
all murderers and prostitutes,' and later in the same book: 'If
I could turn you on, if I could drive you out of your
wretched mind, if I could tell you I would let you know . . .

I am trying to fuck you, dear reader, I am trying to get through.' Adrian Laing confirms that the new philosophy was an amalgam of 'Scotch whisky, Californian grass and Czechoslovakian acid' with, doubtless, more than a soupçon of megalomania sloshed in for good measure. Later came *Knots* and *Do You Love Me*, with such gems as 'Was that a kiss?/or a hiss/ from the abyss?', and in between Laing threw himself into the natural-birth movement, where he was not very much wanted by the likes of Leboyer and other obstetricians who were doing very nicely without him. By the late Seventies he changed tack and found an enthusiasm in re-birthing for adults rather than new birthing for foetuses, taking a troupe of re-birthers (including Adrian) around the country like itinerant soul-midwives. In the Eighties he could be found around Hampstead chanting Tibetan mantras and performing Native American warrior rituals for the greater good of his suburban souls. As his life got smaller and his concerns narrower, he became a hopelessly alcoholic and unreliable shaman/showman who was liable to burst into tears in the middle of a lecture.

But was he one of his own existential heroes? Perhaps, by his own definition, he was. Very likely he would have said so. Possibly he would have settled for being an iconoclast, which lets him off the hook as a reformer. If causing a stir was all he wanted to do, then he succeeded. What you can't help feeling was that there was a terrible waste of talent, though such a thought is nonsensical. He must be credited with provoking psychiatry into rethinking its automatic reliance on drugs, ECT, brain butchery, and what often amounted to the imprisonment of sick people. Though it's tempting, it's too harsh to blame Laing for the callous pragmatism of Thatcher's version of care in the community. Yet as a reformer he never made it clear how, once the mad had been liberated from their chains, he was going to deal with their anguish. Indeed, he made that anguish seem exotic and desirable, which was, perhaps, his most damning fault. A doctor who does not take his patient's pain into account is failing at a most basic level.

One special difficulty for psychiatrists trying to relate to the psychotic is what information theory defines as the signal-to-noise ratio. Mad monologues are filled with random noise, exceptional skill is needed to distinguish between valid signals and meaningless interference. It might make life easier for everyone if shrinks were seen as telephone engineers of the psyche. Ever since Freud, mind-doctoring has been trying to present itself as a science, but the role confusion has always pulled patients in both directions. It's never clear when we settle on the couch or across the desk whether we have put ourselves in the hands of experts or sages. It seems more than likely that doctors have the same problem defining themselves.

Laing was undoubtedly a divided man; a charismatic ill at ease with his own intellect. It often looks as if each part went its own separate way, and his own puzzlement, as well as that of his onlookers, is understandable. Adrian Laing tells the story of his father on a speaking tour of the States in the early Seventies, when doctors in Chicago asked him to examine a young woman who was diagnosed as schizophrenic. She was silent, naked and had done nothing for months but rock back and forth. Laing, the charismatic, stripped off all his clothes and sat with her, rocking in time to her rhythm. After 20 minutes she started talking to Laing and the doctors were stunned. 'Did it never occur to you to do that?' Laing asked afterwards. Even if it had occurred to the Chicago mind-doctors to get naked and rock the young woman back to health, they might have wondered where they were to find the time and resources to deal with all their other patients. We aren't told what exactly the young woman said when she finally spoke. Maybe something like 'Get your sodding clothes on. I'm the madwoman and you're the doctor, Doctor.' Laing continued on to San Diego after performing his Attenborough-among-the-wild-things number; he'd done his stuff. It was a personally creative moment, perhaps, but not a very serviceable one for the development of psychiatry.

Life, Death and the Whole Damn Thing

> *An Anthropologist on Mars*
> by Oliver Sacks
> (PICADOR, LONDON, 1995)
>
> *The Island of the Colour-Blind*
> by Oliver Sacks
> (PICADOR, LONDON, 1996)

Oliver Sacks seeks for meaning in the chaos of neurological deficit. He has that in common with his patient Mr Thompson, one of two Korsakov amnesiacs described in *The Man who Mistook His Wife for a Hat*, who, says Sacks, 'must seek meaning, *make* meaning, in a desperate way, continually inventing, throwing bridges of meaning over abysses of meaninglessness, the chaos that yawns continually beneath him'. Mr Thompson invents personal narratives over and over again with endless variation, but, according to Sacks, they fail to work 'because they *are* confabulations, fictions, which cannot do service for reality while also failing to correspond with reality'.

Oliver Sacks does not trust fiction. Borges's fictions, dripping with parables of memory and identity, are much admired by Sacks, but are not trusted to serve reality without a basis in documentary fact. 'I have often wondered whether Borges's Funes, so uncannily similar to Luria's Mnemonist, may have been based on a personal encounter with such a mnemonist,' he muses in a footnote to Mr Thompson's story. 'Funes the Memorious' is the story of someone inexplicable and astounding: 'A circle drawn on a blackboard, a right triangle, lozenge – all these are forms we can fully and intuitively grasp; Ireneo could do the same with the stormy mane of a pony, with a herd of cattle on a hill, with the changing fire and its innumerable ashes, with the many faces of a dead man throughout a long wake.'

Oliver Sacks and the narrator of 'Funes' are in the same business of delineating the extraordinary, outlining the nearly unthinkable. The difference lies not only in the prose and the overtly fictional form in which Funes is presented, but in the moral tone of the narrator. Borges allows us to judge Funes's tragedy for ourselves, presenting his case without pronouncing a final verdict on the condition of his soul. In the case-history which Dr Sacks provides of his patient Mr Thompson, he does not hold back from pronouncing him damned. Jimmie, the other Korsakov sufferer in the book, is granted a soul because he achieves short periods of concentration and repose during the hospital Mass: Mr Thompson is deemed 'de-souled' by his incapacity for quietness and fellow-feeling. Jimmie – with his occasional capacity for 'genuine emotional relation' – '*can* be redeemed'; he has the possibility of 'salvation' because he 'is in despair'. There is, however, nothing redeeming in Mr Thompson, who is all 'brilliant and brassy surface', which may, Sacks acknowledges, obscure desperation, but only 'a desperation he does not feel'.

Dr P., who mistakes his wife's head for his hat, is compared to Zazetsky, the subject of Luria's other great case, *The Man with a Shattered World*, and found wanting for his inability to recognise and despair over his visual errors. Dr

P. 'was not fighting, did not know what was lost, did not indeed know that anything was lost. But who was the more tragic, or who was more damned – the man who knew it, or the man who did not?' Some of us, forced into such a formulation, might conclude the former, but it is Dr P. who is Sacks's choice. This is not just a personal response on Sacks's part, a private revulsion against the emotionally gutted condition of his patients: it is a judgment embedded in the philosophical soil of Nietzsche's belief that 'only great pain is the ultimate liberator of the spirit'. Will ordinary pain not do?

It's one thing to know, because you are a neurologist, that Mr Thompson is suffering from Korsakov's psychosis and that Dr P. has a massive tumour or degenerative process in the visual parts of his brain: it is, I think, quite another to speculate on the condition of their souls. But that is the contradiction which Sacks fails to resolve, and it is, of course, largely for that reason that he is so read and admired in the literary world. Perhaps it is also the reason his books are almost invariably reviewed by writers and intellectuals rather than his fellow neurologists. He writes with the authority of a medical doctor not just of symptoms and diagnoses, but of intimations of immortality, and of the spiritual significance of remembrance of things past. He is read as a guru who can authenticate neurologically the art of Proust and the visions of Hildegard of Bingen, confirm the veridical aspects of Borges's imagination, and reinforce our belief that salvation can be ours provided our brains are able to connect in the Forsterian way. He acts as the non-fictional conscience of imaginative art. The moral and spiritual diagnoses of his patients serve to reaffirm our metaphysical hankerings in much the same way that a recent television advertisement for medical insurance assured viewers, with a recital of the marvellous complexity of the human body and what it can do, that 'you are amazing'. Something about

Sacks's work similarly flatters his readers. (My God, we are
extraordinary, look how interestingly wrong we can go.)
After a thorough examination of the works of Oliver Sacks,
you come away with the oldish thought that identity matters,
as well as a new conviction that, along with good social
relations, the purchase of a hard hat might be a useful hedge
against soul death.

I don't know whether in the weird world of neurology
there is a condition that makes people profligate with footnotes, but if so Dr Sacks has it in spades. The text of the
revised edition of *Awakenings* is practically doubled by its
footnotes, and *An Anthropologist on Mars* is itself almost a
stand-alone footnote to *The Man who Mistook His Wife
for a Hat*. Many of the case-histories are similar to the cases
in the earlier book or amplifications of them. Greg, 'The Last
Hippie', a Krishna convert whose progressive brain tumour
was mistaken by his fellow worshippers for special spiritual
illumination, has a detachment from his illness similar to
that of Jimmie, the Korsakov amnesiac. Jimmie's memory
came to a dead stop in 1946, while Greg's arrested in 1970,
late enough to permit a continuing devotion to the Grateful
Dead – or rather the music the Grateful Dead played up to
1970. Sacks has the same spiritual concern for him that he
had for Jimmie and Mr Thompson: 'Given this radical lack
of connection and continuity in his inner life, I got the feeling, indeed, that he might not *have* an inner life.' For the
Krishnas, when Greg was living with them, this detachment
indicated an extreme of spiritual development, for Sacks it
meant quite the opposite. Greg, I suppose, expressed no
opinion either way, though he did enjoy the Dead concert to
which Sacks took him, for as long as he could retain the
memory of it.

Another Touretter stands in for Witty Ticcy Ray of *The
Man who Mistook His Wife for a Hat*, a surgeon, this time,
instead of a musician. Sacks goes to stay with Dr Bennett

and wonders at his capacity to perform tic-free operations while spending the rest of his time – which includes some hairy driving – ticcing up a storm. For Sacks, this is an example of the will, the inner life, shining through: the insistence on living a coherent life in spite of the demands disease makes on the personality. Bennett, and later Temple Grandin, a biologist suffering from autism, provide the metaphysically upbeat note to Sacks's meditations on disease. Rather than merely seeing the difference between patients as what they can or cannot manage, Sacks offers a disease-as-personality theory. In *Awakenings* he states: 'There is nothing alive which is not individual: our health is *ours*; our diseases are *ours*; our reactions are *ours* – no less than our minds or our faces.' Our responses to illness, he says, are expressions of our nature, and, quoting Sir Thomas Browne, 'things cannot get out of their natures'. He puts this case to counter modern medicine's inclination to reduce disease to the separate and mechanical, and it is a case that always needs reiterating, but his commitment to the notion that 'diseases have a character of their own, but they also partake of our character' does rather land the Mr Thompsons and Gregs of the neurologically deficient world in a mechanical hole. We would all applaud those who can overcome their disabilities, but it seems impertinent to consign those who are unable to do so – for whatever reason, biology or character (whatever that is) – to a spiritual wasteland. These latter Sacks declares to be 'Humean beings', on the grounds of Hume's declaration that we are 'nothing but a bundle or collection of different sensations, succeeding one another with inconceivable rapidity, and in a perpetual flux and movement'. The others, the fighters, as Sacks puts it, who have retained their sense of identity, are, I suppose, Homo sacksian.

Dr Sacks's point in writing up his patients' histories in the way he does is to liberate them from the loss of identity which occurs with the old-style medical description. He wants to present them, empathetically, in their totality, as persons rather than bundles of neurological symptoms. This is the current thinking, and a great improvement on cold medical authority, but if in their totality, which must include their disease, the patients have become depleted, it would seem decent to consider them more or less ill, rather than more or less persons. But then if your philosophical position is that illness takes its tone from character (again, whatever that is), I suppose the latter view follows logically. As someone free, so far as I know, from neurological insult, I'll listen with interest to any judgment anyone fancies making about the state of my soul; but should I ever be in need of neurological attention, I think I would prefer my physician to confine himself to curing me or making me comfortable.

Of course, Dr Sacks, in his authorial hat, is writing books, not being a medical consultant, but there is a disturbing moment in his examination of Dr P., who is intact musically and abstractly, but so unwittingly damaged in his concrete apprehension of the world that he neither knows nor cares to distinguish his shoe from his foot. Dr Sacks was consulted by Dr P. and his wife on the advice of his optician that there was something wrong with his brain, not his eyes. The fact that the appointment with Sacks was made and kept suggests that someone, if not Dr P. himself, then his wife, recognised something was wrong and was worried about it. After the first examination and the pricking of Dr Sacks's interest, he himself makes a visit to Dr P.'s house, in order to see him in his natural surroundings. He talks to Dr P., has tea with him and his wife, does a variety of tests and accompanies Dr P. on the piano as he sings Schumann. The tests tell nothing, he says, of Dr P.'s inner life, so he asks him to describe *Anna Karenina*. He finds that his patient can relate the plot and even the dialogue, but that his telling of the novel is 'quite empty for him, and lacked sensorial, imaginal or emotional reality'. I'm not really sure what that means, with what kind of passionate involvement one is required to précis a novel, but it is clear from the two examinations that Dr P. is a very sick man. 'Well, Dr Sacks,' says Dr P., 'you find me an interesting case, I perceive. Can you tell me what you find wrong, make recommendations?' Sacks says that he can't tell him what he finds wrong, but adds; 'You are a wonderful musician, and music is your life. What I would prescribe, in a case such as yours, is a life which consists entirely of music. Music has been the centre, now make it the whole, of your life.' That's it; consultation over. We are not told how Dr P. or his wife responded to this and Sacks never saw them again, though it is not explained why he didn't. Had I been the patient, I would have been left confused and deeply alarmed. The humanitarian part of the doctor's role was performed with elegance, but what of his medical function as a diagnostician and physician? Doubtless, something else happened here that Sacks does not write up, but it seems a curious lacuna.

Sacks suggests that one of the reasons some doctors strive for what they hope is an objective distance from their patients is to prevent their own 'subjectivity' from confusing the relationship. This is, we understand these days, a chimera, but it is interesting to see how a more open mutuality between patient and doctor might alter attitudes, though not necessarily for the benefit of the patient, who may find the doctor's personal requirements an extra burden. Agreeing with Freud that a full life – inner and outer – consists of work and love, Sacks finds most disturbing those patients who are most detached, most emotionally deficient. So do we all. Those who cannot connect – that is, those with whom Sacks cannot make a human relationship, to whom he can only relate as physician – are condemned. The two-way relationship needs to work for Sacks to feel comfortable.

In the final essay of *An Anthropologist on Mars*, the autistic Temple Grandin is shown as a highly intelligent woman who has achieved an independent life as a biologist working primarily with cattle. Sacks visits her and she explains how her autism has prevented her from having the normal experiences from which social knowledge is constructed. As a result, she has to 'compute' the intentions and states of mind of others, 'to try and make algorithmic, explicit, what for the rest of us is second nature'. Human interactions of a social and sexual kind she cannot 'get'. She's good with cows: 'When I'm with cattle, it's not at all cognitive. I know what the cow is feeling,' but it's different with people and she has recognised her own needs by designing and building a 'squeeze' machine that holds her in a way that she cannot allow people to do. Sacks is very moved by Grandin, and impressed. He knows as a neurologist the emotional limits of autistic patients and the difficulties living holds for them, even if they are fortunate enough to be highly intelligent. 'My work is my life,' Grandin says. 'There is not that much else.' She took him to the airport at the end of the visit, and 'suddenly faltered and wept', saying that she wanted to leave something behind her, to know that her life has had meaning. Sacks tells us, by way of ending both the essay and the book: 'As I stepped out of the car to say goodbye, I said, "I'm going to hug you. I hope you don't mind." I hugged her – and (I think) she hugged me back.' The romantic in Sacks aches for relationship, even where its neuronal lack has, most heroically, been accommodated to. He *will* hug and wants to feel a reciprocation. Doubtless we all do, but this is the human Oliver Sacks trying to connect, rather than an equally human Dr Sacks respecting the existential reality of his patient. Moreover, the moment provides a moving conclusion to his story.

A story needs a conclusion whereas a case-history may not have one. In fact, stories have all kinds of needs that a case-history will not supply, and Sacks is insistent that he is writing the stories of his patients, not their cases. This is not intended to fudge fact and fiction, but to enlarge patients into people. On the other hand, he is describing people with more or less devastating illnesses – that is his *raison d'être* – and his explicit purpose is to generalise from these, usually unhappy, accidents of life and nature, to a greater understanding of the human condition. In *Awakenings* he states: 'If we seek a "curt epitome" of the human condition – of long-standing sickness, suffering and sadness, of a sudden, complete, almost preternatural "awakening"; and, alas! of entanglements which may follow this "cure" – there is no better one than the story of these patients.' He is offering life, death and the whole damn thing in the metaphor of his patients. And it is true that these patients and others show us what it is like, as he says, 'to be human and stay human in the face of adversity'. But metaphors are not in fact descriptions of people in their totality. They are intentional, and consciously or unconsciously edited tropes, not complete, contained narratives. I don't know any kind of narrative, fictional or otherwise, that can present people in their totality, so perhaps it doesn't matter, but Sacks is offering us people because of their sickness and the manner of their handling it. This is hardly an overturning of the medicalising tendency of doctors. And when we read these stories, as we do, to tell us more about ourselves, we read them as exaggerations of what we are, as metaphors for what we are capable of. Their subjects may not be patients as freaks, but they are patients as emblems. They are, as it were, for our use and our wonderment. Around their illness, the thoughts of Leibniz, Kant, Kierkegaard, Nietzsche and Proust are hoist like scaffolding, as if to stiffen their reality into meaning.

In *The Island of the Colour-Blind* Sacks the romantic is clearly visible, rather than merely inferred. It is a very different kind of book: two accounts of Micronesian island-hopping, based on a six-part television series to be broadcast this autumn. A fascination with islands following a childhood holiday on the Isle of Wight and reading boys' adventure yarns, along with a Wellsian-cum-Darwinian fantasy of isolated mutation that results in a neurologically specialised population, is made concrete when he hears of a Pacific island with a colour-blind population. *The Island of the Colour-Blind* is a somewhat misleading title, as Pingelap turns out to have a population of 800, of whom 57 are congenitally colour-blind. The book parallels neither 'The Country of the Blind', nor *The Voyage of the 'Beagle'*, but functions more as a travelogue of truncated dreams. This would be fine if it was written with self-conscious humour, but Sacks continually tries to redeem the minor key of the story with grand claims for what to the lay reader seems only a mildly interesting situation.

Colour-blindness – the complete achromatopsia, seeing no colour at all, only degrees of luminosity that the colour-sighted would regard as grey, rather than the more common red-green colour-blindness – is also not new territory for Sacks. *An Anthropologist on Mars* included the somewhat Conan-Doyleishly entitled 'Case of the Colour-Blind Painter', who lost all sense of colour after a car accident. The condition was thoroughly described; the histology of achromatopsia was included as well as Goethe and Land's investigation into colour vision. The narrative interest depended on the fact that Jonathan I. was a painter and on the detail of how he coped with a new life devoid of hue. Colour-blindness, however intellectually interesting, does not have the same deep reverberations as the conscious/unconscious story of *Awakenings*, is hardly the 'curt epitome' of the human condition, as Sacks seems to acknowledge: 'On the ultimate question – the question of qualia: why a particular sensation may be perceived as red – the case of Jonathan I. may not be able to help us at all.'

The minority population of achromats on Pingelap have a hard time of it. Not only do they see quite differently from the majority, and suffer, therefore, a degree of social stigma, but their condition carries with it an extreme sensitivity to light, so that they are only able to function fully in twilight and darkness. Although we lose the metaphor of the country of the blind, we do get quite a bit of medical information and develop a sympathy for their lot. Much of the story, however, is travelogue, as Sacks gathers about him a Norwegian achromat, Knut Nordby, an ophthalmologist friend, Bob Wasserman, and all their test equipment. (I presume he also had a film crew from the start, though they aren't mentioned until he lands on Pingelap and we are told 'the island children were fascinated not so much by our cameras as by the sound boom with its woolly muff, and within a day were making their own booms out of banana stalks and coconut wool.')

There's plenty to worry about, as well as plenty to learn about Oliver Sacks and his predilections. Spam, it seems, is devastating the eating habits of Micronesia: they love it, Sacks doesn't, and frets anthropologically that their natural life is at risk as a result of American Spam importations. 'Having a sort of passion for monotony, I greatly enjoyed the unvarying meals on Pingelap, whereas Knut and Bob longed for variety . . . But we were all revolted by the Spam which appeared with each meal – invariably fried; why, I wondered, should the Pingelapese eat this filthy stuff when their own basic diet was both healthy and delicious?' This seems a minor problem compared to the fact that a good many of the islands Sacks and Co land on or pass over on their way are hush-hush American air-bases or have unbreathable air because of the usefulness of the atolls as nuclear testing sites. Still, I'm biased since I have a bit of a fondness for Spam myself.

Sacks's emotions are fully engaged on this journey. As he

lands on Pingelap, children arrive to investigate. 'I felt a wave of love – for the children, for the forest, for the island, for the whole scene . . . I thought, I have arrived. I am here at last. I want to spend the rest of my life here – and some of these beautiful children could be mine.' In fact he spends three weeks here and on other islands, meeting achromats, testing them and handing out sunglasses – a practical result of the doctors' visit, since this simple device enables them to get out and see properly – in the way they can – during the day.

Another neurological mystery is found on Guam. A disease known as lytico-bodig, which has elements of both Parkinsons and motor neurone disease, is endemic and goes back in families to the beginning of the last century. Again, this is old Sacks territory. The variety of the symptoms and their late onset, as well as the Parkinsonian aspects, are reminiscent of his post-encephalitic patients in *Awakenings*. The situation presents a great challenge to the brain investigators who have yet to find the cause. It may be the result of a craving for the seeds of a particular cycad which is used by the locals as flour for tortillas and tamales. The seeds are poisonous unless lengthily prepared. It may also be the result of what seemed to be naturally very low calcium and magnesium levels. The mystery is never quite resolved, but it begins to look, by the end, as if the by now almost expected, and perhaps not very surprising, answer is that it's the result of a combination of hereditary and environmental factors.

In any event, the affected families are suffering greatly, and Sacks visits them, observing and making tests. The disease seems to be self-limiting. No one born after 1960 appears to get it, and though this might be some comfort to the older generations, who know their children will be free of it, it's a nuisance for the neurologists: 'The disease is indeed dying out at last . . . will the quarry, hotly pursued for 40 years now, with all the resources that science can bring, elude them finally, maddeningly, by disappearing at the moment they are about to grasp it?' There is no cure for the disease, as indeed there seems to be no cure for much that neurology takes to be its concern. This is not the first time the locals have met neurologists. The doctor who lives on Guam and tries to make the lives of sufferers more comfortable says: 'The patients ask us, "So what happened to those tests performed on us?" But we have no answers for them, because they are not our tests.'

There is much, towards the end of this book of the television series, on the nature of cycads, ancient palm-like plants that hark back to the Palaeozoic. Cycads are a passion of Oliver Sacks's, and he writes of seeing them in their natural habitat in terms of the primeval sublime. Metaphors for the sublime come readily to Dr Sacks from out-of-the-way places and medical conditions, and perhaps the plethora of them in this book will work better in the visual medium of television, but after my rereadings of his other works, I began to long for someone to come along and fill instances of the mundane everyday with meaning. There must surely, I found myself brooding, be some significance in the ordinary.

Taking Off

Writer in Residence, Palm Island

It's six-thirty, I'm wide awake and all fired up to go to Palm Island. As I'm about to run the bath, a sudden silence breaks over the flat. An electricity blackout. A little urban catastrophe and a personal disaster: no hot water. How can I start the day, let alone go off lotus-eating, without a cup of tea and immersing myself in hot water? I assess my resources, and in the spirit of pioneering self-sufficiency (pre-desert island practice) put three large saucepans of water to boil on the gas stove. I shall have my bath and cup of tea – and go to the ball, too, if I want! But ten minutes later the electricity clicks and hums all the machines back into life, and almost immediately a fax comes through in the study. It is from P., currently out of town, wishing me *bon voyage*. No need to scan it; it'll be deliciously filthy, designed to keep his memory jiggling in my base and basest cells as I idle away my fortnight in paradise. A mistress of the deferred and doubled pleasure, I save it to read with a cup of tea back in bed, while the bath runs.

The saucepans are boiling, and an unaccustomed mood of conservation comes over me: I won't waste the water, I'll use some to fill the teapot. The fax, fairly pulsing with lewd

thoughts, is on the draining-board as I pour the boiling
water from the biggest saucepan without a lip. Some of it
does go in the teapot, but the same amount takes a graceful
and, it seems to me, gleeful leap over it, to splash-land dead
centre on the fax. Time, heat and moisture fade fax paper to
total blackness. The only thing this fax didn't have was time,
and instantly, every delightful, dirty word disappears,
replaced by an A4-sized black hole. I decide philosophical is
the way to go, and tip my hat (happily, already on my head
in case I forget to pack it) to the Old Joker. Easy come, easy
go. Anyway, I know the value of the imagination over the
specifics of language. I'll manage without the words. If I
can't read them, I'll invent them.

Later, unpacking and re-packing less then more T-shirts,
the phone rings. It's a friend, older generation (*even* older
generation), currently doing some digging into her past.

'Do you remember "rumpty tumpty"?' she asks.

'What?' My mind was on the algebra of how many T-
shirts equals two weeks by the sea.

'Rumpty tumpty. Meaning "sex". Or it did when I was
young. Didn't your lot have the phrase?'

I shake my head, confounded.

'No, we didn't. Rumpty tumpty? And still you managed to
win the war?'

'I wondered how long it was used for. It's like "poon
tang". You know *that*, don't you?'

'A Far-Eastern herbal remedy for memory disorders?' I try,
hopefully.

'Sex, dear. You *must* have had *poon tang*.'

'We had "fucking",' I say, dredging up all the laid-back
cool I can recollect from the late Sixties.

'I always said the trouble with your generation was you
didn't know how to have fun.'

I shove *all* my T-shirts into the case and shut the lid.

'A man in Santa Monica wrote to the *LRB* to say what

Dahmer did with his dead heads was *irrumation*, not fellatio.'

'What's that?'

'I don't know, but I don't see why I should be the only one to worry about it. Bye-bye. I'm off to Palm Island.'

And not a moment too soon.

If you stand on one edge of Palm Island and look straight ahead inland, what you see is the other edge of Palm Island, and the same deep turquoise and navy blue of the Caribbean as you would if you turned round and looked behind you. Palm Island may be bigger than Primrose Hill, but I think London Zoo would spill over into the sea if it was moved here.

Mostly, what the handful of people staying here do is lie breathtakingly still in the sun and watch big white boats with tall triangular sails go by – very likely to somewhere else. There's nothing to do, and nothing happens. Except, the plovers fight with the rose-throated doves when I throw them crumbs of the cake which arrives with a pot of tea at my beachside patio at four o'clock.

I know they're plovers and doves because Errol told me. Errol's the head waiter, also apparently having (unofficial, I suppose) responsibility for single women. At any rate, he assures me repeatedly that he wants personally to make sure I have a really good time, and if I need company, just let him know – not so much Man Friday, as a potential Month of Sundays. Though Errol is gorgeous, no doubt about it, I explain that I don't suffer from loneliness, but he could tell me what the birds are called. He is very accommodating and points out the plovers and the doves hanging around the table.

'And the little yellow bird?' I ask.

'It's a yellowbird,' says Errol.

Just like that nice couple Nina and Frederick used to sing about before Nina became the world's worst movie actress and Frederick disappeared without trace.

'And that one?' I point to a small black bird, with absurdly large feet.

'That's a blackbird.'

Well, it's only sometimes a black bird; at certain angles it's definitely midnight blue, and it doesn't look like any blackbird that comes visiting my back garden in Gospel Oak. But I'm not going to argue with Errol, who, after all, is in charge of lunch. I figure out for myself that the white, long-necked bird which wades in the swamp, is, of course a white, long-necked swamp-wading bird.

I am here under false pretences. Arnold, the young man who picks me up from Union Island, a mile across the bay, seems mysteriously over-excited to see me, and asks in the launch: 'You're in the movies, aren't you?' I tell him I'm not. He insists; he knows he's seen me in a movie. I swear to him I've never been in one. Later, I hear he thinks I'm Barbra Streisand. This isn't the first time I've been mistaken for her (I have the profile, but not the vocal chords). The waiter at dinner says he's seen me before. I say it's my first time on the island. 'Oh,' he says with a knowing smile. 'You know, faces . . .' He'll maintain my incognito, his nod suggests, he understands the pressures of fame, but he wants me to know he knows I'm really Barbra Streisand. I'll just have to live with it. I dare say Barbra gets pissed off being mistaken for me.

Meantime, I lie on the beach, face down on my sunbed, brooding about the cassata-coloured sand, which is, I'm told, parrot-fish shit after a meal of coral. I also spend a great deal of time on a float mat, eyes level with the surface of the Caribbean, watching the waves roll and ripple towards me. According to Simone Weil whose biography I'm reading, the movement of the waves is a manifestation of Necessity, that to which we must consent if we're to apprehend the Good. I can go along with that, and for countless hours consent to the Necessity of the waves. I wonder, too, where the current would take me if I let it float me away (a short story here I think, which means I'm doing research as well as consenting to Necessity). I keep an eye open, as I paddle myself farther out and stare down into the water, for sea serpents and the ancient wrecks of buccaneers, barnacle-struck on the bottom. Nothing, so far. Very occasionally I remember I don't know the meaning of 'irrumation'.

After lunch I paddle through the surf on a tour of the island, and settle on one of the four totally empty beaches to read. I alternate between the Weil biography, another of Roy Cohn (McCarthy's henchman) and the *Oedipus* trilogy – the good, the bad and the mightily confused (perm any one of three?). All this indolence is not in vain: it's in preparation for the rigours of my sunset vigil.

It takes tremendous concentration to keep an unblinking and even-eyed watch on the movement of the sinking sun, the long shaft of silver made up of triangular lights on the water, the pinks, mauves and puce of the sky at the horizon, and the darkening, sharpening outline of Union Island across the way. And as if that wasn't enough, there's the sand crab at my feet to follow in my peripheral vision, trying to make it to the water's edge. It makes small rushes of six inches, but, terminally tentative, scurries back to where it started and zips back into the sand. I try, while still holding sun, shaft, horizon and outline in view, to give it moral encouragement from a corner of my eye and mind, but it never makes it. Luckily, however, my attention has not been fatally diverted, and the sun does finally fall below the horizon. It's exhausting, making this happen night after night, but it's worthwhile work, I feel. Certainly, Ricky, the barman, thinks so: he runs me up a congratulatory daiquiri, with, I think, a look of quiet gratitude and relief.

The starwatch project is more difficult. Apart from

having to douse myself with lethal chemicals to keep mos-
quitoes at bay, astronomy and geography are blanks to me.
I never did get the stars straight, and, in truth, I'm not sure
which hemisphere I'm in, nor what difference it would
make if I knew. Still the stars are up there in their millions,
burning holes in the sky, and I've identified some constella-
tions: the Little Peugeot 205, the Great EC Insignia, the Big
Toshiba Laptop With Combined Automatic Eggwhisk, as
well as the pair of Stonewashed Levi's which forever pursue,
but never catch the Seven Very Sensible These Days Virgins.
Stars plummet by the bucketload. If there's anything in this
wishing on a falling star business, then we can all relax,
everything's going to be all right: Eastern Europe, world
recession, spiritual anomie, the British Library, the lot.
There are even enough shooting stars left over to apply to
the wish fairy for an appointment as Writer in Residence to
Palm Island.

After all, there's still the droll and terrible story of the
Caldwell dynasty to relate. I didn't bring *Oedipus* with me
for nothing, it turns out. There is discontent in paradise.
Papa Caldwell, who bought Palm Island for a dollar (for all
I know from Ernest Hemingway) is a Jack London-reading
Texan who believes in only eating when hungry and not
having second helpings. Mary is the wife he collected at the
end of the war from Australia, after building a boat to collect
her in, and go in search of Eden. They separated 20 years
ago (same island, different establishments). One 40-year-old
son glowers dangerously and sails a yacht called *Illusion*.
The other older son manages the hotel, but, as he tells
anyone who'll listen, only when Papa Caldwell lets him. He
lives with his Mum; defeated, overweight and nearly tragic,
skewered on his father's continued shrivelling need for control. Failed husband, diver, businessman, escapee, he talks
mistily about finding a woman and an island of his own,
only he can't quite get to leave. Fortunately, he's become a

spiritualist, and is certain it'll all come right in his next incarnation. Tennessee Williams, anyone? Best, I suppose, to get back to the land of disappearing faxes. Anyway, I've got a lunch date at The Ivy with my publisher: maybe *she* knows what 'irrumation' means.

'Page 120'

It always happens somewhere between pages 120 and 150. This is what they tell me, and I suppose there must be something in it, because I only have to get a certain look on my face and the daughter and ex-husband nod knowingly at one another and say: 'Page 120.' Invariably, between half and two-thirds of the way through a novel, the whole thing turns to dust. The choice is to take a deep breath and re-write, or chuck the whole thing into the dustbin at just the right moment on a Thursday morning so there's no time to retrieve it before the dustmen come and claim it. After the event, with a slab of finished manuscript sitting on my desk, I call it a second draft: now with months of work a heap of ashes, a pile of incoherent words whose meaning I cannot for the life of me fathom, I wring my hands, drag my feet, and announce dully to anyone who'll listen that *this* time (yes, I know last time, and the time before that, but *this* time) it's an irretrievable disaster. And my loved ones yawn as if Karl Popper had never lived.

There's very little leeway for temperament round here. I think of a long-ago lover who stormed out of my distracting bedroom with his manuscript under his arm, saying, 'I have to concentrate on my work,' leaving me entranced by the enormity of the paired pronoun and noun. I've tried it once or twice at home, but seem to provoke very little reverence for the magnitude of my task, unless I misread the cocked eyebrows and suppressed giggles. Things can't be like this for Julian Amis and Kingsley McEwan.

However, this time (page 147) I do not dispose of the current manuscript in the garbage, nor do I roll up my sleeves and just get on with it like a plucky little householder, mother and lady novelist probably ought to. Instead, I pack my laptop into its snappy black case, leave housekeeping money on the kitchen table, give what I hope is an affirmative hug to the daughter, commend her well-being to her father, and bugger off for a fortnight to a place where I don't have to do anything except sort out the random words of my manuscript into something approximating to a novel I once had in mind.

The place is a health farm in Hampshire. Where else can you go on your own, get a sauna and massage each morning, be fed three times a day and have no interruptions? Apart from Julian Kingsley's house, if you're Julian Kingsley, I can't think of anywhere better. In reality, my haven is a place people go to shed fat and get fit, but by avoiding the exercise classes and the after-dinner talks on the uses of colour analysis in physical and mental well-being, what I have is a hotel with full board, unlimited work opportunities and someone to massage the chain-mail knots of anxiety out of my shoulders and neck.

I say 'hotel', but it's more like a nursing home. Actually, it's that place which my shameful psyche has been dreaming about for most of my life: a hospital (specifically a mental hospital, since no one is physically ill) with none of the institutional and moral disadvantages that spoil the real thing. There is no brisk frosty Sister pulling back the covers of my bed/pit crying: 'Up we get, dear, it's not good for us to lie in bed.' No one chases me off to Occupational or Art Therapy, where overalled people with soft voices and understanding eyes produce paint, clay and bits of bendy sticks, so that I can express myself creatively. No doctor sits, fingertips together, forefingers tapping his message out in morse, telling me: 'You have to confront reality.' (I do? Why?) There's none of that here, just crisp sheets, power showers, and a day punctuated by meals. This is the trick, routine without responsibility: institutionalisation in its most morally neutral form. I do the writing, they can do the rest. Take my body, feed it, heat it, cool it, massage it, relax it, and let the rest alone.

My fellow inmates are on the elderly side, which is soothing, and quite cheering in the sauna if I concentrate on the how-it-is-now rather than the what-it-will-become. They are, for the most part, widows, or wives who are taking a break from marriages which have taken a break. There are fewer men, all business types and afraid, what with the lack of exercise and the unavoidability of the business lunch, for their hearts. A handful of couples, hearts at peace or dead in the water, sit respectively in comfortable or sullen silences in the lounge and dining room.

I indulge in one of the great pleasures of life: eating alone and reading. It's not easy, I've discovered over the years, to do this in public without provoking resentment. Luckily, most people eat in the Diet Room, and there are enough tables in the dining room for those who want to be sociable to get together and for me to be left to my book. I've developed a special kind of avid look: deep concentration on the text while forking food absent-mindedly into my mouth, which precludes interruption without seeming actively unfriendly. Putting other people's backs up is stressful and best avoided. Even so, the reading thing is a problem in this bastion of Middle England. 'Still struggling through your reading book?' says a man narrowing his eyes at me. 'Good book?' asks another who barely suppresses a sneer and walks away before I have a chance to answer. No one else reads anything other than a daily newspaper here – generally the *Telegraph*. Books are suspect. In fact, I am not struggling through my reading book, I'm swooning through it. It's my biennial-or-so dip into *Lolita*. I don't know how many times I've read it, but enough for me now to consume it sentence by sentence, word by word, incredibly slowly, like licking a lolly down to the stick. The writing tweaks the delight centres of my brain. Imagine being able to do that . . . and that. I was Lolita's age when I first read it, and now I'm seven years older than Humbert. Charlotte Haze was a mother's age that first time round, now she's a decade younger than I am. By focusing my internal telescope carefully, I can catch sight of the different me's reading this same text over time – even get them to converse if I catch them at the right moment and they're prepared to look up from their book. This time, though, the current incarnation of the word 'abuse', dressed in social-worker drab, lurks in dark corners, threatening care proceedings on the book – which can take care of itself well enough. (My daughter was told recently by her school librarian that it was 'a boring book written by a pervert'.) Anyway, I'm happy as a wasp in jam, and most people are content for me not to bother about them, if they don't need to bother about me.

Even so, a perfect silence isn't achievable. Quite rightly, morses the Ineluctable Doctor stowed away in my superego, reality and all that. The lady who has embarked on a campaign to give me serene shoulders, my 'massoose' she calls herself, asks me what I do and gets the wrong end of the stick. No, really, I'm not here in search of plot ideas. 'I expect you have to travel a lot to get stories to write about.' 'Not at all,' I say. 'I stay at home and make them up.' She doesn't seem to have heard me, and during our daily half-hours together, she offers me her own and her mother's stories, which variously involved destitution, bigamy, illegitimacy, sudden death, marital violence, suicide attempts and kitchen renovation. I wonder if the whole saga isn't cribbed from a Catherine Cookson novel, but, of course, it's just the regular family narrative. 'What kind of novels do you write?' she wants to know. I don't know the answer to this question, though once, in the States, when I answered 'fictional', my questioner nodded, 'Ahh,' and went away satisfied. But my massoose helps me. 'Romances, are they?' 'No, they're more . . . realistic . . .' I don't think it's true, but it's all I can manage covered with almond oil and in a near-trance. 'I know what you mean, more like *EastEnders*?' she says brightly. More like. To the standard questions (Do your characters take you over? Do you make a chart before you begin? Is it all autobiographical? Do you have to be very disciplined?) I answer yes and no in a random order that does as well as any other, and hope she won't forget to do the bit at the bottom of my left shoulder blade.

There are a lot of sadnesses here, which I confess I try to avoid. Most people drift about during the day in their dressing-gowns, which is conducive to that sort of thing. Say what you like about exercise increasing endorphin levels, a day in a dressing-gown will bring it all to nothing. I make a point of getting dressed after my massoose has had her way with me – anyway I find I can't write unless my teeth are brushed and my stocking seams straight. A friend who comes here frequently told me she often finds women doing homeopathic weeping in the swimming pool. I'm rather taken with the idea of the pool of tears in the basement, but find myself reluctant actually to swim in it. I'm not overly fastidious, but don't fancy immersing myself in other people's waste products whichever end of the body they drip from.

Some social intercourse is inevitable, especially as I have to use the small smokers' sitting room at regular intervals. In any case, the Persistent Doctor tells me there's much to be

learned from this gathering of the heart-landers. As the pool
of tears suggests, this is a Looking-Glass Land of sorts. Get
talking and a dreamlike quality settles over me, though occasionally it slips into nightmare.

One evening, after dinner, I'm joined in the sitting room
by my only fellow smoker and her pal, D., a fiercely made-
up, blood-lipped, tailored (even her dressing-gown has darts)
woman in her early fifties, who launches a conversation on
the subject of veal calves. My fellow smoker ventures an
opinion. 'Well, I don't know what all the fuss is about. If
they've never seen daylight, they won't miss it.' All the lights
of North London flicker and dim, philosophy departments
crumble to rubble as we speak. In this world abstract ethical
considerations are entirely absent. Forget Mary Midgley,
expunge all uses of the word 'right' (other than those that
define direction). There are no moral imperatives here. I
don't doubt that the 'if you've never had it, you don't need it'
argument would extend well beyond calves, but I don't feel
like testing it.

I don't have to. D. is already speaking in tabloid headlines
about the demonstrators – 'rent-a-mob' – trying to prevent
the calves from being shipped from Brightlingsea (there's a
name for crated calves to conjure with). Against my own
advice, I say that, as with the poll tax and motorway campaigns, this cause seems to have a middle-class component,
and that I've just seen on the news respectable elderly ladies
shocked rigid at being manhandled by the police. 'Exactly,'
shrieks the Queen of Hearts. 'The media *deliberately* film it,
so people will knock the police. They shouldn't be allowed to
show that kind of thing.' Freedom, inalienable rights? Not
on this side of the looking-glass.

Cruella de Vil is in full flood. 'The trouble is that young
people are so spoiled today. They get everything they want.
Look at children in care.' (At this point I check to see if we
don't have a satirist in our midst, but sincerity is burned

into her expression.) 'They live in luxury, each child has a live-in care worker of their own. They're given computers for Christmas by the local authority.' I say – can't stop myself – that this isn't the way any children in care I've ever come across are treated. Cruella throws me a poisonous look and informs me that she knows, as it happens from experience. 'We've adopted a teenage boy, Jason. He's so materialistic. That's what they teach them, these care workers, that they're entitled to have whatever they want. Well, we were going to adopt, but we've changed it to fostering.' She smirks at my fellow smoker, and it's clear that Jason will soon be back wallowing in the over-indulgent arms of the local authority.

I'm about to stub out my cigarette and flee to my room but I seem to be paralysed. The Wicked Witch of the West slithers on to tell us about her 'black-sheep brother'. Specifically, that she has (giggles) three 'half-caste' nieces. The brother lives in Africa, retreating from country to country as they come under the government of their rightful owners. Along the way, he seeded these three girls with 'native women', telling his sister (who tells us as an example of his wit) that three mistakes in his life is not bad going. My fellow smoker, who may be reaching some kind of limit, asks if he supports these children. 'He sends them a bag of mealie meal from time to time,' chortles the Evil One.

I loathe this woman so much (Yea, yea, moral philosophy and freedom of speech) I decide to kill her. A plan forms in my mind, and, pointing myself in her direction, I light another cigarette. I'm going to passive smoke her to death. Even if I fail and end up actively smoked to death myself, I can't lose; either way I'll be on the opposite bank of the Lethe to her, which is the minimum distance I require.

The next morning my massoose is astonished at the state of my shoulders. All her good work has been undone and we have to start from scratch. While she's pummelling away at me, I ponder about my obligations as a member of society.

The Inescapable Doctor muses on the importance of investigating and understanding the wider world. I dare say he's right, it's probably true that the looking-glass world is inside, not outside my skull. All this I grant in theory. Nonetheless, by way of an answer, I smile sweetly, stuff cotton wool in my ears, and put on a pair of shades cunningly mirrored on the insides. 'That's better,' says my massoose. 'Those muscles are really beginning to relax.'

Downhill
Creativity

It's a bad year for snow in Zermatt. Mont Cervin is mostly bare red rock. The Matterhorn has only a frosting of snow. But the pistes are all right: every few hundred yards bright yellow snow-making machines, like small snub-nosed cannon, soak up water from the lakes and shoot it ten metres into the air to do what God can usually be relied on to achieve, and keep what skiers there are on the move. Still, the shopkeepers and hoteliers are not a happy bunch, and there are nothing but shopkeepers and hoteliers in Zermatt. The lights in this tacky twinkletown flitter merrily, gold watches glisten in the jewellers' windows, but the faces are glum. There is no other point to the place except to enable wealthy folk to slide down the mountain into the shops and bars to spend their crisp Swiss francs. Except, that is, for one long weekend each year when two hundred people gather together in a windowless, air-conditioned hall in the basement of one of the swisher hotels in order to learn how to be creative. The director-generals of Lancôme, Ciba-Geigy, ABB and Nestlé, along with their underling executives, have all paid four thousand or so Swiss francs to discover how to add a mysteriously desirable cache of creativity to their already accumulated, though more concrete, store of wealth and power. Like so many overbred princesses, they still feel the pea, no matter how many feather mattresses they lie on.

The word 'creativity' is bandied about over the four days of the sixth International Zermatt Symposium on Creativity in Economics, Arts and Sciences as if it were an abracadabra. Only give us the wand, the hungry hotshots cry, and we'll be masters of the universe. At one point the super-suits are even prepared to sit manipulating the ends of a metre of rope to learn from a French funambulist how to make a clove hitch knot that unties, if you do it right, as if by magic. They've paid their money, and they will acquire, by hook or by hitch, what seems to be missing from their bag of tricks.

The ISO-Foundation for Creativity and Leadership is the brainchild of Swiss-born Dr Gottlieb Guntern, a one-time medical psychiatrist turned systems-theory proselytiser and consultant to the stars of Swiss mega-corporations. He has written books to explain, as he repeatedly does when introducing the speakers, that we have been living and suffering 'under the sign of the dinosaur'. Only innovative leadership, prepared to break up the dinosaur into a thousand creative butterflies, will enable us to enter the new millennium successfully. 'Creative leadership renounces trailership, which reacts tactically-defensively where strategic-proactive thinking and acting would be necessary.' What this means, I can't say, but the Suits have put their money where Dr Guntern's mouth is, so they have some inkling of what it's all about. They, after all, are rulers of the multinational corporate universe. Never mind that the dinosaurs lived successfully for longer than any other species; never mind that it is in the nature of butterflies to flit aimlessly from one brightly coloured flower to the next, to eat, reproduce and die in the blink of the sun; never mind that it was the small, shifty-eyed ratty mammals, our ancestors, who colonised the planet after the dinosaurs died, not from stupidity but from the effects of a fortuitous meteor shower: surely the powerhouses in the darkened hall would not be sitting here tying knots in pieces of string if they weren't going to get something for the expenditure of their precious time.

The delegates lap up Guntern's brain physiology talk. 'There are five brains,' he keeps saying. The appending of popular biology to the notion of creative leadership gives both a scientific sexiness and a flattering affirmation that this very special audience is ready to learn the secrets of the cosmos. The 'old brain' (the cerebellum), the 'automotive brain', the 'emotional brain' and the two hemispheres of the neo-cortex are Guntern's components. We do not use the correct part for the right task. Before you know it, we receive the news that the left and right halves of the neo-cortex are the key to everything. Right side equals intuitive, creative; left side is rational and linguistic – and heaven help those of us who are left-handed. Right side good, left side bad. Between the two, the corpus callosum represents, of course, the 'information superhighway'. This is all neat and apprehendable. All we have to do is use the right side of the brain and creativity will flow. However, it's been 15 years or so since the notion of an absolute split between the functions of the hemispheres has been regarded as simplistic nonsense by neurobiologists, and no one would suggest that anything but the merest hints has been understood about the way the brain and its chemistry actually function in the macro world of the individual in daily life. But it's so attractive to feel in the know brain-wise. Questioned about his theories, Guntern explains to me that, yes, it is true that brain research is in a very uncertain infancy, but we must use whatever tools we can in order to intervene in the disastrous conduct of modern life and to save companies which are dying from lack of creativity. I suggest this is odd from a man so committed to evolutionary theory. Surely extinction of forms which are no longer appropriate is the very mechanism of evolution? 'Some people, though I know you do not mean it to be so, would find that very cynical.' I explain that I did somewhat mean it to be cynical, and wonder if it is right to intervene with such poorly understood tools. It is criminal, he tells me severely, not to intervene when you have the ability to improve things. I suspect that the unspoken question 'What ability?' is visible in my raised eyebrows. He offers me a quote from Camus, who said that after the age of 45 people are responsible for their faces 'so if there is an expression of arrogance or contempt, it is because the individual has negative inner attitudes.' That deals with me apparently.

Apart from *creative, innovative, leadership* and *brain physiology*, the other concept that seems to get the corporate juices running is *eclecticism*. If the chairman of Nestlé is asked to sit and listen for four days to the chairman of ABB, he's liable to get restless, but ask him to listen to an 'avant-garde' high-wire street performer, the woman who concocted Calvin Klein's Eternity, a Latin American novelist and the American whizzkid who is the current last word in computerised graphic design, and Mr Nestlé is likely to get the feeling that he's really going to learn something. Naturally, he's not planning to wire-walk the twin towers of the World Trade Centre, and he probably knows that he'll never get round to writing that magical realist novel he feels he could if only he had time. But surely he can squeeze the essence from the variety, and find the concentrate that makes all these diverse people entitled to stand on a podium and call themselves that deliciously vague word 'creative'. Want some? Here's a whole handful of the stuff. Creativity in Zermatt is about getting extra. None of the speakers suggests that their audience might have to lose something they already have in order to get what they want. On this journey, all you have to do is learn to juggle with disparately shaped objects.

Mario Vargas Llosa turned out to be something of a juggler, and provided a finely balanced introduction to the world of creativity. A novelist who has also entered the sphere of politics; a very public man, neatly suited and at ease on a platform. He begins by explaining that he does not totally understand or control his creativity, and this cheers me up. A straightforward, accurate statement, it seems to me. So can we all go home now? Apparently not as he explains the wellsprings of his creativity – his childhood, his father. I begin to wonder if the role of writers is not to flatter the world into thinking it is a deeper and more interesting place than it really is as he declares that the novel must always be in rebellion against society while going on without pause to relate the story of his intervention on behalf of sense and sanity in the prickly politics of Peru. London intellectuals are besotted with Fidel Castro, he announces, whereas the real political hero is Mr Christiani, a businessman turned politician (as Christ was a woodworker turned messiah) who single-handedly returned Salvador to moderation and democracy. This Ross Perot of the Latin world is an unsung saviour, and the businessmen are delighted to hear that the chaotic political world awaits their intervention.

The self-congratulation reaches a peak with the next speaker. Eberhard von Koerber is the president of ABB Europe, a multinational electrical engineering company presently employing 220,000 people. In his introduction, Dr Guntern shoots out metaphors as from a snow-maker. Von Koerber is a dolphin, leaping and twisting through the air in an orgy of creativity. The business world he encountered was like a tanker propelled by a paddle, in a world which is like a car driver who speeds up and brakes at the same time. I think jazz and dissonant notes came into it somewhere, but by then I was suffering from a distracting vertigo.

He expresses his admiration for Dr Guntern, who, it turns out, is employed as an adviser to ABB, which was in the dire condition of the dinosaur when von Koerber took over. Drastic, innovative action had to be taken, first by sacking ten per cent of the workforce (downsizing, restructuring, rationalising) who, not realising the creativity of the act, were unconvinced of the long-term benefits (for the company) and chorused their disapproval outside von Koerber's window. It was, he said, a long and stony path, and very distressing, but he persisted even when his secretary, not used to the music of dissent outside her window, had a heart attack. She left the story there. Von Koerber didn't say whether she survived. Older staff members were the first to get the sack, as Dr Guntern advised, along with anyone who showed an inability to accept change. This ten per cent represents 25–30,000 people put out of work, but von Koerber – unlike his secretary – could live with it. Creativity, he told us in a moment of searing honesty, is only a means to an end. Creativity is at the service of profitability. We do not need managers, but leaders, authentic leaders like von Koerber, Guntern says, or we will arrive at the 21st century with a 19th-century mentality.

Von Koerber's story was one of decentralisation, of a company broken up into 5000 'profit centres' responsible to head office as a way of creating local pride and individual responsibility. People, he explained, must be free from anxiety and stress if they are to perform creatively. Actually, this isn't true, and luckily for the profits of ABB he does not follow his own advice. Head office analyses and compares the profits of each profit centre on a three-monthly basis (internal bench-marking), and if there is any falling short of requirements, hit squads – excuse me, teams from head office – are sent in to 'intervene and coach' the offending managers. A German journalist familiar with the practice of decentralising business into profit centres explained to me that this had the useful effect of dispersing the power of the unions, making them much easier to deal with.

ABB snapped up ailing businesses in the former GDR,

but found, surprisingly, some resentment and resistance from East German workers. Von Koerber planned a visit, but was worried about how to present himself until a friend gave him a strategic tip he 'hadn't thought of'. It was that he should appear before the workers 'as a human being who, though now rich, had not started life with a silver spoon in his mouth'. His only real advantage, he told them, was that he had come from a more advanced society than they had. This worked a treat, according to our authentic leader.

After that the oddballs of creativity were mere froth on the cocoa. Sophia Chodosz-Grojsman (aka the Rose) declared America the land of freedom, where anyone could become anything. She became – after what she finally admitted were 30 years of slavery – a master perfumer at International Flavours and Fragrances, New York, and is responsible, some would say culpable, for inventing Trésor and Champagne and for scenting hairsprays and shampoos. She would rather, she said, have used her chemistry degree to find a cure for cancer and Aids.

Phillipe Petit, on the other hand, was genuinely strange. A high-wire walker who is artist in residence at the Cathedral of St John the Divine in New York, he is described, with a simpering smile from Dr Guntern, as a con-quistador of the useless. Petit is a tiny, frail man who looks like a haggard Jean-Louis Barrault. He offers magic tricks and his offences against the social norms to the audience, but off-stage there is a grimness in his expression and some-thing in his eyes that reminds my German journalist friend of death. I wonder, during question time, if he doesn't sometimes experience the temptation to fall. This makes him very angry and he informs me that he is so sure of his technique and dedicated in his practice that there is not the slightest chance of his falling. Given his anger, I do not ask the subsidiary question about why then he doesn't just walk on the ground.

Paul Scott Makela galvanises and alarms the audience on the final morning with a viewing of the video he designed for Michael Jackson's 'Scream', the song Jackson released after the child abuse allegations fell away. Makela acknowledged that $7.5 million was a substantial amount of money for a five-minute video, but was consoled when Jackson donated $4 million worth of Vitamin E to the malnourished children of Bosnia. Even now, I look at my notes just to check: but, yes, it was Vitamin E.

The company is a bit baffled by Makela's work. It is all too fast for them. Most of the questions begin 'Maybe I am too old . . .' But Makela's whizzkid status is nonetheless admired, not least by Makela himself who repeatedly refers to himself as 'very young', though at 36 this sounds more like a plea to the gods than a description. His 'valve' of creativity lies between 'fleeting thoughts where the non-linguistic and non-judgmental lie . . . simple wakefulness and ultimate abandon'. This might be too simple for the gathering who are now getting ready to return to real office life where ultimate abandon may not be easy to come by. Still, over the final coffee a man from Ciba-Geigy ('I am a kind of writer. I write ideas in my office and then send them out to be implemented') feels he has had a thrilling and rare experience. Where else, he asks, can you hear so many different kinds of people talking? Where else could one think about the creative connections between economics, arts and science? He looks suspiciously at me when I suggest a critical, 'wakeful' evening in front of the telly might do the trick.

I arrive home to two not irrelevant pieces of information. There is a report in the *Guardian* that Apple Macintosh is in dire trouble, and that all the desperate innovation of the past few years has failed to give them a survivable share of the computer market, despite having by far the most creatively user-friendly product. Dr Guntern mentioned Apple several times during our long weekend as a lesson in the revival of flagging corporate thinking. Then I phone a friend of mine who, when I ask what he's up to, tells me he is about to spend the next few weeks, or maybe months, scratching his balls. He means, I immediately understand, that he is starting to write his next novel.

A Small Accident

'What do you think of the colour?' Sister Brendan calls down from the top of the ladder where she's painting the gate to the enclosed part of the convent a lurid green. She has to repeat the question because her Irish brogue is so thick I find it hard to understand her.

'A bit bright,' I reply, screwing up my eyes against the glare.

'I know. The sister who bought the paint thought it would be darker. Mother says this is the paint we bought so this is the paint we've got to use. Are you sure you don't do anything to make your hair that colour?'

All week I've been fighting off that Wonderland feeling, now I give up, and allow myself the image of the Abbess arriving, long habit rustling, waving her finger and shrieking 'Off with her head!' at Sister Brendan for the colour of the gate, and me for the colour of my hair.

For the third time during my stay, I explain to Sister Brendan, to whom my hair is a thing of wonder, that it's naturally grey, I don't dye it, honest, it just grows like this. She shakes her head, up her ladder, at me, disbelieving. I want to give her *something*. 'In the early Sixties, I used to iron my hair. It was curly, no one wanted curly hair then, so I used to iron it straight on the ironing board.'

Sister Brendan had already been a nun for 16 years when I was ironing my hair. She'd left school in rural Ireland at 14 ('I wasn't much for schooling'), spent three years having fun ('Oh, nothing wicked, you know, just nice fun') and become a nun the same year I was born. When it's her turn to read aloud from the Bible during mass, she does so with some difficulty. Now her eyes widen in wonder at my revelation. 'You never did? Iron your hair? Well, I've never heard of such a thing.' We both shake our heads over my younger self. She comes halfway down the ladder and confides, 'You know what I've a fancy to do? I'd like to paint a little flower on this gate. Just one, in a corner, to make it prettier.' She's a mite shocked at having such a thought. 'Why not?' I say. 'It wouldn't be wicked or anything.'

'Do you think not?'

'What harm could a flower do?'

She chuckles to herself as she climbs back up the ladder, and I continue walking with the words, 'Curiouser and curiouser' ringing in my inner ear.

On my way to meet Sister Agnes Teresa I run into another nun. I tower over her, all five feet three inches of me. 'I'm Sister Paul,' she shouts up at me, wanting a chat (it's talking time at the convent). 'I'm Mary Paul really, but they call me Paul for short. I'm afraid one of these days I'll just be Sister P.' Even nuns don't have time to call you by your full name, apparently. Sister Mary Paul is in her eighties. She's recently had an operation for mouth cancer and is taking tablets for growths on her uterus which she says, raising her hands to heaven, have turned out to be a blessing because as a side effect they stop her retaining fluid. She's nearly blind, which accounts for why she's virtually standing on top of me, though she should be completely blind according to the doctor. 'But I prayed to the Lord not to make me a trouble to the others, and he answered my prayer, so I can still see a little out of one eye. And I've got a wonderful gadget from

Germany which is a torch and a magnifying glass to read with.' I could swear I hear her say: 'There's glory for you!' but I know it's just another aural hallucination. I've seen her with her reading machine in the chapel, bent over, peering at the prayer book as though she were examining a patient with tonsillitis.

I mention Sister Brendan's floral fancy and Sister Paul's miraculous not-quite-blindness to Sister Agnes Teresa as I settle down in the shabby chair in the nun's sitting room for our chat. She winces at the prospect of a flower on the gate, though the aesthetic pang is mixed with amusement. She's in her mid-fifties and has been a Poor Clare since she was 18, but she's an educational and intellectual world away from Sisters Brendan and Mary Paul. She tells me about overhearing Sister Paul, an innocently beatific smile on her face, telling a recently bereaved mother that God must have wanted her young child and that it was a blessing. Sister Agnes Teresa shudders. 'She sincerely believes it, but what kind of thing is that for a nun, or anyone else, to say to the woman?'

'Do you believe it?'

'No,' she says without a moment's hesitation.

'Then what?'

'I don't know.'

A small look between us suggests we both rather envy them their certainties. Sister Agnes Teresa may also be a theological world away from Sisters Brendan and Paul. But she affirms her choice of vocation.

'This is my place in the dance. I've chosen to be here and I know it's the right place for me, even though it's on the margins of life and I have to miss out on some things.'

I am silent for a bit, watching images trickling past my mind's eye of the kind of things Sister Agnes Teresa had been missing these past 37 years. A child, good food in smart restaurants, Shakespeare at the National, sex, television, digitally

perfect reproduced music, family, fine fabrics made into beautiful clothes, opera, choosing and coming first with one person
(or several persons serially), staying in bed until lunch-time if
she felt like it, alcohol, taking off and basking naked under a
foreign sun, dinner/cocktail/publisher's parties.

'*Have* you missed out on anything unmissable?' I ask. It
was a genuine question. I couldn't think of anything it would
be impossible, or even very terrible to do without.

She made an effort to help me. 'Children?'

'Plenty of people don't have children and have a full life.'

'Sex?' Sister Agnes Teresa tried, though with little enthusiasm.

'Nice, even very nice sometimes, but not essential. It can
be done without.' I thought on for a moment. 'You've missed
some good movies . . .'

Sister Agnes Teresa and I met on three afternoons between
2 and 4.30, during my stay at the Convent of the Poor
Clares. I'd spent time, the previous month, at a Carmelite
Monastery near Oxford, where I talked with Father Pat
every morning. What the Carmelite monks and the Poor
Clare nuns have in common is a life devoted to moderate
silence and a great deal of prayer. They don't do anything
out in the world other than receive retreatants. No teaching,
or nursing; nothing of any obvious social use by which they
might justify their existence to secular society. The nuns pray,
and work (as an aspect of prayer) is teleological; gardening,
cooking, cleaning, making items for sale – whatever is possible within the enclosed life that will maintain it. The monks
(being priests? being men?) seem to do very little else but
pray – cleaners and cooks come in from outside, though I did
see a postulant planting a climber against the wall while I
was there. The Carmelites get money from the Church; the
Poor Clares, severe Franciscans, radical religious that they
have always been, do not, relying on providence to make up
the difference between what they need and what they've got.

It wasn't quite clear to me what I was doing there, other than being idly curious, until on the first morning at the monastery, Father Pat greeted me with, 'You haven't run away yet, then?' Why would I? I had a small comfortable room in the Retreat House adjoining the Monastery, like a study bedroom, with a bed, desk, washbasin, wardrobe. I could, if I chose, do nothing at all during my stay except be in my room, reading, writing, gazing into space. The grounds consisted of 17 acres of woodland and garden to walk in. Three meals a day were provided for me and the three nuns who were also on retreat. I didn't have to talk to anyone if I didn't want to (even mealtimes are silent except for an occasional whisper 'Could you pass the salt, please?'); I could attend Chapel up to five times a day, or not at all. Far from wanting to run away, I was trying to figure out how to become a permanent resident.

'I'm a writer,' I explained to Father Pat. 'Being quiet and alone is what I do for a living.'

To Sister Agnes Teresa, when she asked me the same question, I was a little more honest.

'Neurosis,' I confessed. 'I go a little crazy if I don't spend large chunks of time alone. This suits me down to the ground. I really had to be a writer to justify the hours I've always spent sitting in rooms staring at the ceiling. Now I can call it work and get away with it.'

At a later meeting, I came a tad closer to the truth. I'd been dreaming every night about hospitals, nurses bustling about in uniforms, beds with white sheets, me in one, blissfully sedated. Since late adolescence there's been a part of me hankering to be institutionalised, which meant out of it, some kind of absenteeism, no need to *do* or *be* anything. I spent some time in hospitals in my teens and early twenties, but found it disappointing: they're always getting you out of bed, dragging you off to art therapy, making you join groups to discuss the fact you don't want to join a group. It took a while, but I finally figured writing was a better way to get what I wanted, though it had the drawback of meaning I had to be in charge of my life. *Nothing's perfect*: I think that's the single piece of wisdom I've accumulated over the years. But wisdom doesn't stop you dreaming, and somewhere at the back of my mind, a small white room with a bed, desk, books, silence, meals appearing, no one around, exists as a Platonic form. And the monastery and convent are close.

But only close. There *was* something after all, about the secular life that Agnes Teresa had given up which I thought was essential, unmissable. My Platonic white room is actually a hermit's hole, not a monk's or a nun's cell where you can spend only a very few hours alone, because for most of the time you are part of an inescapable, unchanging community. What's really difficult about being a nun, Agnes Teresa explains, is living and trying to get on with other people *all the time*. If you want to be a solitary, be a writer, not a religious.

Agnes Teresa writes, too. She's had books on prayer and contemplation published, and translated a life of St Clare from the Italian. She has to fit her writing into the couple of hours a day set aside for private study of religious texts. She also digs up onions for the kitchen, and prints mugs with 'I ♥ the Poor Clares' to sell to visitors. The life is so busy, so filled with other people, I feel pangs of empathetic panic as I take down her daily timetable. Between getting up at 5am to pray at 5.45, and going to bed after night prayers at 8.45pm, the day is crammed. Every hour accounted for, and all of those hours, except for half an hour here and there for private prayer, spent in the company of others. It's certainly institutionalised, but more like being a sailor – on a submarine, and no shore leave. *And* they're supposed to love each other. They are, after all, brides of Christ: Jesus's harmonious harem.

'Do you?' I ask, about loving the others.

'I try. But I frequently fail. It's what I most need God's help for.'

I'd almost forgotten about God.

My encounters with formal religion have only been intermittent over the years. Very early on, though not for long, we went to an uncle's Passover *seder*. Sometimes my father would take me to the synagogue at the end of Yom Kipur and sit me on his shoulder so I could see the ram's horn being blown to signify atonement was over and everyone could go and get some good Jewish food down them. That was about it until I was 11, apart from school assemblies, where I sang and enjoyed hymns like 'To be a Pilgrim' that seemed to hunger interestingly after something, though I wasn't clear what (an improvement, surely, on my daughter's primary school assemblies where she warbled 'Blowin' in the Wind' and 'Nowhere Man').

The chummily named Father Pat was actually a gaunt, severe young man in his thirties, all bony angles which twisted uneasily around each other as he sat talking, his eyes focusing hard on a bit of me and then refocusing to another bit (shoulder, knee) as if trying to find the right place to rest his gaze. He never tried my eyes. At the end of our first meeting, he'd suggested I read the Scriptures for the next day. Perversely, I suppose, I started with Job. I said the obvious.

'We cannot know what is in God's mind,' he told me. God had said, finally, to the suppurating Job: '*Where were you when I laid the earth's foundations?*' But we *do* know what's in God's mind; we're told at the beginning, the whole thing is a wager between Yahweh and Satan to see how much suffering an innocent man would put up with before cursing his maker. All right, so he made it up to Job, but when does it get better for – I say, a little embarrassed – Bosnians . . . Somalis . . .?

'There are many more good things happening in Yugoslavia and Somalia than bad,' Father Pat assures me. I stare, open-mouthed, at him. 'The media only shows the terrible things, the suffering, not the other things.' Suddenly, I'm in conference with Martyn Lewis. 'I've never met anyone in my time as a priest who was truly in despair,' he adds. 'Except, of course, the mentally ill.'

Oh, yes, them. I suspect it wouldn't be fruitful to discuss what he means by mentally ill and try another angle if only to keep my lower jaw from dropping off my face altogether.

'What if Job wasn't innocent? What if his friends are right and he's being punished for smugness and complacency?' I know it's not on the list of deadly sins, but perhaps a modern list might have complacency somewhere near the top.

'No,' Father Pat says firmly. 'It says he's completely innocent. The point is that humanity cannot apprehend the Divine.'

There's a wall of faith between us that isn't going to be scalable. I do not like this Old Testament Yahweh, this jealous god that is that he is. Who Aquinas says created humanity so that we would love him. Why would anyone worship such a monster? We would suggest a person like that get help. Then again, if we are the creatures of any god, that one sounds the most closely related.

I slink off back to my room and read Elaine Pagels on the Gnostic gospels. This makes sense: the God of Israel, merely a demiurge, just a hack creator of a universe, an underling who got above himself. A Gnostic text discovered at Nag Hammadi says: 'when Faith saw the impiety of the chief ruler, she was angry . . . she said, "You err, Samael [i.e. 'blind god']. An enlightened, immortal humanity [*anthropos*] exists before you!"'

It seems a little late to become a Gnostic in 1993. I don't mention it to Father Pat. Anyway, as I sit down next morning, he leans towards me and speaks in a tone I find oddly familiar.

'Something new is happening in your life. You must be

open to what has led you here. You seem to be searching . . .'
(I'd explained in my letter I was planning to write an article).

Martyn Lewis turns briefly into a shrink and then makes a final transformation into Gypsy Rose before my very eyes. He's right in a way, mind you, though my search is more that of a dilettante seeking after speculation than the certainties of faith. It's precisely the *insoluble* nature of God that intrigues me. I go back to my room and read John's gospel. 'In the beginning was the Word.' It cheers me up no end.

I enjoy the praying and silent contemplation in the chapel. I feel like I've been dragged on stage at the National to speak Hamlet's soliloquy as I gather up the courage to join in saying: *As it was in the beginning, now and ever shall be, world without end.* I start to look forward to prayer times so I can say it again, and intone, along with the monks, those wonderful lamenting psalms. Not so different really from being six years old in bed and knowing the value of repetition and making signs. Only I don't eat or drink Jesus at Mass; thoughts of the ram's horn prevent me from committing such blasphemy.

Most of the Poor Clares go barefoot during prayers – discalced in foot as well as name, they are. Proof of god-fearing toes as well as a symbol of their poverty. They do an anglicised version of plainchant, rather than just muttering as the monks do, and at night-prayers, the lights are turned off and the 'Salve Regina' is sung in candlelight. I revel in this, a daily treat, and like the marking of the day's passage – but perhaps it just reminds me of the pills schedule in hospital, I tell myself, severely.

'Listen,' I say to Sister Agnes Teresa. 'It's dangerous to believe in God; too easy to slip into the sentimental, to find consolation, to avoid looking hard at what's going on.'

'Have you read Merton?' she asks.

Thomas Merton is more to my taste: spiritual deserts, a deity beyond human imagining who exists in the emptiness of existential doubt. But then Merton was in Japan when he died in 1969, investigating the godless spirituality of Zen. Would he have remained a Christian monk if he'd lived? Buber interests me. God as Thou, utterly other but utterly real; to be confronted but never known. No hippie nonsense about God is me and God is you. 'Go on believe,' says Wittgenstein, 'it does no harm.' This is patently untrue historically, but as a personal decision, why not? What difference would being wrong make, really? Kierkegaard makes some sense: faith as a leap into the dark. Could the absurdity of deity be the very reason for choosing faith? Faith is, by definition, ridiculous, but why not be ridiculous?

Don Cupitt writes in a letter to the *Guardian* that he's a 'non-realist theologian' and that the question is not 'does God exist, but what do we mean by "exist"?' Sister Agnes Teresa and I have a bit of a giggle over this, but I nip off to Cambridge for coffee even though, on the phone, he speaks of himself as being a 'postmodernist' without saying sorry. The talk is of American colour-field painters – Rothko in particular – as representing the divine more appropriately for our time than Michelangelo, which I can see; and there's much said about Wittgenstein and language games. I ought to feel better about this than I do. Language seems to me precisely the problem with religion just as it is with biology. Genetic and theological description is befouled with the language of intentionality: genes are selfish or altruistic; God gives, God wants, God plans. *God* is a meaningless syllable and it's supposed to be. But we can't think outside the concrete. We can't help dreaming up a God who dreams up us in his own image. Cupitt's cultural, anthropological reading of theology can't be faulted, except why be an Anglican, a Christian, a theist? Perhaps, once the deconstructionists have finished with it, the question *is*, after all, does God exist. And the answer to what do we mean by 'exist' is 'not much', or to put a shoe on our head. The question is: why ask the question? Don Cupitt accepts there might be something else than an exclusively materialist world (I think), but I can't see why he needs Christianity as a structure, rather than as just one of all the myths and legends humanity has assembled to share its solitude.

The absurdity of *disbelieve* looks as heroic a leap into the dark as any. To confront a god whose name, by virtue of his/her/its unknowability to us, is Accident, gives us an interesting answer to Einstein's final unsolved problem: God *is* dice. Cupitt is spot on with Wittgenstein: if god could talk we wouldn't understand him; whereof one cannot speak, thereof . . .

There is courage in devoting your life to the meditation of an inexpressible idea, and I can see the point of it. There's nothing (apart from the food) about the Carmelites' and Poor Clares' way of life that I find very problematical, except for the notion of God. Which is to say that to devote a life to a quiet search seems fine to me, what I find abhorrent is the possibility of *finding* something – especially what you think you are looking for. I suspect that Sister Agnes Teresa is not a universe away from this position. She believes in God, but finds the word unhelpful. She says that she no longer thinks in terms of getting a return on her investment of right living. Recompense is not available, nor the point. What has been given up is gone. Religion for her is permanent risk; there are no bargains to be made. She has little fire on the subject of morality, but speaks of sin in terms of behaviour which comes from a place in her that is wounded and is therefore damaging to herself and others. It's a description of human strife I could live with. It is the *Church*, she says, which is infallible, and when Popes issue directives which are not in harmony with the wishes of the Church, they can be, and are, fallible. But what about Christ and all those interceding saints, who, during all the praying, I've come to think of as Rabbit and all Rabbit's friends and relations? She tells me that St Francis believed the incarnation of Christ was in God's mind before the Fall. She's happy to speculate about the crucifixion being an historical accident; that Christ was God joining us, with us and in us, but that it went wrong. Even so, she cherishes the idea of the Madonna as an image of perfect and sorrowing woman, and when I suggest that in a world (which I'm prepared to postulate and in which she believes) of good and evil, it seems evil has the greater power, Agnes Teresa tells me she is sure I am wrong, and such a notion is a modern error which enhances evil in the world. Somehow, she does not start to look like Martyn Lewis, but I remember that she is, after all, a Christian nun and I am not. I ask her if there's room in her beliefs for the purely accidental, and she pauses before she answers with a hesitant no, but then adds that what she's read of chaos theory is interesting about patterns of randomness, so perhaps the random has a part to play.

At the monastery, I ask Father Pat whether anything in the world was, in his view, random. He didn't stop to think for a second before assuring me that nothing was. 'Nothing?' I asked, as shocked by this as a Catholic faced with evidence of Jesus and Mary of Magdala making babies. 'Nothing.' It seems so dull a view, so ungodly, somehow. It doesn't even leave room for the joy of accidental meaning, surely a sign of god, if not God. I don't want to be made to feel better by a personalised God offering me niceness in the hereafter, but I do want to be surprised and to find myself laughing from time to time.

One afternoon, at the monastery, I was reading a book by a bunch of Benedictine monks and nuns, talking about the religious life. There were no surprises; almost all of them had been brought up Catholics, gone to Catholic schools, and becoming a religious was barely a choice for most of them. It didn't seem to have anything much in it for me, and the writing wasn't good. Every essay had its pastoral moment – the joy of nature as an expression of the holy, that kind of thing – and finally, on reading a nun waxing lyrical about the turning of the seasons, making her point by describing a new shoot she'd seen which had pushed its way right up through the centre of a dried-up fallen leaf from the previous year, I got terminally grumpy, slammed the book shut and went out for a walk. I hated the image, and, in any case, I didn't believe in the mechanics of it. Surely the shoot would just have pushed the leaf out of its way. I'd never seen such a thing.

I sat on a bench the monks had made surrounding a great spreading chestnut in the woods and sulked, until I started to enjoy the smell of damp and decay and woodiness. The ground was carpeted with soft rotted humus, a scattering of mushrooms and some still-intact leaves from last autumn. Six inches in front of my right foot, there was a brittle, brown leaf speared straight through its centre by a bright green seedling, just beginning to open its first pair of leaves. 'Oh, for God's sake!' I groaned at it. But I've always been fond of bad jokes, so by the time I got back to the Retreat House and almost bumped into Father Pat at the door, I was chuckling merrily to myself. He wondered what I was laughing at. 'Nothing much,' I smiled. 'Just a small accident.'

Commitment

For some time now, it's been clear to me that consciousness of death is a kindness bestowed on us by the Great Intelligence, so that even if all else succeeded we would always have something to worry about. This, of course, accounts for pussy cats and lions sleeping 18 hours a day and therefore failing to invent the fax machine. Us humans, up and anxious about death, have passed the time thinking up civilisation as a way to distract ourselves, or at least to let others know that we're awake, too. Unfortunately, the fax machine having already been invented, I had to settle simply for being up and anxious all Bank Holiday weekend, brooding darkly and leafing restlessly through the *Gazetteer* of London cemeteries.*

It began when my friend Jenny (not me in my postmodern mode, but someone else entirely) made me the offer of a lifetime. She'd bought a plot in Highgate Cemetery, she told me, which was a mere snip at £700, especially since it accommodated three ex-people. Would I care to share it with her? Not immediately, of course, but when the time

---

* *London Cemeteries: An Illustrated Guide and Gazetteer* by Hugh Meller (Scolar, London, 1994)

came. Highgate Cemetery is a very nice place, and Jenny is an old and dear friend. I was properly honoured; no one else I've known has ever wanted to spend eternity with me – as a rule the occasional supper is sufficient – and I wished to express my gratitude. But at the same time my heart rate began to speed, and my throat to constrict: classic signs of claustrophobia and panic. I've never been any good at long-term commitment.

'Are you sure?' I asked. 'It's a bit perpetual. What about your children?'

'They can make their own arrangements,' she said darkly.

Jenny is known for going off people – even people who are not her children. She keeps a bottle of Tippex beside her address book to deal with those she's no longer on speaking terms with. I felt that apart from my reservations about making a long-term commitment, we ought to be realistic about the eternal prospects of our friendship.

'I know we get on well, but we have to think practically. For ever's, well, a very long time to be side by side.'

'Actually, one on top of the other. It's a vertical plot.'

There was a lot to think about here. Assuming that things went according to the Great Chronologist's plan, Jenny-who-isn't-me would be tucked in first, since she is 20 years older. On the other hand, I smoke several packs a day and eat salami like sweeties. There was, therefore, no guarantee that I'd get top bunk.

While I was wondering if this mattered, the Heir Apparent shuffled into the room and announced that she had something to say about all this, since, after all, she'd be in charge of arrangements. We'd already had a prior conversation about the disposal of my remains because she's a sensible girl and doesn't like to leave things to the last minute. I'd suggested cremation (so they could play 'Smoke Gets In Your Eyes' while the casket slid behind the modesty curtain) and that my ashes should be scattered over the threshold of the Hampstead branch of Nicole Farhi.

The only other really appealing possibility was a monomaniacal plan of the Victorian architect, Thomas Willson, who in 1842 designed a brick and granite sepulchral pyramid with a base area the size of Russell Square to be built on Primrose Hill. Its 94 levels (topped by an observatory) would be 'sufficiently capacious to receive five millions of the dead, where they may repose in perfect security'. The scheme foundered, but if anyone feels like reviving it, I'd be happy to make a contribution in return for a guaranteed place somewhere near the pinnacle. Failing that, I thought I would after all settle for the shared accommodation on offer in Highgate Cemetery.

'God, you're always changing your mind,' the Heir Apparent said impatiently. 'If you're buried you'll have to have a headstone. That's more of my inheritance gone, and what's it going to say on it?'

'*Jenny Diski lies here. But tells the truth over there*', I instructed. 'Also, I'd like a dove, a wing'ed angel, an anchor and an open book, properly carved on a nice piece of granite.'

The Heir's eyes narrowed dangerously.

'You get in for nothing if you've got a relative on site. Otherwise it's a pound a head. So there's a saving,' the other Jenny reassured her. 'And there's much more scope for drama in a proper burial. At the last funeral I went to, the grieving mistress tried to throw herself into the grave. Very satisfactory, and not a thing you can do at a cremation without making a nasty stink.'

It looked like it was decided. I wasn't to go up in smoke, but would instead fatten the worms which feed the birds which keep the London cats sleek, self-satisfied and asleep for 18 hours a day. While the other Jenny went off to spend the holiday weekend in Bradford (which gave more pause for thought about spending eternity in such eccentric company), I hunkered down with my *Gazetteer* to apprise myself of the interment possibilities.

It was not so much the fact of death as the quantity of it that struck me. In 1906 the Angel of Death dropped in on houses in London at the rate of once every six minutes. Oddly, London's population has returned to roughly what it was at the beginning of the century, though I suppose that the death rate (Bottomley notwithstanding) must have fallen. I added to my collection of useless but disturbing thoughts the fact that currently the total land used for burial in London is three thousand acres. Anyone with GCSE maths (three thousand acres ÷ six-foot plot × three bodies deep) could work out how many dead are lying around London. I don't have GCSE maths, so I didn't try, but, according to the *Gazetteer*, Highgate has 51,000 plots containing 166,000 bodies. Do the rest of the arithmetic for yourselves. And if you're very keen, how many people *in total* have died since Homo got to its feet? More than everyone alive today? I only wonder because I like large numbers.

I was troubled by the idea of so many people dying as we wake and sleep and go about our business. It's an astonishing feat of human lack of imagination to be able to ignore all those souls up and down our streets, fluttering off minute by minute, all around us. I remembered an incident in the early Seventies (when else) during a community festival in Camden Square's central patch of railed-off greenery. Perhaps it was midsummer, or Easter, or maybe it was just one of those pseudo-spontaneous street parties that were supposed to weld us all together, before we knew the Eighties were coming. Anyway, we had a great bonfire, a lamb roasting on a spit, rock 'n' roll megawatting through monster speakers and the decidedly mixed inhabitants of the square – the teenage villains, pre-pubescent truants and lawless toddlers of our Free School plus the recent incoming gentry whose houses they regularly broke into. The robbers and the robbed mingled riotously to celebrate the spirit of their community.

Suddenly, someone was standing out on the street, shouting through the railings. 'There's a woman dying at number 65!' he bellowed at us revellers over and over again, and finally made himself heard. 'Hasn't she got the right to die in peace?'

There was a bit of a lull, long enough for any-man's-death-diminishes-me sort of thoughts to start rolling around in my head before a bearded and bejeaned community hero spoke up for the collective will. He was sorry about the woman, he told her son or husband or friend, but there were a couple of hundred people out here, also belonging to this square, and we were celebrating life. Man! The very shade of Jeremy Bentham hovered over Camden Square for a second, and then a roar of affirmation went up. The Utilitarians won the day. The Stones were turned up again to ear-splitting level, and John Donne slunk back with the soon-to-be-bereaved protester to get on with private dying behind closed doors. Logical, of course, but for all that, the lamb tasted raw and rotten to me.

It's possible I take death too seriously. It's always seemed a momentous business, coming, as it generally does, after a lifetime's consideration, unlike, for example, birth, which happens (to the new-born, if not the parents) before one has a chance to consider it, so far as I can tell. For a long time I supposed it only happened to very serious and substantial people, but then my father died when I was 17 and I was amazed to discover that something as weighty as death could be done by someone so dedicated to evading life's trickier realities. I confess I was, and still am, impressed that he could have done something so committed as to die.

The *Gazetteer*, however, kept all such metaphysical thoughts up in the air where they belong, and my feet on the ground. It quotes from the *Builder* in 1879: 'The principles of proportion and of harmony of grace and form which are required by a well-dressed woman in her costume are equally applicable when she comes to choose a tombstone for her husband.' Though not as much fun, I should think, as burying a husband, thoughts about one's own tomb are just as sartorial. What if Armani and Calvin Klein diversified into the undertaking and stone-dressing business? I could fancy an eternity of decomposition under a layered beige, beautifully cut headstone. But could my cheapskate descendant be trusted not to shop around and dump me in the Monsoon cemetery for dead hippies?

Planning the style of one's burial is also a rather cunning way to avoid thinking about its prerequisite, I discovered. The *Gazetteer* has no mention of people dying or the manner of their death, and in an investigative wander around West Hampstead Cemetery (I thought I'd better wait for Jenny's return from sunny Bradford before visiting my prospective plot) there were very few indications of how the interred got there. I suppose it doesn't matter unless something extra special carried them off. I'm rather partial to the idea of being *translated*, myself, but mostly the dear departed, sorely missed, tended to fall asleep or pass away.

Except for Tony. *Tony* was carved in six-inch lettering on a slab of black marble and under it was inscribed: *I Had a Lover's Quarrel with the World 1947–1978*. I was moved. 40-year-old Tony. One of my lot. Post-war Tony, agitated by peace and prosperity, his youth a haze of misremembered sex and drugs and rock and roll, as overfull of romantic aspirations as he was of existential despair, threw in his towel after doing the best he could to compose a resonant if pretty yukky farewell to life. Sadly, when I got home, I found it was a quote from Robert Frost. Even so, Tony didn't just pass away and wanted to be remembered for not doing so. Perhaps he died of disappointment at not even being able to think up an epitaph of his own. Mostly, disappointment of one kind or another is what my generation died young of. If it's any consolation to them, those of us who remain find ourselves with the practicalities of not having died young to attend to.

There is, apparently, a cemetery in Buenos Aires which is a veritable city of the dead, with named avenues lined with scaled-down architected homes for the late-lamented. Relatives come and housekeep on Sundays, dusting, polishing and replacing lace doilies while chatting to neighbouring survivors over the fence. This set me brooding about my one-up-one-down resting place in Highgate. What about a mausoleum, I began to wonder. It could be fitted with a wood-burning stove and comfy chairs. I'd leave funds so that a bottle of Scotch and packs of cards would be available in perpetuity, so friends and well-wishers could drop by on gloomy Sundays for a game of poker. The Heir Apparent was not keen on this idea. Quite apart from the drain on her inheritance ('To hell with the expense,' I cried. 'You're so selfish,' she hissed), there was the matter of the earth's resources to consider. She pointed severely to an article on natural death.

'There is some other kind?' I queried.

It turns out there's no legal reason not to bury your dead in the back garden. I was delighted.

'Darling, you can have me around always. Sod Highgate. You can just dig me a nice big hole and pop me under the yucca.'

She explained this wasn't a good idea because it would very likely lower the value of the house when she came to sell it, and she certainly wasn't going to dig me up and take me with her every time she moved.

I called the Natural Death Centre* and a Mr Albery explained that their idea is to use European Union set-aside land to inter bodies and create lovely nature reserves full of you and me, while the farmers get paid for not growing anything useful on it. Instead of gravestones, they'll have trees. I could have a plaque if I wanted it, though he didn't sound enthusiastic. No need for embalming. All those chemicals are just to stop what's going to happen anyway from happening for a while. It seems it's perfectly all right to keep an unembalmed body at home for up to three days, and frankly who wants one around longer? And forget about coffins. Mr Albery advises the use of a simple sheet. By now the Heir was smiling broadly: it was all beginning to look like a pretty thrifty exercise.

However, it turned out that for £85 a specially woven natural woollen shroud can be purchased, which has a plank along the middle (to stop that nasty wobbling corpse effect) and four ropes at each corner for lowering it into the grave. A bargain, I thought, though the Heir muttered that one of our old sheets would do perfectly well. Still, I have a terrible dislike of the cold, especially when it gets into the bones. There was something comforting about the prospect of a woollen shroud, and I think she would have relented if just then I hadn't remembered that I have no desire in this life or after it to conserve resources, that I am and always have been an urban dweller and I didn't see why a detail like death should mean I have to end up in some draughty, disorganised, naturally set-aside bit of rustic. What I fancied was a proper old-fashioned pollution-filled London cemetery to rest my wearied bones, and if I couldn't have it, along with an expensively carved headstone and a very long and elaborate funeral, with hymns

* *Green Burial: The DIY Guide to Law and Practice* (Natural Death Centre, London, 1994)

and popular hits of the Sixties sung, a certain amount of dancing, and my deeds recounted for the edification of all, then the Heir could whistle for her inheritance and I'd leave everything to the Natural Death Centre including my clothes. That did it. A proper interment at Highgate is assured.

THEN AGAIN

A powerful novel exploring the nature of belief, the boundaries between madness and sanity, revelation and delusion, and good and evil.

'Diski shows how closed our open-mindedness really is.' *Sunday Times*

'Diski writes with flair and precision.' *Evening Standard*

SKATING TO ANTARCTICA

'This strange and brilliant book recounts Jenny Diski's journey to Antarctica . . . intercut with another journey into her own heart and soul . . . a book of dazzling variety . . . Diski's writing is laconic, her images are haunting.' Elspeth Barker, *Independent on Sunday*

'Astonishing, harrowing, very funny, and always completely enthralling and brilliantly written.' Harry Ritchie, *Mail on Sunday*

LIKE MOTHER

Chillingly original, *Like Mother* is the spellbinding story of Frances told to us in the voice of her ultimate fictional creation and means of self-expression, Nonentity, a baby without a brain.

'Diski's writing is at its best: imaginative, taut yet elegant.' *Times Literary Supplement*

'She writes with enterprise and cunning.' *Observer*

For further information about Granta Books
and a full list of titles, please write to us at

Granta Books

2/3 HANOVER YARD

NOEL ROAD

LONDON

N1 8BE

enclosing a stamped, addressed envelope

———————————

You can visit our website at

http://www.granta.com